THE MISSING SEASON

HARPER TEEN

An Imprint of HarperCollins*Publishers*

GILLIAN FRENCH

HarperTeen is an imprint of HarperCollins Publishers.

The Missing Season
Copyright © 2019 by Gillian French
All rights reserved. Printed in the United States of America.
No part of this book may be used or reproduced in any manner
whatsoever without written permission except in the case of brief
quotations embodied in critical articles and reviews. For information
address HarperCollins Children's Books, a division of HarperCollins
Publishers, 195 Broadway, New York, NY 10007.
www.epicreads.com

Library of Congress Control Number: 2019933063
ISBN 978-0-06-280333-7

Typography by Erin Fitzsimmons
19 20 21 22 23   PC/LSCH   10 9 8 7 6 5 4 3 2 1
❖
First Edition

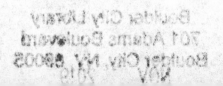

For Lucas

Traditional children's rhyme, Hancock County, Maine

Mumbler, Mumbler, in your bed,
Mumbler, Mumbler, take your head,
Eat your nose, gobble your toes,
And bury you where the milkweed grows.

ONE

HOODIES COME OUT of the rain, four of them, coasting down the Birchwood Terraces slope on stunt bikes. Green hood leads, followed by blue, yellow, and white, their knees up around their ears, steering with one hand, letting the other dangle.

My jacket's zipped to my chin, but if I could, I'd pull my whole head inside, tortoise-style, and wait out this ritual. Got to wear the old stone face, though. Prove I'm hard.

They hang a left, straying across both lanes toward the school-bus-stop shelter where I stand. Some of the other kids shift, tensing here beneath the corrugated plastic roof, where the sound of raindrops is amplified to a snare drum backbeat.

Green Hood circles the shelter, gone, back, gone, back, the other hoodies trailing behind. Scoping the new-kid situation. I focus on the sign across the street, peeling and faded, welcoming people to the Birchwood Terraces development—*Affordable Family Housing*—ready to eat my ration of shit so they can forget about me.

"Who's that?" Green Hood says.

"Dunno." Blue Hood reappears.

"Hey. Who are you?" Green Hood flashes by. "Hello-o-o? You speak-ay Engleesh?" Something bounces off my chest, and my gaze follows it to the mud. A balled-up gum wrapper. Back to the sign. *Affordablefamilyhousing. Affordablefamilyhousing.* I'm going to make it here. I am.

"What's up with her hair?" Blue.

"Looks like Christmas barfed on her head." Green.

Laughter, from the hoodies and the other kids. Take it. Take it. My jaw clenches so tightly that the tendons jump in my neck.

A girl speaks in a low monotone: "Aidan?"

Green Hood puts his foot down to brake when he sees who's talking.

She stands to my right, tallish, rangy, wearing a charcoal-colored fleece, her blond hair in a brief ponytail. A middle-of-the-classroom type, average, nothing to see here. Only her gaze—shrewd, eyes a barely-there shade of gray—makes her something more. She twitches her head once. "No."

She could be telling a cat not to play with her shoelaces. I expect f-bombs, but Green Hood just sniffs, wipes his nose on his hand, and shoves off down the street, letting the rest of them play catch-up.

She turns to me. "Goddamn hoodies make everybody look bad." Her expression's deadpan, a real stone face, not like the mask I wear. "We aren't all assholes, I swear."

I don't thank her—I can tell she wouldn't like that—and I don't ruin everything by saying that she should've let the ritual play out, that now they'll only wait until they can get me alone. I search for chitchat. "They left fast. You must be scary."

A slight nod, no softening in her expression. "So, I'm Bree." She points to the girl beside her. "That's Sage."

Sage. A gymnast's build, tortoiseshell glasses, her hair a lob ombré'd from deep brown to platinum. She wears trendy hot-girl clothes—skinny jeans, a lace-trim cami—and a flannel boyfriend shirt over it all. Boyfriend because it's huge on her, maybe XL, in shades of brown and green, washed and worn to a soft patina.

When Sage grins, it's forthright, devilish. "How're you liking the Terraces so far?"

"It's"—I scan the identical cube houses lining the cul-de-sac, shabby little three-family units, each with a shared parking area and a strip of backyard facing the woods—"very beige."

They laugh, a relief, but Bree's gaze is still sharp. "Why'd you come here?"

Typical accusatory question. One thing I've learned, moving from one dying town to the next: everybody in a place like this thinks they're being held hostage. "My dad's working the mill demolition." Their dads are probably on unemployment, now that Pender isn't making paper anymore.

"Oh. The wicked-built guy with all the tats?" Bree bumps shoulders with Sage, says to me, "We were watching out the window when you moved in."

"No shit. You get to call him daddy?" Sage cackles. "Luck-y. He could tuck me into bed anytime." She sees me flinch, glances at Bree. "Too far?"

Bree measures a half inch between thumb and forefinger as the school bus stops at the curb, all shrieking brakes and groaning hydraulics. We clomp on board into a funk of stale air, old vinyl, and spectral puke from bus rides past. I swing into the first empty seat. The girls choose the seat across the aisle. Bree raises her voice over the din: "What's your name?"

"Clara."

She considers. "How about Clarabelle?" She glances at Sage, who shrugs approval.

I can't tell if they're joking. I look at the floor, Sage's block-heel mules and Bree's canvas sneakers together, my leopard-print skimmers keeping their distance.

◗ ● ◖

Pender District High is a cinder-block bunker with low, grimy windows that open on cranks, and rows of battered purple lockers. A mural of the sweater-wearing, steam-snorting mascot consumes the wall by the office, gift of the class of '18. Go-o-o, Raging Elks.

Bree and Sage are sucked away into the major artery of the place, and then there's just me, Clara Morrison, Human Conversation Piece, the girl who's starting school on a Friday, over a month late, with her hair a dye-kit disaster, a mess of reddish-green streaks in hair faded yellow with lightener. I pretend I can't feel the eyes on me as I circulate through the usual manic pre-homeroom buzz, searching for room six so I can be marked present. In body, never in spirit.

First-day highlight reel:

Mr. Spille, second-period American history, is PDHS's resident drunk teacher. Never straying far from his desk, he delivers his lecture to us on gusts of minty breath spray with base notes of bourbon. We learn about Harpers Ferry for fifteen minutes until an earnest-faced boy diverts him into a period-long conversation about the Patriots' draft picks. I doodle in my notebook until the bell rings. It's restful.

Hot lunch is slices of anemic turkey, a scoop of instant potatoes with gravy, and green beans drowning in their own bodily fluids. Thank God I brown-bag it. I peel back the tinfoil on my sandwich, the crust an inch from my mouth when I notice the white specks. Bread's gone bad.

Someone put a sticker on my back. Elmo, holding a gold star, smiling gapingly, with the words *Good Job!* underneath. I have no idea how long it's been there.

My study hall is in Mrs. Klatts's room, which has a western exposure, facing an overgrown field bleeding into woods. I'm about to open *A Clockwork Orange*—the rest of my junior English class has already read through page one hundred—when instinct flicks my ear, making me look up at the exact second Bree and Sage sprint across the field, legs pumping, heading for the cover of a single stand of yew trees.

I glance at Klatts, buried in her planner, the bowed heads of the other kids. I'm the only one seeing this, at least in room twelve.

Bree and Sage crouch out of sight, then pelt toward the woods. A moment later, they're gone. I wait for teachers to give chase, for sirens and searchlights. Nothing. The clock over the whiteboard ticks on.

I spend the rest of study hall with my chin resting on my folded arms, staring after them.

Shocker: Bree and Sage don't get on the bus at the end of the day.

I slouch in my seat. Decompression. Or maybe decomposition? Gazing out the rain-speckled window, I register a transition from light to shadow as we drive beneath an overpass. That's when I notice the writing.

Four feet tall, somehow spray-painted across the underside of the pass; the tagger must've hung upside down from the girders like a bat. The message makes me turn even though it's too late, we're through, back in the gray light.

The words said *Fear Him*.

TWO

I'M OUTSIDE AND Ma's in. From where I sit on the back stoop with *A Clockwork Orange*, I hear canned TV laughter, then silence; a song and a half from the radio before she shuts it off, too keyed up about her first day on the job to settle. Probably ironing her uniform shirt, one pink curler rolled into her bangs, reaching for a cup of coffee on the end table each time she checks out the window for Dad's old Suburban pulling into the lot. He's late, and she won't leave until he's here. She worries about me being alone in a new place.

Ma's ringtone sounds. A minute later, the screen door creaks open on its metal arm. "He's on his way." Another creak as she shifts her weight, gauging me. "Think you can handle taking the meat loaf out when the timer goes off?"

"I'll give it my all."

Her foot meets the top of my butt, *bump*. "Miserable brat." She wedges in beside me, smelling like that vanilla perfume she asks me to get her for her birthday every year because it's cheap and easy to find. "School so bad you can't talk about it?"

I glance over; she hasn't asked all afternoon, not even when we ate microwave popcorn and watched the end of a cooking show together. On the other side of the Terraces, a kid screams in play. I swear I've been here before. Not Birchwood Terraces, exactly, but other developments like it, named after the trees cut down to build the place: Oakfield, Elm Park, Spruce Way. We've moved three times in four years, and twice when I was in elementary school, following Dad's construction work, but somehow, we always end up right here.

"Figured I'd let you bring it up." She waits. "Let me guess. Waterboarding. The rack."

I shrug. "Your words, not mine."

She studies me, then *A Clockwork Orange*, and exhales. "Try, Clara. That's all a smart girl like you has to do. If I'd brought home grades like yours, think I'd be hanging around here? Hell no. I'd be in Paris or someplace, getting waited on." Paris is the dream, so far away and impossible that she can imagine anything there, any kind of life. She gives my hair the side-eye, maybe waiting for it to leap like a tarantula. It was supposed to be a pastel rainbow: the picture on the dye kit showed a sexy, up-for-anything girl with a sleek bob of teal, pink, and baby blue. I wanted to be that girl. Self-reinvention in six easy steps. I bought it on the sly with the birthday money my grandma mailed me, lightened and dyed on the second-to-last day before we left our old apartment. If Ma's hurt that I did it while she was at work, fumbling with instructions and bottles and alligator clips, she hasn't let on. "How'd your new look go over?"

"Does Christmas Barf mean anything to you?" She snorts, ducks her head to her knees, and laughs down at her toes. I can't help laughing, too, even though it won't be funny the next time I run into the hoodies. "Right. Mock me. Maybe tomorrow you can come to school and pants me in the cafeteria."

Dad's coming up the walk from the parking lot to the back stoop now, carrying his lunch cooler. His boots are heavy, steel-toed, his jeans coated in pale dust, the powdered remains of walls and foundations. Maybe asbestos. You never know what's lurking inside these paper mills that have been standing for fifty, sixty years. It's a long day, driving a fork-lift, shifting scrap. He shoots a finger-gun at me, and I flop against the railing, hand to my shoulder, a game so old I could play my part in my sleep. He blows invisible smoke from his fingertip. "Deadeye."

"Just a flesh wound."

Ma smiles as he kisses her head. Then he flips the curler, saying, "This is nice."

"Oh God." She pulls it out, hurriedly fluffing her bangs. Ma's got great hair, thick, black, and shiny, her Italian heritage showing through; if I took after her, I'd never even look at a box of dye. Pre–Christmas Barf, mine was a dead-mouse shade of brown, same as Dad's, which is probably why he keeps it buzzed short. So, this is me—pale-ish, medium-ish, a face that never launched any ships. But I'm good at bullshitting an English theme. And I make a bitchin' ham and cheese on moldy rye.

Ma runs inside, comes out heaving her big purse over her shoulder, every zipper jangling with rings and pulls. "Wish me luck."

"Luck," Dad and I say in a monotone. Ma's new job is cashiering at a truck stop out by the interstate in Brewer. She'll hate it in a week. Who wouldn't?

Dad showers, dresses in his around-the-house sweats and Dropkick Murphys tee, joins me at the table. We eat the meat loaf; smothered in ketchup, it's not too bad. "Should probably keep unpacking," he says around a sip of Shipyard.

"Probably." We glance at the stacks of beat-up cardboard boxes in the living room—the U-Haul box guarantee says they'll survive four moves, and it looks like only just—then we each go for another slice of loaf.

Packing sucks, but unpacking is the worst. It's basically life's way of saying, hey, in case you were hoping for a fresh start, here are your scratchy bath towels and the lamp nobody likes, to remind you how impossible that is. Unless you've got a million dollars. And a Milton Bradley Facial Reconstruction Kit for Beginners.

After clearing the table, I return to the stoop with my book. I'm a big reader, total escape artist, but this time, it's a prop; I haven't cracked the cover yet. I'm waiting for somebody, testing a theory. If Bree and Sage watched us unload the Penske truck, one of them must live close, with a view of the paved walkway and parking lot. From what I've seen, nobody uses their street entrances here. The real living's done out back, where the woods wait beyond the neighbors' charcoal grills and plastic playhouses. Dense woods, mostly pitch pines, those trees that don't seem to be able to sustain their own limbs, multiple amputees with black, scabrous bark.

Ten minutes later, Bree proves me right, walking between our house and the one next door. From this angle, she looks spare, straight up and down, a raw frame bulked with loose clothing. She senses me and stops dead, glancing over. I'd been mentally rehearsing what I would say, but now I just stare back at her, gripping my book.

She comes over to the edge of our unit's walkway. "Hey."

"Hey." I haven't been able to get the sight of her and Sage escaping into the woods out of my head. That was almost five hours ago. Wonder what that's like, having a partner in crime. Mine's been mostly a solo act so far. Not by choice. It's just tough to commit while wondering if you'll even be around long enough for these people to sign your yearbook. I never quite fit in our last town, Astley, over in Western Maine; I tried the no-friends thing there, and I'm here to tell you, it sucks. The label of Desperate Loner Chick holds zero mystique. "What's up?"

"Nothing." Matter-of-factly. A pause. "What'd you think of school?"

I copy her deadpan expression. "Nonstop thrill ride." She laughs; it's a good laugh, unexpected, a little harsh. "I didn't see you." Such a liar.

"Then it's working. I strive for invisibility." She glances at our door. "Are you locked out?"

"No. My dad's in there."

Bree steps back. Silence. "Well. Come over, if you want. My mom isn't home."

She says it like, *we have cookies*. This is what I wanted—I think. To know more. To make it here. My stomach knots up anyway as I rap on our door, calling, "Be right back," to Dad, who's probably already dozing off on the futon—we do that, buy a Walmart futon when we move in, dumpster it when we move out—his feet propped on a box, TV whispering like the ocean in a conch shell.

Bree lives right next door, 8A, which has a window facing

13

the side of our building, a perfect clone of hers—single-story, a back stoop for each of the three apartments it contains. She pulls a key from the little hip pocket of her jeans and lets us in.

Every light is on. Techno's pumping. Somebody's left their hot-pink Asics on the welcome mat and Bree side-swipes them without even looking. The kitchen's identical to ours—bottom-of-the-line appliances, patterned linoleum, frosted ceiling fixture—but the surfaces are stacked with cat-alogs and unopened bills, the fridge collaged with alphabet magnets and school photos. Lots of life accumulated here. In the living room, a girl in yoga pants does the stanky leg, her back to us, following some dance routine on TV, so deafened by the music that she doesn't hear us come in. As we head down the hallway, she pops, locks, drops it, and says, "Ow."

Bree's bedroom is the same one I chose, end of the hall, left of the master; her window is the one that looks out on our stoop. I'm caught off guard by her slate-blue walls. Dad says you're not supposed to paint a rental. Compared to the rest of the place, her room is a tidy, muted oasis: ecru cur-tains and bedspread, blue throw pillows, a shag rug tossed down over the ugly high-traffic carpeting, stack of novels on the nightstand. She perches on the bed, shows a flicker of impatience when I don't sit right away, and pats the spot beside her. I sit, feeling stupid. "Saw you reading the book for Hyde's class," she says. "What's it about?"

"You're in that class?"

"Occasionally." Bree reaches into her bedside table drawer,

pulls out a gallon ziplock bag of candy, and drops it between us. "Hope you're not diabetic."

"Whoa." It's Halloween candy: mini boxes of Nerds, Mary Janes, those little fruit-flavored Tootsies. I choose a chocolate tombstone. "When the zombie apocalypse comes, I know where I'm holing up."

She cuts her eyes at me, checking my expression, and a thin smile crosses her lips, which look kind of chapped, like she bites them. "What do you know about Halloween here?"

She says it the way she says everything, making it impossible to read her meaning.

"Um . . . nothing. Why?"

She completes her smile, untwisting a Jolly Rancher wrapper. "You better be ready. We got over two hundred trick-or-treaters last year. And everyone called it a bust Halloween."

"You're kidding me."

"Nope." The Rancher clicks in her teeth. "It's a Pender thing. Everybody decorates, the businesses get into it. People bring their kids from hick towns like Derby to take them door-to-door, because we have, like, sidewalks. You'll see." She lifts a shoulder. "But I don't know, maybe not so much this year. With the mill closed and everything, lots of people have moved away."

I take another piece of candy and concentrate on gluing my jaws together. My dad worked the paper mill demolition in Astley, too, and it felt just like this: like we were scavengers, coming to clean up after a town died. Bree's watching, and it's like she's in my head with me, because she says, "How come you started school so late?"

"It took us a while to find a place to live here. Everything was either way too expensive or too long a commute for my dad. Then this place opened up."

"Will you move again when they're finished tearing the mill down?"

I shrug. "Depends. My dad works for Cuso Construction—they won the bid for the demolition and everything. They've got jobs going all over New England. I mean, he'll try to get something close to here so we don't have to leave so soon, but sometimes"—just talking about moving brings discomfort back, the thought of packing up, cleaning up, that last swift walk out the front door with the keys left behind for the landlord—"there just isn't anything." I stuff the wrapper into my pocket. "Anyway. Nobody ever trick-or-treated at our old apartments. Guess they were too sketchy-looking. Everybody's mom probably thought we'd give their precious pumpkin a razor blade in a Mr. Goodbar or something."

I earn another rough laugh. Feels like such a win—you can tell she doesn't give them out much. Bree checks the time on her phone. Maybe hinting for me to go. But then she says, without lifting her gaze, "Can I ask you something?" I say yes. "Do you want your hair like that?"

I brace up, like maybe she lured me here just to give me shit. "Obviously."

Footsteps stop outside the doorway, and the girl from the

living room peeks in. Bree's little sister: same eyes and hair, except mini-Bree wears hers longer, and her style is totally girly. A glitter appliqué on her tank top, pink polish on her toenails. She's maybe twelve.

"Yes?" Bree bites off the *s*.

"Heard you talking." Mini-Bree looks at me curiously. "I thought it was Sage."

"Well, it's not. It's Clara. Bye."

I wave. She keeps looking.

Bree sighs. "God, Hazel, it's customary to say hello. Is there a reason you came down here?"

"Mom's going to be late. They're slammed tonight, and then she's going out for drinks after." She traces her toe over the carpet. "Thought you'd want to know."

Bree glances at me, nods.

Hazel tugs the drawstrings of her pants, taking a few steps into the room, her attention on me again. Upon closer inspection, her eyes are nothing like Bree's; they're dove gray, not a hint of steel about them. "Have you ever heard of FreshStepz?" I don't have a chance to say no. "It's this dance troupe I'm in."

Bree looks at her from beneath her brows. "It's a class at the rec department."

"So? Same thing." Hazel stops at the foot of the bed, blows her bangs off her forehead. "We have a show next month. I'm practicing really hard."

"Cool," I say.

She drops onto the mattress beside me, pulling one knee up. "Your mom lets you wear fishnets? You are *so* lucky. Where'd you get your shoes? I had some like that once, only they had silver sequins on them and they—" Bree clears her throat, makes walking legs with her fingers. Hazel rolls her eyes. "Fine. Forget it. See ya."

Once I hear her bedroom door bang shut across the hall, I stand to go, but Bree catches me with "The reason I asked about your hair?" I half turn, gaze trained on a framed poster print of swirling blues and yellows, some surreal starry night, ready to take it on the chin. "I think it's cool. I mean . . . that you weren't afraid to show up at school like that."

Fearless. That sounds way better than too broke to buy another box of dye, and too stubborn to ask Mom to bail me out. "Um. Thanks, I guess."

A pause. "Look, if you're ever bored or whatever . . . sometimes Sage and I hang out at the skate park." She fidgets with her phone. "Boys go there."

Full turn. Her face is guarded, like I'm the one who could do the hurting. "Boys are good."

THREE

I THINK I surprise them, Bree and Sage.

It's Monday, Columbus Day, around six p.m. They get points for waiting for me at the streetlight in front of Unit Eight like Bree said they would, but I doubt they would've hung out long. Nervous energy crackles around them in electric halos, mixing with smells of Tommy Girl, fruity lip gloss, and fresh deodorant. Whoever these boys are, they're getting the full treatment, and the butterflies in my stomach turn to ravens, talons dragging down my insides. Despite all my "boys are good" talk, I've never actually done this, met up with some like an almost-date, and what the hell made me think I'd be able to fake it?

Sage is already moving, bouncing on the balls of her feet, walking backward to face me. "Your mom's cool with this?"

"She's at work now. I'm good until nine-ish." Ma's probably still in shock; I waited until she was almost out the door to ask if I could go to the park with the girls, leaving her speechless for a full three seconds, looking at Dad, who'd stopped at the stove, a stolen forkful of spaghetti halfway to his mouth. Shocked I've already met kids in the neighborhood, I guess. Complex coded messages shot between those two, making me wonder what they say about me behind their bedroom door at night, especially since the hair-dyeing incident. I've overheard enough when they think I'm sleeping—*feel so bad, putting Clara through it again*—to know that they worry about it, our three-person caravan in perpetual motion.

Now, I tug my long cardigan around me. The temperature's dropped—it's the third week of October and feels every bit of it.

Bree leads the way down the hill to the development's coin-op laundry building, where fluorescent light glows through steamed windows. Beyond, in the woods, a trailhead waits for us, the ground carpeted in dried pine needles. Those pitch pines are everywhere, splintered limbs, trunks jeweled with streams of hardened sap.

Bree sees me hesitate at the sight of that shadowy opening. "It's okay. We take the trails all the time. This cuts right over to Maple."

We walk the trail three abreast, hands in our pockets, footsteps crunching. It's dark here, patches of fading daylight showing through branches like cutouts in a black valentine doily. Nobody speaks until Sage says, "Wait till you see Trace."

"Please." Bree hip-checks her. "It's all about Kincaid."

Sage giggle-snorts, and we all laugh. Their giddiness is catching, like riding whiffs of nitrous oxide down the trail, and I don't pay much attention as they choose a fork here or there, because it all looks so much the same: walls of brambles grown spindly with the colder evenings, tiers of black evergreen branches stirring in the slight breeze.

And then we're there, stepping out onto the fringes of a public park.

The grass is mostly dead, mowed bald in patches. We pass a covered picnic area shedding brown paint, a playground with jungle gyms and swings tossed up over the frame, and, beside that, a skate park.

It's all concrete, like a drained swimming pool with rails and half-pipes. That's where everybody is, a small crowd beneath the streetlights, perched or sharing benches or ollie-ing boards off ramps. Reminds me of when we lived in Berlin, New Hampshire, where I spent most afternoons with my best friend at the time, Nica Pleck, eating Popsicles and watching her brother practice stunts on his board in their driveway. When I had to move the summer before eighth grade, Nica and I made the usual promise to visit each other over school breaks. Tough to keep when you're thirteen and your life is ruled by your parents' schedules and whether they're willing to drive across state lines just to ensure that your BFF doesn't find somebody else to eat blue Icee Freezes and share Raina Telgemeier books with. We drifted. Four years later, Nica's a vaguely familiar profile pic on my social media feed, shrunken, without detail.

Now, Bree's fingers work the hem of her shirt, itching to tug it down. "Shitshitshit*shit*. Why didn't I change—"

"You look hot, okay? Quit messing with—" Sage's last word hiccups off as he collides with her, this boy-shaped bullet who seems to come from nowhere, catching her around the waist and tossing her up in the air, nearly knocking me on my ass in the process.

No time to shriek—she's over his shoulder, laughing crazily, carried off as if by a pillaging Celt, which he sort of looks like: six and a half feet tall, his hair a ragged carroty-red Mohawk, the flannel around his waist streaming back like a clan tartan.

I shoot a *WTF* look at Bree, but it bounces off her back. She doesn't even slow down, totally focused on finding a strategic position along the edge of the park, only a few feet from where the concrete dips down into the flat bottom, where the skaters do their thing. I run to catch up.

Bree seems to want distance from the cluster of girls who chat on the benches nearby, so we stake our own territory close enough to catch the wind off the passing skaters. There's a carnival vibe here, the smell of cigarette smoke and overfilled trash barrels, and music, somebody blasting vintage Beastie Boys from iPhone speakers.

After charging her in mad circles around the parking lot, the Celt brings Sage back clamped upside down under his big arm, letting go every few seconds like he's going to drop her on her head, and saying, "*OhmyGod—ohJesusChrist—*" while she screams like she needs saving. People only laugh and catcall, so I guess this is normal.

"That's Trace," Bree says. "Don't ask."

A girl on the nearest bench appraises me with cooler-than-thou stoner eyes, and I force a laugh, turning my back on her. *Act like you're having the best time, brazen through it*—my own good advice, hard to take. "Where's yours?"

She inclines her head slightly to the left. "Black coat. Don't look."

Lots of boys and a few girls on boards out there, hitting the ramps, grinding over the rail, swirling together like leaves in an updraft; I track pairs of sneakers just to sort them out. Vans, DCs; my eyes finally land on a pair of black Converse high-tops with dirty skull laces coasting on a battle-scarred Polar board, somehow hardly having to push off to keep momentum. His jeans won't survive another wash cycle—both knees are out—and his black wool topcoat falls at mid-thigh, a bottle of Jolt sticking out of the pocket. He slaps and scoops the tail of his board, catches a moment of air to pop shove-it, then slams down, rolling away like business as usual.

"Right?" Bree waits.

Heat rises from some magma chamber inside me, and I forget about wanting my coat, may never want for anything again, because I've just seen the most incredible face.

Not a perfect face. It looks like his nose might've been broken once, and he has some acne at his jawline, aggravated by shaving, and scattered at his temples, where I get it, too. His hair is long, the color of straw, with a few thin braids that snake around whenever he lifts off on his board. He wears a wallet chain. I can't stop looking.

And I need to, because Bree is waiting for my answer, starting to take offense, one eyebrow raised. "Wow. Nice." I sound vague and half-assed, too stunned to say the right thing, and I think I've pissed her off.

Now, Trace finally flips Sage and sets her on her feet. She whirls, pounding his bicep, swearing at him as he laughs, drawing all eyes their way except mine. I watch Kincaid, following his motion to the top of a plywood ramp, where he decides to sit on the edge, hanging his board off the side and drinking his Jolt, wearing a thousand-yard stare as the other skaters bomb past him. From here, his eyes look dark, but not brown; maybe a muddy green. Beneath his dangling feet, half buried by swirls of spray-painted initials and X-rated cartoons, are those words again: *Fear Him.*

"I've seen that." I was mostly thinking out loud, but I've got Bree's attention. "That message, 'Fear Him.' It's under the overpass by school."

"It's everywhere. All over town." She watches me, gaze intent. "What do you think it means?"

"I don't know. Like, God, maybe?"

She gives one of those laughs, 90 percent cacao, bitter and rich. "No. Not God."

Sage comes over to us, struggling to walk with Trace draped over her like a bearskin rug, his chin resting on her head, arms slung around her neck. "Hey, psycho, you're pulling my hair—" He kisses down the side of her throat, nibbling, making her laugh and wrinkle her nose. "You're so gross."

"Clarabelle wants to know about the Mumbler," Bree says.

Trace keeps nuzzling. "No, she doesn't."

He hasn't even looked at me yet. "Yeah, I do." My voice carries like Bree's, getting the attention of some of the skaters.

Trace lifts his head. Pale eyes, cinnamon freckles, earlobes pierced with half-inch stainless-steel tunnels, wide enough to fit your thumb through. I brace up, half-afraid he'll bull-rush me. "You'll be sorry." Sage lets him pull her back with him in staggering steps. "What is known cannot be unknown."

"Wow. So wise." One of the bench girls turns to face us. "Is that like a quote?"

"Book of Trace. Mumbler Three, Verse Sixteen." Trace presses his nose into Sage's hair, watching me with eyes that remind me of a coyote's, something feral. He holds up a finger. "Whoever believes in him shall perish, and never find eternal life."

Bree folds her arms. "Scared yet?"

"Nah. She doesn't get it. She's not feeling it here." He thumps his fist to Sage's heart like it was his own. "You know who needs to tell it?" He glances back, says, "Kincaid! Get over here, ya skinny bastid." Trace looks at me and raises his eyebrows. "Trust me. This dude will scare you."

I thought I had time to observe, to take in every detail of him, but he's coming, and there's no chance for me to hide myself and how much I do/don't want him to look at me. Kincaid stops maybe four feet from us, giving Trace a dimly amused *yeah, what?* look, and I can't remember how to act casual.

Trace jerks his chin toward me. "Chick wants to know about the Man with the Sweet Tooth."

"Chick's name is Clarabelle." Bree avoids Kincaid's eyes, like there could be something better to look at, and now I'm not sure who they are to each other. Kincaid's gaze keeps right on traveling, and Bree scuffs her sneaker over the dirt, pendulum-style. For some reason, she's put her crush in a killing jar. It must be slamming from one side to the other, iridescent wings pummeling the glass.

Kincaid looks at me; my lips part, but nothing comes out. *He'll scare you*, Trace said. But Kincaid smiles, his eyes creasing into these cute half-moons. "Where'd you come from?" His voice is teasing, and a little hoarse, like he might be getting over a cold.

Say something witty, anything. My words come out tinny and distant, like I'm reading cue cards over an old-timey radio: "Astley. Outside of Skowhegan." Nice.

"New blood," says Trace.

"Fresh meat," says one of the bench girls, and somebody wolf-howls.

"It's sad, you coming here." Kincaid takes me in, his smile fading. "Now you've got no chance."

No chance. Like he read it in my tea leaves or the lines of my palm. "Why?"

"Because he only takes Pender kids. Likes our taste, I guess." Kincaid drops his board, glides backward on one foot, never breaking eye contact. "Like . . . hopelessness."

"And Steak-umms from the caf," somebody says, making people snicker.

"Liver." Trace shows his teeth. "God, I love that shit."

"What about Gavin Cotswold?" Sage says. "Have they figured out how he died yet?"

"Mumbler got him." Trace.

"He OD'd." Bree gives Trace a withering look. "He went out in the woods, got fucked up, and died. His own mom thinks so."

"I heard the animals didn't leave enough of him behind

to be sure," Trace says. Then, to Kincaid, "Tell her about the first boy. Ricky Whoever."

"Sartain. Ricky Sartain." Behind Kincaid, most of the activity has stopped, everybody pulling up some concrete to listen. He's holding court, a storyteller who knows his audience. "It all started, like, twenty years ago. Kid went missing two days before they found him on the banks of the marsh, way out by the railroad bridge." Kincaid nods slowly, easing into it. "Somebody put their hands all over him."

More covert laughter, Trace's whisper: "Loved to death."

Kincaid entwines his fingers, working his palms together in sinuous rhythm. "Squeezed him, crushed him. Mashed his spine, smashed his belly."

A voice speaks up: "My mom said that kid got hit by the train."

"Of course she did." Kincaid doesn't turn. "She also told you that Santa Claus is real and honesty is the best policy and if you're good, you'll get into heaven, right?"

Snorts. Somebody mimics, "But my mommy said," whacking the boy who interrupted with a baseball cap.

"He was folded in half." Sage grips Trace's forearm. "That's what I heard."

"No." Kincaid's hands are tai chi slow. "Lengthwise."

"Stop." Bree says it under her breath; I'm the only one who hears.

"Ricky disappeared right around Halloween. That's the

pattern." Kincaid skates a circuit around us, dismounts, and slaps the tail of the board so it pops into his hand again, all one smooth movement that I wish I could watch again frame by frame. "Truth. After, Ricky's friends told everybody how they'd all gone out to the railroad bridge to smash pumpkins one night, and there was somebody hiding under there. Too dark to see, but they heard him, mumbling and yammering away."

Yip, yip, yip! I look up to see audience participation, lumbering shapes aping around the others, sounding like a zoo after hours—*Ahhh-ah-ah-ah! Mwaaa-hoohoo!*

"Next time anybody saw Ricky, he was red guacamole." Kincaid pauses, smiling faintly, but he's not really seeing me now. "Ever since, Mumbler's been around. Takes a bad kid every few years, always in October. Grown-ups have some bullshit excuse for what happened to them, but we know."

Nods pass around the circle. I watch for inside looks—they'll drop the act when they see I'm not taken in—but the quiet drags on. "What's the Mumbler look like?" I hold Kincaid's gaze, willing him to let me in on this, let me prove I don't scare easy. "So I'll know him if I see him."

Kincaid looks to Trace, again with the smile that creases his eyes into merry slits, a kid showing his little sister where Mom hides the Christmas presents. "We can take you to him."

29

FOUR

DAYLIGHT'S ALMOST GONE, stranding us in murky charcoal twilight that blurs perception in the woods. Pines press close, their smell sharp and cloying, and it's too dark for this, but we're going anyway, a small band of us, because the boys made the dare, and how could we respect ourselves in the morning without putting our heads in the same lion's mouth?

Kincaid's down the trail somewhere, wearing his question-mark smile, sheer magnetism pulling me through the dark after him, my feet catching on unseen roots, risking a branch snapping back in my face. My hands imagine finding his shoulder blades, my fingertips exploring the rough wool of his coat, discovering what he smells like. Bree is here beside me, silent, and I wonder if she's feeling half of what I'm feeling, even a quarter.

A yell, and someone grabs us both. I'm so amped up that I scream, a real girly scream I didn't know I had inside me. Humiliating. Bass laughter and a gust of Trace—draft horse sweat, shock of peppermint—as he shoulders between.

"Asshole, how'd you get behind us?" Bree turns on her phone flashlight, shining it in his face.

He winces. "Jesus. That's not fair." He grabs the phone, holding it easily out of her reach. "I don't have a light."

"Give me my phone."

Giggle. "You get so mad." He tosses; she fumbles; it lands on the ground. Not that Trace is there to see—he's already barreling off, trying a leapfrog boost on the shoulders of a boy with hair spiking out from under a knit cap and drumsticks in his back pocket, who laughs, nearly falling.

Bree wipes her phone on her fleece, swearing. "I am so buying a tranq gun and putting him down."

"Do you think they sell, like, extra-large-rhino strength?" I ask. We look at each other and laugh, and *click*, I fit a little more, in this night with these people, with Bree, whose humor is a little off, a little black like mine.

This was a real trail system once. The phone flashlight catches an occasional stripe of blaze orange on a tree trunk, left by some Ranger Rick for wholesome hiker types, and there are offshoots everywhere, footpaths through the under-growth beaten down by use. But there are bags of trash here and there, too, ditched by people who didn't want to pay for a dump sticker. Bedsprings, wadded paper towels, beer cans scattered through the brush. Sage's laughter carries back to us, and somebody's singing, or calling out a rhyme.

The stink is the first sign that we've arrived: a dark, sul-furous blossom that brings our hands to our noses. The trees have thinned out, and I catch glimpses of open area, dusky sky. This must be the marsh.

It's tidal, this place, the water at low ebb, baring acres of muddy flats fringed by more pitch pines and mountain holly, wooded hills in silhouette against the sky. Footpaths wind down the weedy, crumbling embankment all the way to the flats, though I can't imagine walking down there or why anyone would want to try.

Bree says, "That's one of the better ones," pointing up.

Above us, the ledge has turned to granite. A broad slab to our left is marked with hot-pink paint, old, faded by the elements. A three-foot-high anatomical picture of a heart, done with a brush, ventricles spurting fat drops of pink blood. The words beside it read *Bury my heart at Mumbler's marsh.*

Bree trains her phone on the embankment as we follow the sloping grade; the light catches more graffiti crisscross-ing the rocks, more paintings, a few so good they must be by the same artist who drew the heart. An interpretation of *The Scream* with green pot leaves where the figure's eyes should be; a jack-o'-lantern with a mouthful of vicious teeth and a rat lifting the lid by the stem, revealing a glimpse of a human brain inside. I want a closer look—but not badly enough to fall behind.

Everyone's gathered up ahead, multiple phones glowing in a vigil.

Kincaid leans against the rock. He doesn't hold a phone, so his face is lost, only a glimpse of his hair and the sinew of his neck visible as he inclines his head. "Here."

Everyone trains their phone on the rock face. What at first looked like a broad, shadowed crevice flattens, revealing a mural taller than any of us, maybe twelve feet high, black paint spread into a hulking silhouette.

A hunched man—something like a man, anyway—in profile, stooping as if to pick up the whole wooded ledge. Only the slightest indication of a head, the hair wild. It's the man's hands that make me stare: squiggling, wriggling fingers like a nest of eels, each fingertip a ball of splattered, dripping paint, like the artist held the spray can in place and just blasted.

Beside it, the message again, tall, spindly letters like I'd seen on the overpass. *Fear Him.*

It takes me a second to find words. "Who did this?"

"Nobody knows. Nobody's supposed to know." The

smile in Kincaid's voice is like an electrical current, raising fine hairs on my arms and neck, unseen coils warming to orange, then red. "Guerrilla art. Make your mark and bounce, right?" As he turns, that precious sliver of him vanishes into ink. It's nearly full dark now, and the only bright spots are the faces of the people holding phones: Sage, Trace's arm around her shoulders again; Bree; two girls who look like identical twins in combat boots and kohl liner; and the drumsticks boy, standing in a carolers' semicircle on the path. "It's a signpost." Kincaid's voice travels behind them, and I turn slowly, tracking him. "Here there be monsters."

"You think he lives in the marsh?"

"Some people think so. Under the bridge, or in the woods. I say he burrows in the mud like a big-ass catfish. Hibernates eleven months out of the year, then *hwwwaahh*"—he makes a rushing, roaring sound, a whoosh of his arms ripping the air—"comes busting out in October, hunting kid meat."

Sage starts the song, spoken-word style, glancing at the others, and I recognize the rhyme I caught snatches of on the walk here: "Mumbler, Mumbler, in your bed."

Bree picks it up, holding Sage's gaze as she sings: "Mumbler, Mumbler, take your head."

"Eat your *nose*—"

"Gobble your *toes*—"

All of them, in a chorus: "And bury you where the milkweed grows!" They laugh, whistling past the graveyard, all of them, but not Kincaid. He doesn't laugh; he smiles. I can feel it.

The name of the game is chase. I have foggy memories of something like it from elementary school recess, boys and girls running after each other on the playground, exploring first crushes, any excuse to touch. This is that game on 'roids.

First, the boys blow past us on the trail, taking off into the dark, whooping and yelling and being so ridiculous Bree and Sage and I collapse against one another with crazy giggles, even with the foul breath of that place at our backs, and the fact that I think none of us can get out of there fast enough. Then they swoop out at us again, no faces, just hands and warmth and boy-smell, somebody tickling my side, making me yell, "Hey!" face burning in the night and wondering, *Who?*

"Oh, it is *so* on—" With a rebel yell, Sage charges the trees, swallowed up by the night, leaving us.

Bree links her arm through mine. "This way. Hurry—"

I can barely see my feet hitting the overgrown side trail, but Bree holds her phone out and we glue together, stumbling and laughing, hearts pounding so hard it seems like they must echo through the woods, giving us away as we hear what sounds like the boys ahead. Bree switches off her phone, and we blitz attack with a scream.

Bree's braver, colliding with someone, while I waver in

the dark, breathing hard, wanting Kincaid but hearing Trace instead—"Body slam! Body slam! Ohhh"— and a mad crunching of dried leaves and brush.

"Bree?" My voice sounds shrill, and I fumble for my phone, *are you okay* on the tip of my tongue, but thank God it never escapes because I hear her swear, half laughing, to my left, which gets me laughing, too, and the danger is fun again.

She takes my offer of a hand-up, wiping her face with her sleeve. She says, "Let's kick their asses," and we're off down the trail, witches on broomsticks, propelling down a tree tunnel faster than we have any right, faster than our feet could ever take us.

FIVE

TURNS OUT THERE'S truth to Ma's old love songs. She listens to weird stuff, the Ladies of Country Gold, hits from the 1960s and '70s—think beehive hairdos and snap shirts, all about standing by your man even though he cheats and drinks and shot your old yeller dog. If my dad tried anything like that, she'd kill him.

But right now, I'm in touch with some of those clichés. Can't eat, can't sleep, up half the night trying to calm the thrumming energy in my limbs—kicking off the covers, pulling them back—can't stop seeing him, remembering five hot pinpoints tickling my side, wondering if it was Kincaid's hand doing the climbing.

● ● ◐

Still caught in the cyclone of last night, I don't really mind getting up for school today, taking a couple bites of generic frosted wheat squares before pushing the bowl away, watching Ma use her reflection in the microwave door to fluff and spray her bangs. Her work schedule is all over the place: a morning here, three nights there. The usual: her managers know she's desperate for hours, so they drop her into whatever sucky shifts need coverage.

"So, I'm on eleven to seven. Probably be late if I'm working with the same little peckerwood as last night—you know I counted the drawer and mopped by myself while he hid out back sexting his girlfriend?" I snort, and she looks over, gaze trailing to the floor as she opens that ultra-sweet coffee creamer she loves, one of the few splurges on our grocery list. "Make sure you've got your key on you, okay?" Longer pause. "You and Dad will have to figure out supper."

"It's all good."

Ma gives me a narrow-eyed look from the counter, watching me put on my sweater. "It is, huh?"

I tug my hair free of my collar, focusing on the door. Talking about boys isn't something Ma and I have ever really done—frankly, there's never been a need, since my longest relationship to date lasted three days (freshman year, with a kid who I'm pretty sure only got the nerve to ask me out once he heard I was moving away at the end of the week)—and it feels awkward now, not something I'm quite ready for. "What, I can't be an optimist for one day?"

"You?" She follows me, standing on the top step, watching me take the steps with more spring than I should, aiming for the corner of the building, where I can disappear from her view. "Not likely."

In the parking area, a black Jeep pulls into the spot beside Mom's RAV4, stopping so abruptly that it rocks on its springs, black fuzzy dice swinging from the rearview. A tall, thin woman with ash-blond hair climbs out, wearing a cracked leather jacket and jeans so tight you could probably trace the lines of her underwear, assuming she's wearing any. I can't help staring, and she turns her head to look at me as we pass, her eyes lost behind round retro shades, perfect circles of darkness carved from her face. I look down fast, then glance back at her once I think it's safe.

She takes the steps to Bree's apartment and unlocks the door gingerly, hesitating a moment before going inside, like she's afraid of waking someone, even though both girls would be at the bus stop by now. Bree's mom, just getting in.

It's against the rules to sit three to a seat, but the bus driver's locked in rage blackout mode and doesn't pay us any mind, too busy bellowing at the freshmen pelting each other with spitballs and bitten-off pencil erasers. Having a place to sit, where you're *expected*—this, I could get used to.

Sage produces essentials—lip gloss, a bag of chocolate-covered espresso beans—and we rotate them, Bree talking rapid-fire, everything good between us now that we're a team, raiders of the dark, the wildness of last night mingling like some exotic perfume, and I know exactly what I'm going to do at school today, exactly who I'll be hunting the halls for: "—and he doesn't have a girlfriend, I'm sure of it, because the girl everyone said was his girlfriend doesn't come around anymore, and he never talks about her—"

"Ask Annaliese." Sage jots digits on math homework, signs her name in giant, swirly letters. She doesn't wear the flannel shirt today; Trace must've reclaimed it. "They talk sometimes. She'd know."

"She hates me. All those girls do. Which is fine." I catch Sage's tolerant eye roll as Bree crunches the last bean in her molars, flicks the bag to the floor. "I followed him once." My attention jerks back, and Bree smiles, a slow expression. "From the skate park."

Sage angles herself against the window. "How did I not hear about this?"

"Because I didn't tell you. It was this summer. One of the times you went in the woods with Trace." Hint of accusation. "Figured, why not." Bree sinks back against the seat, watching her own reflection in the bus driver's circular spy mirror mounted up front, her lashes lowered. "It started raining, like this warm rain, and everybody left. But he stayed.

He was soaked, all his clothes and everything, streams running off his hair. Then he skated down Maple. Just coasting, you know?"

"What's his house like?" I picture a split-level ranch, struggling flower garden out front, maybe a gnome or a plaster angel by the steps.

"Never found out. He turned right onto Summer, picked up his board, and cut through somebody's backyard. There's a path worn through there, like kids do it all the time. When I came out on the other side of the garage, he was gone."

Sage snorts. "He saw you stalking him and gave your ass the slip."

"He didn't see. Nobody did." Bree pauses, biting her lip, then seems to come back to us. "Anyhow. Zero intel collected, other than he lives close." A slap across Sage's bare arm, startling her. "Don't you dare tell Trace."

"Like I would." Sage settles back, saying under her breath, "Even though he could just *tell* us where—"

"No. Let's find out on our own." I look between them. "We must get this information."

Bree nods. "Must."

"So, he didn't grow up with you guys?"

"He moved here . . . four years ago?"

Sage thinks. "More like three. He's older. A senior."

"Is Kincaid his first name or his last?"

Bree grins. "I'm not sure. Even the teachers call him that."

"That's so *weird*."

"I know." And we're giddy.

There's a soft sniff behind us. Bree stiffens, rises to look over the back of the seat, ignoring the driver's voice, worn to sandpaper, *face front face front*. "How long have you been back there?"

"Just a couple seconds." Hazel's defensive. I look around the edge of the seat and find her pinned by Bree's stare, a blue-mascaraed friend seated beside her, smiling nervously around a nibbled hangnail. "We didn't hear anything."

"Then how do you know there was anything to hear?" Without breaking eye contact, Bree slides slowly back onto our seat. "Curiosity killed the cat, Hazel Mae."

"Satisfaction brought him back."

"No, it didn't."

In the school hallway, congestion, suffocation. Bree and Sage pair off against the masses, already in private conversation, not needing me now, and I want so badly to follow. The words I should've said on the bus—*Will you cut again today?*—*Are you going to the skate park?*—and most definitely *Take me with you*—sit on my tongue like something Ma would've forced me to eat as a little kid—creamed spinach, cauliflower—bringing tears to my eyes and bitterness to my mouth because I won't swallow them. I'll just walk around like this all day, tongue-tied.

● ● ●

I'm called in for the usual guidance office meet-and-greet first thing. After two days without a summons, I thought I'd gotten out of it. Guidance is a closet-size space reserved for someone named Mrs. Mac, according to the bright quilted sign hanging from a tack on the door. I knock, hear a muffled reply.

Inside is lamplit—a Tiffany-style stained-glass number on the filing cabinet used in favor of the overhead light—and there are enough potted plants and climbing vines to give the room a cool, shadowed feel.

She's too big for the room, the woman sitting at the desk, though a large part of it may be her hair, a platinum-blond cloud framing a plump face behind pearlized glasses. She beams at me. "Clara! Has to be Clara Morrison. I know everybody around here, but you're a new one on me." She takes off the glasses and waves me in, adjusting her position at the cluttered desk. "Please, come right in, take a seat."

The seat is padded, egg-shaped, covered in geometric-patterned fabric, obviously something she brought from home. I sink in until I'm looking at her from an odd half-reclining angle, one hand still gripping my backpack strap like a lifeline.

She clasps her hands on the desk. Her pink sweater pattern involves pom-pom balls. "Let's have a proper introduction. I'm Mrs. Macintyre, head of guidance." She laughs. "I just like saying that. I'm the whole department." She rests her elbow on the desk, chin on fist. "How are you settling in so far?"

"Pretty well." I shift my butt around, trying to scoot up.

Mrs. Mac's smile fixes, not sure how to take me—probably trying to figure out how much trouble I'm going to give her, if my epic hair fail is a cry for help, if I'll be a daily-visit drama queen or just one of the faceless multitude who don't need her at all. "Are your teachers helping you catch up on classwork? I know that you came to us a little late." When you've had as many get-to-know-you meetings with guidance counselors as I have, that air of client-attorney privilege takes on a distinct aroma of bull. If I mentioned that, uh, actually, my teachers hardly seem to register that I've missed five solid weeks of the first quarter, she'd be scheduling a conference faster than you can say *college brochure*, which she has a nice collection of, fanned out on the blotter within easy reach.

"Everything's going good so far." Bulletproof answer. Reassuring, without necessarily ruling out the possibility of us meeting again.

A little movement of her chin, a quirk of her mouth. Translation: I'm a tough nut, but she likes a challenge. "Well. I just wanted to check in and let you know where I am. My door's always open." Except when it's not? "Also . . . you should know that we recently lost a student. A sopho- more. Gavin Cotswold." She clears her throat. "There's a good chance it was drug-related." Shifts a pad of sticky notes three inches to the left. "So, don't be surprised if things seem a bit off." Her gaze returns to me. "Can we chat again in a couple weeks? I'd really like to get to know you better, Clara. Touch base about your plans for after graduation, that kind of thing. Sound okay?" I nod. My plans involve a state university, major undeclared. Right now, all I'm sure of is that I don't want to work at a quickie mart for the rest of my life, and that Ma and Dad will kill me if I don't put my grades to use. Ambition, thy name is Clarabelle. "Lovely." She holds out a wicker basket, gives it a shake, like calling a cat for yum-yums.

With effort, I lean forward. Inside are pin-back buttons featuring the PDHS Raging Elk. Hooves raised in combat, upper lip curled. Mrs. Mac smiles over the rim. "I think you're really going to like it here."

They find me at lunch. I spot Trace immediately, table-hopping, eating everyone's chocolate pudding. *Bang* onto a stool, talking while he shovels, plucking the plastic cups from every reachable tray, then moving on to the next empty seat before his victims know what hit them. He demolishes both freshman tables in under five minutes; by the time he reaches the upperclassmen, the pudding cups are piled and waiting for him. His "*Yes*. You are my *people*" rises above the cafeteria buzz to the rafters.

The scrape of a tray touching down, and Bree and Sage sit across from me at the flotsam table. I pinpointed it easily on my first day: sparsely populated, large gaps between occupants, obviously the place where people wash up when the social current doesn't pull them in any direction. Sage brings the hot-lunch tray, but Bree has nothing, sitting sideways on the stool with one knee bouncing in the aisle, keeping a watch on the room at large. Kincaid-watching.

"Look at you, bringing your own." Sage takes a bite of mystery meat potpie, points at my paper bag with her spork. "Bet you've got a little box of raisins in there."

"Right next to my Power Rangers thermos." A *bang* as Trace reaches the far end of our table, palming a girl's pudding cup with a "Hi," not bothering to make small talk; everybody knows this table takes the path of least resistance. "You guys have this lunch period?" I ask.

"Occasionally." Bree looks at me. "Have you been sitting here alone every day?"

"Didn't know I had a choice." *Why haven't I seen you?* is the real question, and I'm not surprised when Bree doesn't acknowledge the subtext, instead going back to staking out the double doors. I didn't notice which door they came in, from which part of the school. Dropped in via the gym class ropes, maybe.

Trace lands in the empty space beside me, the table vibrating with force. "S'up."

"I'm curious. Do you know how disgusting you are?" Bree swings around to tuck both legs under the table, pulling a can of diet soda and half a plastic-wrapped BLT from the à la carte counter out of her fleece pockets. "Because I can break it down into small words for you."

Trace gazes back. He looks marginally less crazy than he did in the streetlight glow last night, but apparently, he spent the morning drawing on the backs of his hands with a Sharpie. A smiley face with a scribble of hair and a soul patch stares at me from his knuckles. "Look who's trying to ruin pudding day now. Little Miss Buzzkill. Is it my fault they hand that stuff out in shot glasses?"

"Pretty sure you're not supposed to ingest it by the pound, either."

Trace grins. "Hey, I'm a growing boy." He reaches across the table, gathering Sage's free hand into his. Fake out—his other hand goes for her pudding. Sage slaps it away faster than a cobra strike, making him suck air and shake out his fingers in pain.

"Do I have 'dumbass' tattooed on my forehead?" Sage bangs her pudding cup down on the edge of the table, away from him, flips her hair over her shoulder. "Please."

He leans forward on his elbows. "Why are we over here? It's lonely. This place is for sad people."

Sage nods to me. "Clarabelle exiled herself."

Trace seems to notice me for the first time, a smile

beginning. "Oh, yeah. The girl who isn't scared of the Mumbler." Did I say that last night? "You better be careful, talking like that." Hushed tone: "Has he come into your room yet?"

I whisper, "Who?"

"The man with the hands. The master of ceremonies. The *candy man*, dude, the Mumbler!" He laughs. "He listens, you know." Taps the tunnel in his lobe. "Always has an ear to the ground." Voice goes up, pastor-mode: "He shall bring every deed into judgment, every secret thing, whether it be good or bad." People glance over, then turn back to their lunches, obviously used to him. "Today's the fifteenth. Only sixteen more shopping days until he devours your soul. Will you be ready?"

"I'll get my affairs in order."

Trace flicks a look at the girls. "Still doesn't believe."

Not easy, walking the line between being a good sport and nobody's fool. "Guess I need more proof. Where's your Mumbler expert today?" I suck at sounding casual. Bree gives me a sharp look.

"Skipping, probably. Kincaid doesn't really do school anymore." Trace smacks the table with his palm, making me and my lunch bag jump. "Got it. Landon/Ivy." You can hear the slash between their names. "They have proof. They knew Dabney Kirk."

"No. No-no-no." Sage sits back. "Not that story. I'm eating here."

"Sorry. We've got to strike the fear of the Mumbler into Clarabelle. Otherwise . . . shit, she might not live to see November." He stands. "Let's move out. Cool table."

Bree almost manages to hide a smile behind her sandwich. "We do not sit at the cool table."

"*Pffft*, yeah, you do. If I'm there. Senior. King of the school!" Both fists in the air.

Someone materializes on the extreme edge of my vision, a wavering line, so tall and thin he looks like a mirage. Brown tweedy suit, mustard tie, his face a mournful death's-head. The teacher—make that Principal Crackenback, I see by his name tag—stops a few feet back from our table, hands clasped behind him. A yellow carnation protrudes from his buttonhole, incongruously fresh, like it's worked its roots into his circulatory system and is slowly sucking him dry. "Mr. Savage."

"Yeah?"

"If we could keep it to a dull roar, please."

"Yeah." Crackenback recedes to wherever he appeared from—I picture a tweed-lined spring-action casket—and Trace dissolves into laughter, leading us across the lunch-room.

Sage checks back over her shoulder. "Crack's going to come down on you one of these days."

"Never happen. He and I have an understanding. I don't blow his cover, he doesn't suspend me." At our looks, Trace lowers his voice. "He's El Chupacabra. Goat sucker?"

Bree brushes Sage's shoulder with her own, nodding at Trace. "And you're seen with him. I ask you."

Trace gives up on them and faces me as we walk, hands in the pockets of his worn-out Carhartts. "Why do you think he looks like that? He's starving. Hates what he is. Only feeds when he can't stand it anymore." A sigh. "Yep. Caught him in our back pasture one night. Like, in flagrante delicto. But I told him, look, man, we all got our stuff. I'm not here to judge."

At the cool table, we sit across from the two girls I mistook for identical twins the night before. Now I can see that they're probably not even related. It's their Tim Burton–esque makeup—white powder, eyeliner, red lips—and their matching outfits: black denim jackets with popped collars, buttons, and patches; band logo tees; boots visible beneath the table.

When Trace asks his question, the twin with her hair twisted into a crown of little buns reaches into their shared sandwich bag of carrot and celery sticks. "Dabney?" She gazes at me as she chews. "Yeah. She's dead."

Her twin swirls a celery stick in ranch dressing. Her hair's trimmed close to her head, a smooth dark cap. "Four years ago, now."

"I thought it was five," Bree says.

The first girl, who I see by the dog tags around her neck is Landon, stares coolly back. "I oughta know. She lived next

door to my cousin. We played Barbies when we were little."
Bree snorts. "Anyway. It was pretty harsh."

"Tell Clarabelle about the . . ." Trace draws his finger
across his throat.

"How about not." Sage pushes her tray away, eyes squeezed
shut.

"She was walking home from a party," Landon says.
"Late. Autopsy showed her blood alcohol level was insane.
More Orloff than plasma, you know?"

Ivy: "Probably never knew what hit her."

"Only explanation, right? Hit-and-run. She lost it somewhere between Randall Road and Wright Way." When I
look blank, Landon gestures. "Her head."

That word again: *lost.* Like Gavin Cotswold. I laugh, but
they don't. "Lost it? Like it just fell off?"

"Like severed. Not clean."

Ivy crunches through celery. "Ripped."

I watch their nearly twin faces, giving nothing away as
they solemnly chew their roughage. "How?"

"Cops said it was probably one of the logging trucks headed
to the mill. They used to come and go twenty-four-seven.
A chain or something could've whipped out and caught her
under the chin without the driver even knowing." Landon
shrugs. "Or."

"Or." Trace leans into me. "You know, they never found
the head."

"Don't say it like that. 'The head.' Like it didn't belong to anyone." Landon exhales through her nose. "Her parents had to bury her without it."

Now there's an image. "So . . . it's still in the woods some-where?"

Landon nods. "They brought in cadaver dogs and every-thing." She twists her mouth to the side, laying her half-eaten carrot stick on a napkin and folding it carefully over. "Poor Dab."

SIX

ALONE AGAIN ON the bus ride home.

I look up, waiting for the message under the overpass—
Fear Him. I don't think I'll ever be able to unsee it, unknow
it. Trying not to care that Bree and Sage didn't wait for me
after school. Going to the skate park together once isn't
exactly a blood bond.

Still. Damn it.

Instead, the Terraces wait, slumbering beneath a low,
cotton-batting sky, most everyone at work, little kids still
at school. I start the hike to our unit—feels like I'm always
walking uphill in this town, my quads in a permanent state
of lactic acid buildup—when, at the crest ahead, the hoodies

pop out between Units Eleven and Twelve on their bikes, swerving toward the center of the street.

I dart to the left, knowing there's a chance they saw me. Press up against the vinyl siding of Unit Six, straining to hear. Approaching voices, an occasional too-loud laugh, a shout of "Asshole!," trying to shock some neighbor lady. If they'd seen me, they'd be on me by now.

I peer around the edge of the building and watch Green Hood, wearing a pair of gold shutter shades, lead the pack down the hill, popping an occasional wheelie to the general amazement of no one.

When I'm sure they're really gone, I cut through the strip of backyards until I reach our stoop, rattling the doorknob before I remember that Mom's not home. I have my key, but what's inside—mostly bare walls, boxes of my books still waiting to be unpacked and shelved, nothing good in the fridge because it's almost shopping day—doesn't really call to me.

But the woods. They call.

Why can't I take the trails to the skate park on my own? It doesn't seem like you need an engraved invitation, and I wasted enough afternoons over the past year in Astley doing homework with the TV on for company, wondering what everybody else is up to. If Bree and Sage want a break from the welcome wagon, maybe I'll snag myself a bench and start Kincaid surveillance. I leave my bag inside, then walk back down the hill.

I pass the laundry building—a dryer's whumping around off-balance inside, sneakers in a heavy-duty cycle—and hesitate at the entrance to the trail, remembering Dabney Kirk and her missing head. What it might be like to look down and see a skull, gone gray and porous from years in the elements, jaw unhinged, the molded pearls of some girl's teeth poised around my foot as if to bite.

I step gingerly after that, following the trail until I lose all sense of how long we walked last night before the girls guided me down the first turn to the park. Five minutes? Ten?

I push on through the disorientation, the growing unease. There are bread crumbs here and there, signs of kids having passed this way—a hair elastic, a cigarette butt. I walk by the first blaze-orange tree marker, then a familiar pile of rusty bedsprings in the weeds, where somebody must've ditched an old mattress once upon a time. I'm on the path to the marsh.

Eventually, I step out into the open. The tide is in. Shallow, murky water, islands of reeds and gone-to-seed cattails creating a piecework pattern over to the opposite wooded shore. As I look out, I notice a large, impossibly long-legged white bird on the shore below, still as a spear of birch. I watch it, willing it to move, prove to me it's alive, but I get the feeling it could outlast an ice age.

The murals are even more impressive in daylight, painted in broad strokes by a sure hand. Other, less talented artists have contributed standard graffiti, coating the granite in bright colors so alien to this muted place. I stop, get eye-to-eye with the jack-o'-lantern, running my fingertips over the razor-toothed smile.

Instinct draws my gaze up to the top of the ledge. I spot him there, among the trees and brambles, hunkered down, his face like some brownie's or woods elf's, peering out from a mosaic of branches and leaves. Kincaid.

I jerk back from the mural. He stands, holding a low branch for balance because he's so close to the edge that bits of moss and earth crumble down to me.

He takes the descent ledge by ledge, and I think of last night, slamming through the woods with Bree, how Kincaid always seemed to slip away from us, evaporate into laughter somewhere down the trail. How we could never seem to get a piece of him like we could the other boys.

He hops the last four feet and walks over to me, hands stuffed in his coat pockets, looking taller than I remember, maybe emphasized by his lankiness and the mid-thigh length of his coat. "Found your way back alone, huh? Not easy to do." He leans into the jack-o'-lantern's face. "Makes you wonder about him, doesn't it? The one who started this. Carrying paint and brushes all the way out here to paint for the trees."

"What makes you think it was a him?" A little surprised at how confrontational I sound.

He laughs, glancing over, taking a quick study of me with

those murky green eyes. "Sounds like you've got a theory."

"Maybe it was you."

A pause, then he gestures to something at the base of the rock, his arm winglike in the coat, flashing a worn satin lining. Below *The Scream* is a small date, written in the same green paint as the pot leaves: *'11*. Which would've made Kincaid about nine years old. Clara Morrison, master of deductive reasoning.

He walks away from me down the path, but his word carries back: "Egret."

Right. Big white bird. I follow. "I wasn't sure if he was real at first."

"They're good at that." Kincaid stops beside his board and a woven Baja backpack left in the weeds. "Hold so still that the fish think they're safe, swimming around a couple of tall reeds, not a pair of predator legs. They're going, 'Doo-doo-doo, it's a normal day, eating shit smaller than we are,' then"—with a snarl, whips his fingers down, cupped into a beak—"instant death. Nature's cruel balancing act." He gives this little laugh in the back of his throat.

I watch as he takes a box of cold meds and a nearly empty bottle of soda from his bag, washing a couple capsules down. There's more than congestion affecting the way he talks, though. It's like he had a speech impediment as a kid, one he had to go to therapy for, one they could never quite break him of. A tendency to cluster words together, cram them into a space where they scarcely fit. "What're you doing out here?" All laughter is gone from my voice.

He shrugs. "Good a place as any."

"Plenty better."

"Not if you want some space. This whole marsh is a preserve. Over three hundred acres."

"Just you, the egrets, and Dabney Kirk's severed head." I'm not imagining how his eyes light up, smile creeping back.

"You know about that?"

"Your buddy—El Chupapudding—made sure I found out today."

Kincaid laughs, rocking back on his heels. "Damn, I missed pudding day? They didn't have the Friday French bread pizza, too, did they? That's, like, all wet?"

"Today's Tuesday."

He considers this, thoughtful again. "They brought dogs in. Nobody could find her. How far could a head really roll?"

"Now there's a PSAT question. If a logging truck is traveling southeast at forty-five miles per hour, and a head is traveling northwest . . ." He looks back, maybe amused, maybe tolerant, not giving me much. Not letting me in on the joke. Again. "You don't think it was an accident."

"I think he took her with him. I think Dabney Kirk is hanging in the Mumbler's trophy room right now. He's got armchair, fireplace, Dabney's head."

I watch him, biting the inside of my cheek, fists tucked

inside my sleeves. "You can stop now. Okay? I'm sufficiently pranked." Nothing. "I'm new, so you guys think you need to break me in or something, right? But you're never going to sell me on this boogeyman stuff."

He straightens, shoulders his bag, hooks his fingers under his board's truck. "That's what you think? That I'm being, like, mean to you?" He considers the concept before shaking his head, totally unoffended. "I wouldn't do that."

"Then . . . ?" I lift my shoulders.

"Did you google them? Ricky, Dabney, Gavin?"

"Gavin OD'd."

"Nobody knows that. He'd disappeared last October. They just found his body two weeks ago. There wasn't much left." He watches as I reach for my phone. "Won't work out here. It's a dead spot."

"Of course it is."

"Later. Look it up. You'll see."

"I'll be reading later." I was thinking out loud, but Kincaid looks a question. "*A Clockwork Orange.* For Hyde's class."

"Nice. 'Duality is the ultimate reality.'"

"What?"

"Anthony Burgess. He said that. Man's a visionary." I nod, hoping it doesn't show that I didn't recognize the author's name. Better dig myself a hole and turn some serious pages before Hyde drops the next quiz. "I can take you to the railroad bridge sometime."

I grab on to that *I*—not *we*—and don't let go. "What's out there?"

He smiles, slings his hand back to hang the board over his shoulder. "Make a believer out of you." He ambles down the trail in the direction of town, passing beneath the tree canopy, his coat becoming shadow, his hair birch bark. I don't move, thinking this is the end, he'll fade into nonexistence again, but his voice carries: "You coming?"

We don't walk together, but fall just short of it, Kincaid knowing the way, me moving at my own pace, not sure what this is, us together. Trying to gauge if he's at all nervous to be alone with me, if he even remembers that I'm here.

As he walks, he slides his hand over tree trunks, touchstones somehow confirming that we're following his invisible path. We've lost the trail, or so it seems. Even when we come out on a footpath, we don't stay on it, instead crunching off into brush and brambles, my clothes snagging on branches heavy with berries so shiny and red they must be poisonous. A small maple leaf, burnished half-gold, half-green, falls into his hair and snags. I like how it looks, so I leave it.

Skate park.

No Sage or Bree. I watch Kincaid hit the concrete on his board and coast over to run the circuit with the others. Not as big a crowd as last night, but something tells me it'll grow as darkness falls and parents come home from work, flushing kids out into the neighborhood for breathing room.

I snag an empty bench, pulling out my phone to see if I've got bars. Over at the playground, a weird whining sound comes from the play tunnel, where a few stoners block either end, leaning and smoking and giving each other shit.

Ricky, Dabney, Gavin. Their names googled with "Pender" bring up a flurry of articles, photos hinting at horror: a roadside ditch with rescue vehicles parked up and down it, first responders' faces bleached paper white in camera flash. The most recent update on Gavin Cotswold is from last week, a brief squib from the local paper accompanied by a selfie of a skinny dark-haired boy, smirking, eyes heavy-lidded. After a year of family and police believing he'd run away from home, his skeleton was discovered by a partridge hunter in the woods just over the Derby town line. Skeletal trauma tests are currently being run to determine cause of death.

I'm doubled over, staring at an endlessly buffering WABI-TV video clip when Landon and Ivy come up, arm in arm.

We nod. They part, Landon taking off for the ramps on a Santa Cruz board, Ivy sitting cross-legged on the pavement with a leather tote bag that turns out to hold her knitting. She withdraws a lethal-looking pair of stainless-steel needles, saying without turning, "The benches are for girlfriends. Just so you know."

"Oh. Okay." I glance around, expecting to see a flock of them standing around, looking huffy.

"It's stupid. But if you're still there when they show up later, they'll hate you forever. Word to the wise and all."

"Gotcha. Thanks." Not interested in having a pissing contest with the girlfriends, I sit on the ground near Ivy, prime location by a trash barrel and a streetlight. A metal sign stands nearby, reading *Warning! Neighborhood Watch—We Look Out for Each Other!* Doubtful; the house across the street has a *For Sale* sign in the overgrown yard. Ditto for the yards on either side. "Anything else I should know about this place?"

"Hmm." She touches her needles to her chin. "Don't forget anything here that you don't want to lose. Pretty strict finders, keepers rule." Her hair's only a couple inches long, fitted snugly around her ears, a slight fringe across her brow; I've never worn mine that short. Takes guts to leave yourself nothing to hide behind. "And the cops don't drive by much, but it happens. So, anything you don't want an audience for, take it into the woods."

Another whine from the play tunnel, and now it's obvious they have someone trapped in there; the skaters lean down now and then to peer at their prisoner, and I hear a scratchy little voice say, "You guys? Come *on*."

My video has started in jerky movements, a somber-faced news anchor shuffling her notes. Ivy's needles click rhythmically on her project. "What're you making?" I tap my knuckles against the pavement, ready to chuck my phone.

"A cat cozy." She holds it up, three-quarters of a cable-knit sack, unsurprisingly black. "For Mr. Crowley. When it's done, I can wear him."

She hands me her phone. The wallpaper is a photo of a massive tabby cat sprawled on its back in a comma shape, eyes wide and mesmerizing. "Wow. That'll be a workout."

She smiles. "He's such a snuggle-muffin. He'll probably fall asleep in there and be, like, drooling."

A horn sounds, and a long, brown, old-man car pulls into the nearly empty parking lot, shocks squeaking, flashing its brights a few times to yells and wolf whistles. Trace gets out of the driver's seat, followed by Sage and Bree. I get up to meet them, looking over at Kincaid, who's coasting the boundary of the flat bottom, gaze focused but turned inward.

Bree doesn't seem surprised to see me as she splits off from Sage and Trace. "We would've been here sooner, but we had to check in with his mom first." Her eye roll has layers and meanings I can't decipher before Sage's fist lands on my shoulder, her light steps crunching over dried leaves as she moves around me.

"Clarabelle! You came." She hands me her phone. "Put your number in. We couldn't text or anything to let you know what was up."

So they weren't blowing me off on purpose. Here's my cue to speak, tell them about Kincaid, our run-in at the marsh— but for some reason, I don't. I'm still sorting it out myself, that weird conversation, our walk through the woods that should've been awkward but wasn't. The moment is passing, gone, and all I do is save my info in her contacts and follow Bree's methodical steps through the cedar chips scattering the playground, my smile fading to consternation, gaze on my shoes. I should've said something. Now my silence feels next door to a lie.

The boy with the drumsticks, who everybody calls Moon, is performing machine-gun bursts on top of the tunnel, the others practically falling over laughing. Trace goes to them and leans way, way down to look inside. From where we stand, I see a face appear like a smudgy orb; a boy, on his hands and knees. "Deacon." Trace, all patience and gravity. "Got one question for you. What's black, white, and red all over?"

"Um . . ." The boy bites his lip, then brightens. "A newspaper?"

Trace holds his gaze for a long moment. *"Bahhhh!"* Wrong-buzzer sound; Trace throws his finger in Deacon's face. "You shall not pass!"

"You shall not pass!" The others take it up. *"You shall not pass!"* They close over the tunnel opening again and Deacon wails.

I look at Bree. "Um . . . should we do something?"

She pulls her gaze away from the tunnel. "Nah. He loves it."

"Kid's gotta learn." Trace shakes his head as he comes

back to us. Sage makes a sad face at him. "Hey, when I was his age, if I'd come down here with my little baby board? Skaters would've kicked the shit out of me and dropped my ass in the river with a couple bricks in my Underoos. We're going easy on him." He drives each word home with his forefinger: "Little kids. Skate. In. Their driveways. Everybody knows that." He literally throws his board and jumps on it. "Probably the most attention he'll get all day, anyway."

SEVEN

IT'S LATE. AND there's a sound in my room.

It starts—a tiny *tick-tick*—when I'm in bed reading *A Clockwork Orange*. The book's insane, told in some made-up language, one you can almost understand but not quite, and it's all just so damned Kincaid that I won't let myself put it down, as if it could be some kind of instruction manual for him, complete with diagrams.

Tick-tickatick. Coming from my closet, where the door stands partially open. Mouse in the wall; wouldn't be the first place we've lived that had them. Why do these things only happen at night? I bear down on every sentence, ignoring the words I don't know and grabbing on to the ones I do until meaning rises to the top, the whole thing weirdly like deciphering Shakespeare. An image forms: guys hanging out in a milk bar—I guess people drink milk for fun in this world. Droogs looking for a fight, hoodies who wear bowlers.

A flurry of *ticks*; the thing is in here, with me, not in the wall. I set the book down, go to the closet doorway, turn on the light, and peer inside.

Nothing. Some clothes on hangers, a high shelf, empty except for a single shoebox with my leopard-prints inside. A stain on the carpet in the back corner that I hadn't noticed before, like some kid stashed their science project on mold in here a little too long.

I catch it from the corner of my eye as I turn. From this angle, it looks like dead skin, a big flake peeling from the wall.

I stare, and it takes shape. A pair of wings, antennae. A sepia-toned moth, lying flat against white paint, basking in the glow of the bulb.

Its frothy wings have two dark dots on them, like slightly off-kilter eyes. A disguise, I've read, to fool predators, make them think they're looking at the face of a bigger animal. A scrap of face on my wall, staring back, waiting to see what I'll do.

I'm not above asking Dad to get rid of a bug for me—not proud, either—but they're asleep, turned in to watch a movie on the laptop over an hour ago, which means Ma was probably dead to the world by nine thirty, rolled over on her side with her pillow stuffed between her arm and head. She wasn't in a great mood tonight; I think hope's fading fast that her job might not be too awful, that the same old stuff—jerk coworkers, mind-numbing tasks, managers who are never around—might not have followed her here.

I grab a notebook and reach out toward the moth, not sure if I'm offering a ride to freedom or preparing to smack. It slides on without resistance, paper on paper. Those pantomime eyes never waver.

Dark trek through the hallway and kitchen, lit only by occasional swaths of streetlight spilling across our linoleum. Some neighbor has their music up loud, and there are muffled voices out there, probably a party.

Slide the chain lock, lean out the back door to shake the moth free. A blink-and-you'll-miss-it loop-the-loop and it's gone, part of the night. I stand for a moment, trying to make out the dark scribble of treetops against the sky, imagining the marsh. I wonder if somebody else is trying to catch Kincaid on the trails tonight. I had to leave early to get home in time for supper with Dad, Bree walking through the woods with me, the two of us talking Kincaid rapid-fire, my memory of finding him alone in the marsh glowing like an ember inside me, flickering, buried deep. Telling her now would be impossible, would make it look like I was hoarding secrets and afraid of getting caught. Bree would smell betrayal. I can't risk that, not with her.

Bang. I flinch back, pulling the door shut. Nothing more. I peer out the window that faces on the next unit, seeing a light burning behind Bree's window shade. Their back door hangs open, swaying. The music is coming from their place.

More voices. Raised in laughter or anger—funny how they sound the same through the thickness of a single wall. Silhouettes move past Bree's shade. The bass is pounding, pounding, and not Hazel's dance music, either. Something heavier, older. Metallica, maybe Pantera.

The back door is shoved wide open again, bouncing off the side of the house. A woman's voice—"What do you *want* from me?" Tense, charged silence. "Well?"

Bree says something in her quiet, cutting tone. I can't make out what.

Then her mom comes down the steps, jacket in hand, boots clopping sharply as she passes by our windows on the way to the parking lot.

After her Jeep pulls away, I stand a moment longer, looking at Bree's window. The music shuts off. In time, a silhouette forms, passing the shade once or twice before sinking to half height, motionless. Bree is sitting on the edge of her bed the way we did the other night, in her room of cream and slate blue, maybe with a book in front of her, unread.

"Tell me about Gavin Cotswold."

It's the first thing I say to Bree at the bus stop Thursday morning. She and Hazel weren't in school yesterday; taking a mental health day, maybe. Bree doesn't look destroyed or anything—actually, not a trace of Tuesday night's argument shows on her face—and I want to cover my own guilt over watching, listening, doing nothing. I lay in bed for a long time after her mom left, torn between going next door to make sure Bree was okay and respecting her five-mile perimeter of personal space. But the next morning, I knew: if it were me, I would've appreciated the pop-in. Guess I'm out of practice with this friendship thing. Before I left for the bus stop this morning, I did a quick search for Nica Pleck on my followers lists. She has a different profile pic now, different haircut. Same smile. I tried to remember exactly how it felt, having somebody I spent almost every day with, when being a bestie was once second nature for me.

Now, at my words, Sage stops eating her Pop-Tart and glances at Hazel, who's being allowed closer to us than usual. Hazel's zipped into a pink insulated jacket, completely absorbed in Toy Blast on her phone. She's the proof of Tuesday night's argument: tired eyes, no attempt at her usual starter makeup.

"It's all online," Bree says, watching a chip bag blow around the posts of the *Affordable Family Housing* sign like a half-blind dog looking for a place to lift its leg.

"I'd rather hear it from you. That way I know it's not bullshit."

Bree glances at her sister. "Hazel, cover your ears."

"But I already—"

"Cover." Hazel sighs, puts her phone away, and obeys, glancing around to see who's staring. "Did you look him up?"

"I watched, like, half a video."

"He lived here," Sage says musingly. "Unit Three. Right across the street from me." She wears a navy-blue peacoat in the morning chill, with a snowflake-patterned trapper cap, scarf, and mitten set that would make me look like a preschooler; Sage rocks it like a model in an Abercrombie ad. "Pretty sure if you look up 'hot mess,' there's a pic of Gavin. Sad."

"I can't believe he was dead that whole time. Rotting out there." Bree's expression is cool, no change. "Everybody kept saying it was the Mumbler, cleaning house. I figured the cops would drag him out of a meth bust down in Portland or something. Remember how he had his stomach pumped twice freshman year because they caught him popping pills?"

From the corner of my eye, I see green, blue, white, and yellow, cruising downhill: the hoodies. Green Hood is doing some white-boy rapping, the latest song you can't get away from, freestyling here and there, stupid stuff to make his crew laugh. He drags his heels, doing a slow drive-by past the enclosure, pointing to each girl, including Hazel, and a few of the boys, "What up, bitch—bitch—bitch—bitch—"

Bree's sneaker meets his back wheel, hard. He swivels, almost spills. Planting his feet, he whips around to face us, just in time to see me laugh. Loud.

Bree stares back at him, her mouth a hard line that doesn't quite qualify as a smile. "Aidan." His name is a quiet, condescending dare, all of us waiting to see what he'll do. "Be good. Or I'll drive a stick so far in your spokes you'll never get it out."

Everybody's seeing this, even middle schoolers. Eager eyes, laughter barely held behind bitten lips. Green Hood's sophomore status, manhood, everything's on the line. He'll retaliate, has to, but instead, some intense, Jupiter-like gravity drags him back into the saddle. One final, inadequate, "Bitch," and then he pedals off, low over the handlebars, his boys following at a distance, like maybe if they hang back, nobody will think they're together.

Cloudburst of giggles and whispers. Sage watches the hoodies go. "Damn. He's not going to do wheelies outside your house anymore."

"I'll live." Bree looks at me, shrugs. "Aidan knows Sage goes out with Trace."

"And he knows Trace will stomp his ass if he messes with us." Sage finishes her breakfast, brushes off her mittens as the bus turns into the drive. "So. Think he killed himself? Gavin?"

Bree watches as the doors accordion open, the driver a stolid, humped shape swathed in a PDHS purple sateen baseball jacket. "I think he was killing himself for a long time."

I have the closest thing to an in-school Kincaid sighting yet. I'm using the old bathroom in the math-science wing, a place that feels left over from some 1950s incarnation of PDHS: metal trough sink with rust stains; a long mirror flecked with corrosion. I study my reflection as I wash my hands; after days of rinse-and-repeat shampooing, my hair looks less Christmas Barf and more My Little Pony. In a month, I may reach Cotton Candy in a Drainage Ditch.

A teacher raises her voice in the hallway, followed by the unmistakable *clack-rollll* of a skateboard's hard plastic wheels hitting the floor, heading in the direction of the steps down to the English wing and east exit. As I look over, a colorful distortion streams across the pebbled glass pane in the bathroom door; maybe the black, red, green, and yellow of a Baja backpack. Kincaid.

I'm there in an instant, staring out into a now empty hallway, dappled with echoes like rings on a pond. Moments later, there comes the distant sound of a door closing.

Old-man car is idling in the student lot as I'm swept outside in the rush after the final bell. A shave-and-a-haircut honk, flashing brights, wipers scraping over a dry windshield: Trace's version of a subtle come-hither.

I glance over at my bus, where kids are piling on fast— there won't be any empty seats left soon—then jog over to the car. Trace hangs his arm out the window, beating a rhythm against the door with his hand, saluting in the side-view as other upperclassmen honk their horns and pull around us, yelling insults. Sage leans across Trace's lap, waving me in.

Giving Trace a suspicious look, I climb into the backseat, finding Bree, sitting with her feet pulled up to keep them clear of the fast-food takeout bags and soda bottles covering the floor. I fasten the heavy lap belt and settle back, looking at her across yards of tan upholstery. "You seem really far away."

We laugh as Trace cuts off a Prius and guns out of the lot before we get stuck behind the buses. His eyes find me in the rearview mirror. "What's it gonna be, Clarabelle? Ass, gas, or grass? Nobody rides for free."

"I do," says Bree.

"Yeah, but I'm scared of you." He honks again, throwing his hand out the window as we pass a group of kids walking home. "Okay. Quickie mart first to pick up 'the goods.'" He lets go of the wheel to do air quotes.

Sage snorts. "You are such a dork."

"Yeah, but I'm the 'only one' who 'has connections' to 'get the merchandise'—"

"Will you steer?" Bree waits until his hands are back at ten and two, then turns to me. "Sorry if we were downers this morning. With Gavin and everything."

"Hey, I asked. Not like I was expecting warm fuzzies."

"Damn it, you told her already?" Trace spins the search button on the radio, settles on some spit-spraying talk-show host having an aneurysm over tax hikes and the minimum wage. "I wanted to tell her."

I watch the town flow by like a strip of drab ribbon as we turn onto a side street: brick post office; a Chinese restaurant called Song's Banquet, with sagging green awnings and a gold dragon over the door; a gas station with old-school pumps that scroll gallons and cents past you like a one-armed bandit. Lots of empty shop windows, apartment buildings papered with *For Rent* signs. When a mill goes under, it takes everything: jobs, money for schools, community stuff. What you're left with is this, a slow evacuation, people moving on, looking for anything better.

Trace pulls into the side lot of a run-down little convenience store on the far end of Main Street called D&M, parking beside a mud-splattered Blazer and saying under his breath, "Yesss. Owen. I heart you, bro."

You can see the mill from here, a gigantic battleship-gray complex sprawling along the Penobscot, only a few telltale signs to hint that it's closed: no smoke from the stacks, parking lot a quarter full. Dad's in there somewhere, piling steel and rebar to be carried upriver by barge to a scrapyard. Not breathing asbestos. They wouldn't let that happen. Somebody must check.

Trace gets into the Blazer's backseat, emerging with a heavy paper bag. Catches us watching and does a Grinch tiptoe that gets even Bree laughing.

He stashes the bag in the trunk before thumping back into the driver's seat, texting somebody as he says, "We get pulled over, they can't search the vehicle without cause. So don't flash your piece at 'em, Bree-Bree."

She looks out the window. "As long as you hide the crack you're obviously on."

We pull back onto Main Street and hang a right. Sage glances at him. "Uh, babe? Where are we going?"

Trace starts whistling: loud, exactly on pitch, like somebody's grandpa. The tune might even be "Moon River."

"Perfect Street. Am I right?" When he slides Sage a sidelong look, she sighs, folding her arms. "There's no point."

"What? I want to take a nice drive through a nice neighborhood. Don't you think that sounds nice?" But he's distracted, focusing on our destination, what turns out to be a simple left onto an average street.

The sign actually reads *Prefect Street*—but it *is* perfect, a slice of small-town Americana, oozing white clapboards and lemonade porches and two-car garages. Everybody has real curtains—no bedsheets or towels tacked up to block the light like you sometimes see in the Terraces. We're all hushed as Trace rolls along at five miles per. No reason to hurry; the street's dead. A few mom-mobiles in driveways, most everybody else at their nine-to-fiver, I guess, their kids at football or soccer practice.

Sage presses the tip of her nose to the window. "I bet everybody here has a washer and dryer. No hauling laundry bags around." Pause. "Bastards."

"You know who lives on this street?" Trace, suddenly incensed. "That toolbox Spicer. Assface Spicer."

"Good name," I say. "'I dub thee Assface.'"

"Freakin' chumbait turned me in for putting plastic wrap over the locker room toilets and making Nick Humboldt piss on his new Jordans. Goddamn it."

"Did you do it?" I say.

"Obviously. But he didn't have to say anything." A long silence, broken again by Trace: "See, now, *that* is wrong."

We've come to a full stop in front of a house like the others, a small porch with rocking chairs, pots of mums. "You can't put them out there naked." He's staring at the pumpkins on the steps, scraping his thumbnail musingly across his chin. "The whole point of pumpkins is making jack-o'-lanterns. The whole point of making jack-o'-lanterns is smashing them. What the hell's the matter with these people?" He releases a pent-up breath. "I really want to steal one now."

Sage glances over, checks his expression, looks back at the houses with a soft laugh. "Mumbler's gonna get ya."

"I'll do it," Bree says.

"The Mumbler"—Trace cups the back of Sage's neck, rubs the muscles there—"would pin a medal on me."

"I said, I'll do it," Bree says.

Trace locks eyes with her in the rearview. Bree unbuckles her seat belt, shoves the straps aside. Drawing six guns.

His gaze goes to the driveway: no car, but the garage door

is closed. "Okay," he says. "Let's see it."

Bree shoves her door open, sprints around the tailgate, up the steps, and grabs the first pumpkin she sees. A second's hesitation, then she bundles the other four into her arms, a huge load she can barely see over, almost dropping them as she runs for the car.

I make room so she can spill into the backseat, pumpkins tumbling all over the floor as Trace stomps the gas and we sail off down the street, cab full of our disbelieving laughter. Bree's pretty like I've never seen her, laughing so hard she can't breathe, released.

EIGHT

IT'S WILD NIGHT, Thirsty Thursday, and the drinking starts as soon as we get to the skate park, tiny fifty-milliliter bottles of Fireball Cinnamon Whisky sold at a slight markup from Trace's brown bag in exchange for crumpled ones and fives. Bottles vanish into pockets, cup easily inside hands, the bloodred demon on the label breathing flame down everyone's throats but mine, so I'm digging in my backpack for change even though I know I've got supper with Dad in a few hours. Just want to blend, and it's not like I'm planning on getting sloshed or anything.

Bree gets two bottles on the house for her badassery with the pumpkins. Trace makes the story huge, larger than life, while Bree bites back a smile and shakes her head. We're notorious, trumping the girlfriends and their bench; everybody can get behind bashing the Perfects on Prefect Street.

Kincaid is here, doing his pendulum thing on the halfpipe, hair and baggy jeans and wallet chain rising and slapping like sailcloth. He slows to listen to our story, then hops off his board, waiting until the rest of the crowd has bought their demons to get one for himself.

Kincaid looks at Bree. "You stole pumpkins?" *Sheer delight* sounds so cornball, but his voice is full of it. Bree reddens and glances down. "Can I see?"

Trace opens his car door, showing him the backseat. When Kincaid straightens up from the cab, he's wiping his mouth on his hand, post–Fireball nip. "How the hell did you carry all those?"

Bree shrugs. "Wasn't that hard." At least this time she lets her expression warm a little, like a smile could happen. I don't get it; when Kincaid's around, my insides throw a holiday, big-city Chinatown-style, all swirling colors and lights and firecrackers. I can't even hide it. At this point, her crush must be nearly dead inside that killing jar, twitching. Going dark.

I slap my pile of coins into Trace's hand. "One, please."

He gives a mock-solemn shake of his head. "Weak, Clarabelle. So weak." I feel like an ass, but at least the focus has shifted my way instead of hovering between Bree and

Kincaid, who's probably wondering why the Pumpkin Thief hates him so much.

I glance at the street, then crack the seal on my bottle, hoping no one will be able to tell that I've only ever tried sips of my parents' beer and wine before. I've overheard so much party bragging at the schools I've gone to—who got wasted, who got laid, whose parents don't have the slightest clue— that it feels like about damn time I make a story of my own. The first swallow leaves a trail of fire down my throat, a taste like Red Hots and rubbing alcohol. I wince, but nobody's looking—the boys are unloading the pumpkins, lining them up on the car roof according to size.

Trace takes out his folding clip knife, opens the serrated blade. "This sucker's mine." *Thok*, drives it up to the hilt in the biggest pumpkin, splattering juice.

They're hack-and-slash jobs, the five jack-o'-lanterns staring back at us. Eight of us went into the trees to carve, with only two knives between us—Trace's and Moon's—so a lot was done by hand, cringing as we tossed away slimy, stringy guts, clearing gristle and seeds from eye sockets and gap-toothed grins until they leer or wink or make O's of surprise.

We're all buzzed, and it's nice. Nobody's reeling around, barfing, like so many of these stories end. I drained my bottle, even though it was gross, and now I'm wrapped in a warm, cinnamon-hazy quilt, layers of downy filler insulating my brain against things like awkwardness and worry—making this possibly the most fun I've ever had in my life. Giggling with Bree and Sage, flicking seeds at the boys, whispering about Kincaid, how cute it is that he takes his pumpkin carving so seriously, making a way better face than any of us, full of character, with a nose and eyebrows and everything, smoothing the edges with his fingertips.

Trace snaps a slim branch off an oak and whittles one end into a point, stabbing it through the bottom of a jack-o'-lantern, hefting it over his head. "Check it out. Vlad the Impaler, Vegetable Edition."

Kincaid grins slowly. "Staked on the castle gate as a warning to other gourds."

"Obey or—be carved with a kitty-cat face? Holy lameness, Ivy." Trace aims a kick at her creation, whiffing just a few inches shy. "That's not scary."

"So?" She cradles it to her, stroking the lid. "Black cats are totally Halloween-y."

Kincaid stands. "We need candles." Is it me, or do his hand gestures get even more floaty and trippy when he's been drinking? He takes nips when I'm not looking, always slipping the bottle away just as I turn. "We'll need light on our pilgrimage."

Pilgrimage? Bree, Sage, and I burst out laughing, Sage flops onto her back in the dead leaves to catch her breath, saying, "Where are we going?"

Kincaid's watching me. And like that, I know.

● ● ◑

We wait until around five thirty—twilight—to start our journey. Almost everybody from the skate park joins us. One of the holdout girlfriends, abandoned on her bench, calls, "It's too early for jack-o'-lanterns," but we ignore her.

Because the boys are coming with us.

The last bit of orange sunset peeks through knotted tree branches as Trace leads the way with Sage and the Jack on a Stick, its mouth glowing with a key-chain flashlight I had in my backpack. The rest of the jack-o'-lanterns are dark, cradled in our arms, grinning secretively down at the path.

"Call him," Bree says to me, almost done with her second demon. She drinks like you'd expect, fast, direct, swallowing like it's an assignment. "You won't have reception in a second. Tell him you're hanging with Sage and me and you'll be a little late."

My phone feels heavy in my pocket. "Well, I'm supposed to make supper tonight. My mom's working." Given that Dad always gets out late, I've got maybe half an hour before I need to be home. Kincaid said it takes a while to reach the railroad bridge, like over twenty minutes.

"You want to go home smelling like alcohol?" She finishes the bottle, flips it into the bushes, her face angled away from me. "He's an adult, isn't he? I think he can cook his own frozen pizza." Feels my look, relaxes her tone a bit. "I mean, right?"

I make the call, the boy in front of me giving me this dirty look, like I'm the only one here with parents who expect them to check in sometimes. Dad's voice mail saves me, his message crackly and distant, barely reaching me out here, like I'm launching off in a lunar probe or something. I keep my voice as low as I can, hoping he won't pick up on my buzz. "So, I'll be home by nine . . . hope that's okay"— pause, feel Bree listening—"love you, see ya." End call. We always say *I love you*—on the phone, before bed; Ma's really big on that. I don't care how babyish Mr. Staring Problem thinks it is.

Bree looks straight ahead as I tuck my phone away, holding our jack-o'-lantern in my other arm. My hands still radiate that gone-over-pumpkin stink, no matter how many times I wipe them on the grass. "Do you know how to make GIFs?" Maybe not the best icebreaker ever, but I need to say something to melt whatever's frozen into the space between us just now. "Because we need one of Kincaid's smile. The eye-crinkle thing? So we can watch it on repeat."

The corner of her mouth moves. We're okay. I think.

Our group passes through the marsh, where the sky opens up to our right, the horizon streaked with lavender and flame. The giant Mumbler mural—*Fear Him*—lies in wait, fingers lashing across the rock, face a maddening blank. The path slopes down, growing wetter, muckier, shoulder-high cattails everywhere, flower spikes gone to seed like heavy lumps of brownish wool.

It takes fifteen minutes of following the footpath along the circumference of the marsh, hopping puddles, skirting places where the salt tide rises over the trail, until we're hiking, up, up, into the trees, people complaining about tired legs and sore feet, spitting out their cigarettes or Juicy Fruit.

Then the bridge is there, three arches in silhouette against the vibrant sky.

I follow the rest of them over the rusty railroad tracks leading to it, where the ties have crumbled into loose chunks. The bridge is made of stone—I didn't expect that—big granite blocks spanning a seventy-foot space between landmasses, where water streams through the dark arch tunnels, churning yellow foam.

There's a steel guardrail along either side, a small concession to anybody crossing on foot. The gaps between posts are so wide anybody but maybe Trace would tumble right through if they lost their footing.

It's more than a bridge, though: it's a shrine. Candles have been burned all down the length of the stone ledge on either side, streaks of wax hardened into shiny pools that splinter at the pressure of a foot. Broken beer-bottle glass here and there, and lots of candy wrappers, some stuck in the wax, others scattering in the breeze. The graffiti here is different—sexual, ultra-graphic. Guy parts, girl parts, scrawled requests for things, one picture that looks like it was drawn by a fourth grader copying from *Hustler*. I ask, "When was the last time a train ran through here?" just so nobody catches me blushing.

Kincaid tucks his pumpkin under one arm and leans on the railing. "Maybe twenty years ago. Before the state turned this into protected land. People used it as an excuse for what happened to Ricky, so it must've been running back then."

Trace lays his pike down and sweeps Sage off her feet, spinning her, making her shriek. "Time to check out the ol' swimming hole!"

When he sets her down, she smacks him across the chest. "Dick! Don't do that!"

"Come on, like I'd really let go."

"Uh, yeah, you really would."

He palms the top of her head, pulling her against him in a hug. "I'm not going to throw you down there with the ghost of Ricky Sartain, all gutted and ripped up—" He laughs as she beats him; then he calls in a falsetto, "Helll-ooo, Mumbler? Hungry, dawg? Got something for you—" With his free hand, he grabs Moon by the back of the neck, mimes heaving him over the side. Both boys bust up laughing, throwing punches at each other, shoving.

Ignoring all of it, Kincaid balances his jack-o'-lantern on the railing and takes a couple slow steps back, his face totally still, studying how it looks against the dusky backdrop. He still has a cold—I can see it in the glassiness of his eyes, hear him sniff now and then; skating around outside all the time probably makes it tough to shake. After a minute, everybody notices him and follows suit, the laughter dying down to a few stray giggles, staggering their jack-o'-lanterns along the railing so that the carved faces stare back at us in a row. I'm aware of Kincaid's gaze on me, and the humiliating word for a girl part spray-painted just beneath my jack-o'-lantern, which I didn't notice until right now. My face gets even hotter.

"Make the offering, guys," Kincaid says quietly. Everybody reaches into their pockets like they knew this was coming, and I think of the candy wrappers hardened into the wax, evidence of other supplicants, other pilgrimages.

Bree produces some Jolly Ranchers, a half-pack of gum; Landon and Ivy have caramel creams, Starlight mints; a girl whose name I don't know has a travel-size tube of Tylenol, cold sore treatment. It all goes into the pumpkins, stuffed under the lids, pushed in through the mouths so that wrappers poke out through uneven teeth.

Kincaid surveys the scene, says again, softly, "There should be candles."

I've got nothing in my pockets but the dust of some long-ago cough drop. A second of panic, then Kincaid is there, pressing something into my palm without drawing attention. A plastic spider ring, the kind you get from a treat bag at a little kid's Halloween party. I take it, still warm from his hand, and push it through my pumpkin's eye socket.

"They're just going to rot." Bree hugs herself, sounding a little wistful. "They never last once you carve them."

"Then you can steal us some more." Kincaid smiles, and I'm pretty sure her night's just been made.

Trace and Sage start it, the separating. People pairing off, splitting from the group like gauzy tissue caught in the wind. Footsteps moving over stone; hands slide down arms to link fingers. I see Landon and Ivy slip through the trees at the opposite end of the bridge, a few other shadows moving together in the same direction. Bree and I turn back, the way we came, slow footsteps speeding up, turning to a run.

Tonight, it's hide-and-seek instead of chase, a silent, creeping game. I think I'll be okay even when Bree chooses her own path; I can do this myself. Everybody except maybe Kincaid must feel lost out here. I crouch for a while behind a thicket, listening to other sneaking footsteps moving around me, a cry and a wild giggle as somebody gets pounced on.

I hide until I'm stiff and chilled, then turn on my phone flashlight and move on, half hoping Bree will find me even though I think it's every woman for herself in this. I keep going, following the slope of the forest floor, hiding behind a tree here and there.

When I finally stop, I'm not sure where the path is. I've lost track of time. Maybe nobody's looking for me, or they think I gave up, went back to the park on my own.

It hits me then, wandering alone in these dead-kid woods. My Fireball bravado fades to cold, damp, the feeling of sulfurous mud sucking at my shoes. I've strayed too far down the slope—this is turning into salt flats—and I start to run, wishing I could text *where r u guys*, but it wouldn't send, and what could they even say? *In woods. U?*

Shadow trees, brambles, my hair snagging on a branch and ripping loose, sticky with pitch. I see my clueless face in grainy newsprint, maybe sophomore year's school picture, caught in a permanent blink, *A junior at Pender District High School, Morrison was last seen in a nearby salt marsh* captioned beneath, just another footnote in the news anchor's nightly spiel. I could scream for help; the couples who crossed the bridge might hear. Or call Sage's phone, interrupting her make-out session with Trace so I can whimper about being lost? I'd rather sleep in the mud.

I crash into a clearing so suddenly it scatters all thought.

I've reached the banks, the water so close and so wide that all I can do is stare at the tiny ripples threading the surface, the steely color it takes on in the twilight, something so separate and industrious about it, this living thing that doesn't give a damn about me or my problems. To my left, I can see the bridge, quite a distance away now, three black arches crowned by the silhouettes of our jack-o'-lanterns.

I'm surrounded by cattails. They jog the memory of the egret, tall and reed-thin. Something not quite right about those spindly legs, the curved beak tucked to its breast, the eyes like beads of volcanic glass.

I turn slightly, and it's there: tall, dark egret shape, the head cocked in study of me. I jolt, flashes of thought (*egret—Mumbler—run*) slamming through me, but my feet are rooted, and I nearly fall.

"It's okay." Kincaid's voice. Couldn't mistake it for anyone else's. The egret-thing comes over, long legs, slow steps. Adrenaline won't quite let me believe it's really him yet. "Did I jump you?" He doesn't sound sorry.

"Yeah." My heartbeat's still in my ears.

"Everybody else went that way." He gestures vaguely down shore in the direction of town.

"I kinda figured." He doesn't speak for a moment, and I shift my feet, or try to, sunken in the mud up to my shoelaces, wanting to dislodge myself without being obvious. "Did you come looking for me?" Something in me leaps at that, but I hate the thought of him witnessing my crazy lab-rat-in-a-maze route through the trees.

A shrug. "It can get dangerous out here, if you don't know where you're going. You know how to swim, right?"

"Doggy paddle."

"That works. But everything looks the same. You can get

turned around pretty easy, and if you panic, and end up in the water . . ." Soft laugh. "Glub, glub."

I force a laugh, too, managing to get a foot free and step back. "Sounds like the trick is, don't fall in." Never mind how close I came to doing that. "I'm surprised a true believer like you even comes out here. Isn't this tempting the Mumbler? All this kid flesh in one place?" No answer. I tug the other foot free with an embarrassing squelch, saying in a stage whisper, "Do you think he's watching us right now?"

"He's out there." Mildly, like I'd asked him the direction of the sky. "He's basically nocturnal. You're probably okay if you come here during the day, but at night, you're rare steak on two legs. And you left the herd. Went off on your own." He shakes his head. "Practically culled yourself."

"Then why aren't you more scared?"

He stares at the opposite bank. "When you're scared so much, it gets to be part of you. You know? You wake up, it's there. You go to sleep, it's there. Sometimes, it's better to look it in the face. Know where you're at." His voice is like an echo of his kid-self, hiding under the covers, holding his breath, listening for monster sounds, the skitter of clawed feet over his bedroom floor.

I follow his gaze across the water again, to those reeds, the woods beyond. "Do you see something?" My voice is sharp, almost sounding like Ma when she's mad at me, but it's freaking me out, his not moving.

"Don't you?" He points. "There. In that shadowy place, by the fallen-down tree. You look hard enough, you can see him."

"Look hard enough and you can see anything." But I hold my phone up higher, trying to shine the light to that distant bank. Too far to make out much.

"Then close your eyes." His fingers circle my wrist and he draws me to him, tucking my arm under his. I've never been held quite like this before. Gentle enough, I could pull away—but I don't want to lose this sense of being linked together, side by side, his hand on my wrist, my fingers out-stretched, as if straining to touch something just out of reach. "You can feel him." I'm still looking, spotting the fallen tree, the reeds broken and crushed into a hollow around it, where there could be anything, any hidden thing. "Go ahead, close 'em. He's just standing there."

I shut my eyes. Kincaid sounds hushed, close to my ear, words running together like they do when he's excited. "You can make out his head right there, under those branches, and his shoulders . . . Jesus, he's huge. It's like he's ready to charge us, but he's not moving." A pause. "That long, scraggly stuff like moss, or willow leaves? That's his hair. See it?"

In my mind's eye, I do. A memory, imprinted seconds ago, of something blowing softly in the wind, barely visible in the darkness. I stiffen slightly.

"You can't see his face. You can never see his face. Not

until he's on top of you. The last thing you ever see." His grip shifts on my wrist, and I feel my fingers move on their own, stroking a texture that isn't there. "One look would probably drive you crazy, anyhow."

"Why?"

"Because he's something that shouldn't be. What our brains say can't be real. When you have to believe—when you have no choice because he's there, in front of you—" He breaks off, and I wait, listening, straining for what comes next. "I can hear him breathing. All the way over here. Listen. All whistle-y and dry, like—"

Cornstalks. Dead leaves over a sidewalk. I suck air through my teeth, then hold my breath, eyes squeezed shut. "It's the wind."

"Then open your eyes."

"I don't want to." My arm in the warm hollow under his, the only thing keeping me from running. "I don't want to see."

"He sees you. He smells you. Us." Kincaid's grip tightens, but his voice is soft. "I wonder what he's waiting for."

"Clarabelle!" The call echoes down through the trees, and my eyes snap open, faced with the hollow of darkness across from us—a tree, some reeds, some shadows—then I'm leaving, crunching back through the overgrowth in the direction of the voice, my skin alive with gooseflesh, feeling the nighttime chill all at once now that I'm unlocked from him.

I don't wait to make sure Kincaid is following, but I hear his footsteps, behind me, to the right, like he's only there to see that I don't get lost again. Like he would've stayed on that bank alone, staring down his made-up monster in the darkness. A fresh wave of gooseflesh washes over me, and I walk even faster, calling, "Here! Coming!" the next time the searchers shout my name.

NINE

WE DON'T TALK with the others around. I go over to Bree and Sage, and Kincaid fades back in with the rest, the charge built between us on the banks returning to the atmosphere, leaving no proof it ever existed except for a numbness in my left arm, a minor loss of circulation, like he's still holding it, my senses still full of the marsh and an unseen something that was probably, almost certainly, nothing.

Bree sent everybody out to look for me when I didn't end up back on the main trail; now they're all asking me questions as we reach the park, telling their own versions of when and how I must've gotten lost, nobody laughing at me like I'd expected.

Trace digs for his keys. "You girls want a ride?" Not making a big deal of the fact that the night is obviously over for me, that the last thing I want to do is set foot on those trails again to walk home.

Sage rides shotgun, Bree and I climb in back. As Trace starts the engine, I look out the windshield and see Kincaid sitting on top of the jungle gym, watching us, arms draped loosely around his bent knees, the center vent of his coat hanging like a pair of folded crow wings. One hand grips his opposite wrist; he's still holding me.

Everything I'm feeling—guilt, relief, some sense of a lost chance I'm not even sure I wanted to take—hits me at once, and I rest back against the seat, just grateful for the warmth pumping from the heater and the fact that these guys aren't the type to force small talk.

When we pull into our lot at the Terraces, Sage turns, giving a buh-bye wave. "Sweet dreams, girlies." She looks at Bree, nods to me. "Keep an eye on her. No more search and rescue tonight."

As soon as they back out into the street, Bree says, "Did Kincaid find you?" The words burst out in a rush, contents under pressure.

I hesitate—brief, but there—hearing his words again: *when you're scared so much, it gets to be part of you.* "Yeah." Again, time's eating my chance to tell her about standing with Kincaid on the banks, about seeing the Mumbler with my eyes closed. Even though Bree and I are in this crush together, on this odd-duck boy who makes monsters out of shadows and marsh woods, I feel my fist tightening on this night, this memory, and know that I'm not ready to share. Not until I know what to make of it myself.

"What did Kincaid say? Did he ask if you were okay or anything?"

"Kind of." She keeps looking and I shrug. "You know. In Kincaid-speak."

She laughs at that, a relief. "Lucky slag."

"That's my name."

We start down the walkway. "So how did you not fake a sprained ankle or something and make him carry you?"

I watch my feet. "I'm not sure he could. He looks sort of . . . malnourished, I guess?"

"Yeah. His parents must've really slacked on the Flint-stones vitamins." She nods to the next unit. "Come over. We've got ramen and stuff."

I shrug okay, even though passing the lit windows of my apartment makes me a little lonesome for our sparse living room. Dad's home, probably checking to see if we've got anything worth snacking on.

Bree no sooner kicks the pink Asics against the wall than we see Hazel, sitting on the kitchen floor, a blanket tucked around her legs. Crying.

Phone in hand, she stands, swiping at her nose. "Where were you?"

Bree doesn't answer right away. "Doing stuff. What's—?"

"You're supposed to text! If you're going to be late, you're supposed to text, or call, or something!"

"It's not even seven thirty yet—"

"I don't care." Hazel sniffs, eyes wet, accusatory. "She still hasn't come home. I left a message and she hasn't called back."

"So?" Bree shuts the door with a single push, gaze focused on her sneakers as she pulls them off without bending, toe prying heel. "She probably decided to work a double or something. Not like she doesn't know her way back here."

Hazel shakes her head, lips pressed together, then turns and goes down the hall, her hair bouncing across her back. Bree stares after, listening to the sounds of drawers opening, things being slammed around; then she follows, with me trailing behind.

Bree goes into Hazel's room—blindingly pink, spontaneous princess combustion—watching her sister dump clothes into her dance bag. "What're you doing?"

Hazel keeps packing. "Going to Dad's."

"No. You're not." Deadly precise diction.

"At least he comes home! And makes supper and does dishes and stuff!"

"Two days a week, Hazel. Saturday and Sunday he can keep his shit together long enough to remember you're alive, and you want to go running to him?"

"Well, you can come, too!"

"I'm not going there!" Bree's shout makes my shoulders

jump involuntarily; it rips out of her, foreign from those controlled lips.

Hazel keeps her gaze down, reaching back for more clothes. Bree yanks Hazel's hand from the drawer, pulls the bag away, throws it.

Hazel sobs, shoving at her, and Bree uses her off-balance attempt to force Hazel back onto the bed so hard the springs shriek— "*Bree*," I hear myself say, starting forward—

But Bree doesn't hit her. She pulls Hazel into a sitting position, gripping her upper arms, and gets in her face, speaking low and fast: "You cannot go to Dad's. Even if you called him for a ride, he probably wouldn't come. He works nights, and it's a long drive. So forget it."

Hazel weeps, her shoulders shaking, hair falling into her face. I step forward, sick with how much I want to help. Bree stares at her, letting seconds tick by, then reaches over and pulls a handful of tissues from the box on the nightstand, holding them under Hazel's nose, no softening in her expression. "Blow. Before you drown."

After a stubborn moment, Hazel takes them, making a couple delicate honks before she tries to speak. "You guys are *never* home. If I'm not at dance or Jasmine's, I'm stuck here by myself, and it sucks."

"So hang out at Jasmine's more. Her mom loves you. She won't care."

"I don't want to be there more! I want to be home." I get

what she's saying, but Bree sinks onto the bed with deliberate slowness, like she's barely keeping her frustration in check. "Will you *please* call Mom, please?" Hazel asks. "Say you're sorry, and maybe she'll come back."

"Hazel, I promise, she's either working or at one of her friends' houses. She will be. Home. Later." Bree exhales through her nose, studying her sister's slumped posture, her little bird-bone clavicles jutting against the scoop neck of her T-shirt. "Maybe it would be okay if you came with me after school. Sometimes. Not every day."

Hazel sniffs, glancing over. "I thought you said I'm not old enough."

"You're not. But if it'll keep you from losing your mind over nothing . . ." Bree glances at me. Not sure if I should give a thumbs-up or something; I'm just glad the fighting's over, that nobody's on the brink of explosion anymore. "Dad is not an option. I need you to be clear on that." Hazel nods a little. "Say okay."

"Okay, okay." She kicks halfheartedly at a fuzzy slipper poking out from under the bed skirt.

Bree kicks it, too, making it flop over. She presses her shoulder against Hazel's.

I try to leave without them noticing, reaching the back door before I hear Bree behind me. "You don't have to go." She stands at the end of the hallway.

"It's cool. I should get home." I smile. "Maybe there's some frozen pizza left."

Bree goes to a drawer, hands me a piece of gum from a pack. "For your breath." It takes me a second—oh, yeah. The whiskey.

Dad left the light on above the stoop for me. Something flutters there, ticking against the glass globe; something big, agitated. I don't look, ducking through the door and shutting it hard behind me. Being stalked by Mothra is a little too much for one night.

I turn, and Dad's sitting at the kitchen table, staring, like my entrance has left him speechless. "Hi." Remembering my mud-caked sneakers, I stay on the mat, carefully pulling them off with one finger.

Dad's got a coffee cup on the place mat, a stack of bills, and the checkbook. "Everything okay?"

"Yeah. Yeah." I'm so glad Ma's not home: her radar would be pinging like crazy right now. Dad's range is smaller, less intrusive.

"You eat yet?" he says.

When I shake my head, he gets up and takes a tinfoil-wrapped plate out of the fridge. I think of my breath and don't get too close. "Next time, give me a heads-up if you're not going to be home for supper. I'll give you some money before you leave for school. You gotta eat."

"Okay." The words *it's not even seven thirty yet* want to bolt from my lips, but I bite down on them. Don't need an instant replay of the scene at Bree's house. Dad isn't acting mad, just not normal, like he's biting down on stuff he wants to say, too. I take the plate. "Thanks."

I'm about to go to the couch when he says, "Home by eight on school nights from now on. Okay?"

I hesitate. "All right." Only slightly defensive.

"And it's too cold to go outside without a coat. So start wearing yours." A scrape as he sits and scoots the chair back up to the table. And I still don't know if I'm in trouble.

Later, I lie in bed, lights off, surrounded by my familiar stuff. Worn-out comforter, bookshelf still waiting for me to cram it with my tired old favorites, nightstand with a gooseneck lamp. No matter what apartment we're living in, I always put my bed in the center, posters in the same formation. Making sure there are no surprises in the dark, I guess.

But you can never quite control how the light comes through the blinds, how shadows move across your walls. Because it *is* a different room, a new place, and it's all so completely out of your control.

So tonight, I use the shadows. Relax my eyes, letting the slight variations in blackness run together like watercolors, painting my memory of the marsh. Kincaid beside me, our arms locked. Was there anything across the water from us? Maybe the indication of a head, massive shoulders, but way, way up among the branches, too tall for my brain to even register what they were, because, like Kincaid said—he's something that shouldn't be?

I look, but it's all fragments, abstract shapes and shadows that fall apart when I try to force the jigsaw together, pounding tab A into slot D with my fist like a frustrated five-year-old. I roll over, letting it all dissolve into nothingness again, bringing out the prize I'd claimed from this strange night. I know what Kincaid smells like now. Cold outdoor air. Wood smoke. Demon whiskey, but only a hint of it, like he was trying to make his bottle last.

I breathe, pretending I still smell him, and it leads me to the brink of sleep, where I balance, eyelids heavy, getting one final impression of my closet door, standing open. It bothers me; I want it closed while I sleep. But I'm over the brink now, sinking, and know nothing more until my alarm goes off at six a.m. Bang my hand on the snooze button, gazing at the same angle of the room I drifted off to. Comprehension sinks in.

The door is closed.

TEN

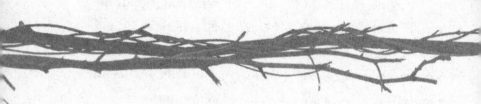

AT THE START of second period, the intercom gives a burst of nasal kazoo buzzes, like they've got a gigantic fly stuck on a pest strip in the office—"Assembly," Mr. Spille translates—and it's Friday, so the herd is rabid. None of the teachers brought their cattle prods; they're shouting, drowning in the rush, soon to be trampled into unrecognizable smears that the custodians will have to sort out later, a pocket protector here, a shard of bridgework there. I'm slammed and bumped so many times between history and the gym that I fight for sheer survival, scraping shins with my heel, stabbing my elbows indiscriminately.

The wooden bleachers are swarming, but Bree, Sage, and

I find one another like we're magnetized, heads together, chatting hard and fast and snarling at anybody who steps on our fingers or drives their knees into our backs. At one point, I see Landon sitting up above, legs crossed, foot bobbing as she scans the crowd. I give a half wave, but she doesn't seem to see.

Crackenback's walk to the podium is achingly slow, like all the cartilage has worn from his joints; today, his carnation is white. He talks for nearly a minute, with us shouting, "What?" at him before someone realizes the mic is unplugged. Whine of feedback; then his dry, funeral-dirge voice: "—ever vandalized the boys' bathroom to come forward to either myself or a teacher you trust. We want to get you the help you need." Clears his throat. "We've had another trash-can fire on school grounds. Fortunately for you all, Ms. Hyde was swift with a bottle of Dasani and the school was saved. If you, or anyone you know . . ."

Someone nudges me, and a thick triangle of paper with Sage's name scrawled on it is stuffed into my hand. I pass it to her, and she unfolds it in her lap, below the line of teachers' vision, a full sheet of notebook paper with only two words written on it that I can see: *Song's run.* Sage smiles, folds the note away.

Crackenback stands, head bent over the podium, before stiffening back to life. "Now, my cherubs, if you could give Mr. Mac your undivided attention, he has a few reminders about homecoming weekend"—bellows and whoops—"which is almost upon us."

I think I misheard the name until a beefy middle-aged guy with short-buzzed hair, wire-framed glasses, and a casual-Friday outfit of polo shirt, wind pants, and squeaky-clean running shoes gets up from the front bleacher. I can totally see him being married to Mrs. Mac. I can also see him playing gin rummy for toothpicks and keeping issues of *Reader's Digest* on the back of his toilet. He has actual notes, which he taps against the surface of the podium until they're nicely edged. "First of all, I'd like to say"—he pauses, his voice quiet—"rage on, Elks."

Dull, pin-drop silence. Then somebody—sounds like Trace—roars, "*Yeeeaahh!*" and stomps the bleachers. Everybody joins in, making our own stampede until the response is deafening. Sage, Bree, and I lean together, laughing, covering our ears.

When the storm breaks, Mr. Mac is flushed, warily pleased. "Right. Good. Thanks. So, we'll be hosting the Brewer Witches this weekend, and I hope you'll all turn out to watch our Lady Elks beat the tapioca out of them on the soccer field Saturday." Another pause. "Oh, yeah. And the football game, too."

Silence. Poor Mr. Mac. Rode the high of his opener a little too close to the sun.

"But"—shuffle, shuffle, flush deepening, brows drawn—"speaking not just as an assistant coach, but as a member of the PTA and the neighborhood watch committee, some stuff has happened at past homecoming games that we don't want to see again. No alcohol or controlled substances on school grounds. Park your cars only in the provided spaces at the athletic fields or here in the student lot. No foul language or fighting in the stands. I'll be there, of course, but so will other volunteers from neighborhood watch, and they will be paying attention. Okay? We love you guys, and we want you to be safe."

Trace's voice from somewhere, low and crooning: "Wuv ooo tooo . . ."

Mr. Mac collects his notes and returns to the bleachers, applauded only by the soft friction of his pant legs. I spot Mrs. Mac in the corner of the room, shooting him an enthusiastic double thumbs-up.

Crackenback reclaims the floor. "Allow me to second Mr. Mac. Please try your darnedest to be the soul of courtesy and good sportsmanship as we host the Witches. Not like last year. Or the year before that. Or any in memory." Finally, he raises his eyes to us, a nearsighted gaze that somehow manages to be penetrating. Sage's fingers go to her jeans pocket where the note is, her expression kept carefully blank as she looks back at him. "That's all. Back to class."

Our exodus is the opposite of our arrival: molasses-slow, clotting around the double doors, barely moving, bodies pressed against bodies. Sage catches my elbow, whispering in my ear. "Feel like Chinese food?"

◗ ● ◖

We run, frosty wind ripping back our hair. *Five seconds to make the trees or somebody'll see*, Bree told me as we hid in an empty classroom close to the English wing exit, waiting for the hallways to clear out for first lunch.

Don't trip, Sage said. *If you fall, you're a dead soldier, and we can't stop for you. Sorry.*

My pulse is cranked bass, my throat pounding with it as we fly over dead grass, the copse of yew trees ahead, the only cover from view of the classroom windows on this wing. So this is cutting. Never done it, wanted to ever since we spent three whole months learning how to hold a pencil in kindergarten. I'm scared, psyched, a million worries taking a backseat to how badly I want to be in on this, part of them, the third weird sister.

Bree makes the trees first. Sage and I tie for second, all of us flattening ourselves back against the trunks, breathing hard. "Kincaid won't come," Bree says. "I know it. We'll get all the way down there, risk our asses, and he won't show."

Sage shakes her head, sucking wind. "That's what you guys get. Falling in love with a ghost."

Bree bolts. We race after her. I can't help but take one backward glance at the school, the image bouncing with every step like the final scene in a found-footage horror movie.

◗ ● ◖

Downtown. Song's Banquet waits quietly, the lot mostly empty before the noontime rush. We pass beneath the gold dragon into synth waves flowing from a radio behind the unmanned counter. Smells of hot oil and soy sauce, walls decorated with silken embroidered hangings. *It Will Be Our Pleasure to Seat You*, the sign says, but nerves and guilt stretch two minutes into ten, so when the hostess doesn't turn up, we go in search of the boys ourselves.

Trace and Moon are at a booth in back, Trace with his shoulder pressed against the wall, one bent arm shielding whatever he's working on. Moon balances on the edge of his bench, using his phone while they talk. "Damn it," Bree says under her breath: no Kincaid. Part of me settles back to earth, deflated, but maybe it's not such a bad thing. He really got in my head last night. Looked around, rearranged things, left a closet door open behind him to let all the bad things in. I should be pissed at him, and I am, a little, but then I think of his hand, gripping his own wrist in place of mine, like he needed someone to hold on to that badly. Kind of takes the wind out of the sails of the Good Ship Resentment.

Bree and I slide in with Moon while Sage bounces in next to Trace, planting a kiss on his cheek, which he returns with quadruple enthusiasm, saying, "Anybody see you guys?"

"Just some random people downtown." Sage sits back and takes a breath, grinning at me. "Clarabelle can really haul ass. And she didn't even get lost."

I laugh, flipping her off. Bree cuts in with, "Is this everybody who's coming?" glancing back at the entrance.

Trace smiles, about to speak, when our waitress comes around the corner of the dining room and slides a few menus onto our tabletop. She has that uncanny flawless beauty reserved mostly for models in cosmetic ads; twentysomething, her long black hair pulled into a ponytail, her lips penciled red with laser precision. Her name tag reads *Daisy.* "It's you." She folds her arms, leveling a look at Trace.

"It is."

"No school again, huh."

He takes a menu. "Teachers' conference."

"They have a lot of those."

"They certainly do." The rest of us study the tabletop, the floor, the window, but Trace gazes back at her in his best impression of a plaster saint. "Hate to lose valuable class time, but it is what it is, Daze."

She pulls her mouth to the side, nodding slowly. "You're lucky I don't give a shit about your ignorance." She takes the menu out of his hand. "Buffet, I'm assuming."

"Naturally. And some of your finest bubbly for my friends." Trace teepees his fingers as she walks away.

Sage shakes her head. "If the crab Rangoon weren't so amazing, no way would I let you come here to flirt with her."

"Flirt? I'm covering our asses. Can't hurt to be on good

terms with the people who can turn you in, right? Right?"
But Sage is going to load up at the buffet table. Raising his
eyebrows, Trace follows her, and we slide out, too, letting
Moon leave the booth, jamming to whatever's in his earbuds.

"You coming?" Bree looks back at me.

"That's okay. I'm good." I start to slide into the booth.

"Don't worry about the money." Bree waits. "Seriously.
You're covered."

She doesn't elaborate. I have a hard time believing she has
the cash to pay for us both, but I'm learning, with Bree, that
if she says it, she means it. By the time we sit down with our
lunch, Daisy's back with our bubbly, soda in plastic pebbled
glasses.

A flash of motion outside the window. I look up in time
to watch Kincaid glide by the glass on the next wall, then
push up the wheelchair ramp to the entrance. Bree squeezes
my forearm under the table, almost painfully. Like I needed a
signal. Seeing him is an adrenaline shot to the heart.

I'll never get tired of the way he doesn't fit into a room, his
slow mosey accompanied with the jingle of his wallet chain
on the rare occasions when he has his feet on the ground.

Kincaid drags a chair over—a couple old ladies stop eating
their early-bird lunches to stare at him like he has horns and a
spaded tail—and drops it backward at the foot of our booth,
straddling it with his arms folded on top of the backrest, gazing in that unfocused, possibly stoned way of his while Daisy

gives his board a look, saying after a pause, "I suppose you want something."

He glances up, not obviously sucked in by the tractor beam of her hotness, which earns him points. "Can you bring some of that tea? That red tea, that comes in the pot?" He makes the pot shape with his hands.

Bree and I sneak a look at each other. Daisy studies the ceiling. "Tea in a pot. Let me see what we have." Steps elaborately around his board as she goes.

Trace talks while shoveling. "I got questions for you, bud." Waits as Daisy brings the tea, leaves again. "Dude. Eat, for chrissake," he says to Kincaid. "You're more than covered for an eight-ninety-nine buffet. Man cannot live on Fireball alone. You'll get gut rot and die."

Kincaid smiles, taking a sweet-and-sour wonton from Moon's plate with his fingers. Still hasn't looked at me, as if last night never happened. "Questions about what?"

Moon grabs the paper napkin by Trace's elbow, holding it up. "Attack plan for tomorrow night."

Trace swears, jerking his arm down, glancing over his shoulder at the old ladies. "It's called discretion, man. Jesus. The Golden Girls over there probably live on Perfect." Trace flattens the napkin, which serves as a canvas for a crude map drawn in ballpoint. Intersecting lines. A street grid. "You know in-town way better than I do." He stabs his finger at one of the lines, a row of squares down either side, representing houses. "If you follow Perfect, you hit Oak, right? Where does Oak let out if you go east?"

"Anson Pond Road." Kincaid sucks sauce off his thumb. "Takes you over the town line into Derby, if you keep going."

Sage stares at the map. "What is this?"

"This"—Trace vibrates his hands above it—"is a siege. Of epic proportions." Pastor voice, at low volume, high malice; if there was a congregation present, they'd be shaking: "Their day of disaster is near, and their doom rushes upon them."

"Meaning?"

"Nuke the block." Moon smiles, one earbud dangling.

Sage bites into a crab Rangoon, chewing with a slow and steady gaze. Trace releases a breath, tries again. "We need you guys. That's why I wanted everybody in the war room today. Got a list for you." Pulls a scrap of paper out of his pocket and tosses it to Bree. "Read it, know it, swallow the evidence." Checks his phone. "Shit. Ten minutes."

Bree looks at the list. "Why would we have these things?"

"You're girls. You're resourceful. If you don't have it, you'll find it." He gestures to Kincaid and Moon. "We're men. We don't know shit."

We girls look at one another. I say, "He's totally been practicing that in front of a mirror."

Bree eats her last bite of rice. "Sounds like a kiss-ass way to get us to do all the work."

"Nope. We have our own list. Way more challenging."

She flicks the note. "Jell-O. Really? Stick the girls in the kitchen, right, while you guys get to go out and do all the cool stuff?"

Trace glances at Moon, then back at Bree. "You want to come? Because we kinda figured—"

"If I'm making the artillery, I sure as hell want a chance to throw it." Bree looks at us, and I nod, still not sure what I'm agreeing to. "What's it gonna be? Are we in on your little siege or not?"

Trace's grin grows by degrees. Drains his glass, bangs it down. "Okay, Pumpkin Stealer. Ground floor. But no wussing out. Anybody who chokes has to buy Song's for the rest of the year, and I'll never tell them anything again."

Kincaid holds his hand out to Bree for the list. "What's on there?"

Bree gives it over without a word. Trace watches with a smug, knowing look, and suddenly it's way too hot in here, wedged into this booth side by side. Kincaid hands it back, laughing his rusty laugh. "Sounds messed up. I'm there." When Bree folds the paper small and closes it in her palm, I know what she's doing—transferring the warmth from his fingers to her skin.

"You'd better be," Trace says. "We're counting on you to bring the mud."

● ● ●

Outside into the crisp, blinding day, puffy clouds surfing a sky so clear it looks chlorinated. Kincaid holds the door for us, arm hooked through the handle, hanging off it like a tire swing as he watches traffic. I think again of my closed closet door, the definite knowledge that it wasn't right, what I was seeing; how that spooked feeling trailed me clear through my morning classes. Ma must've come in before my alarm went off for some reason and pushed it shut on her way out, I know that, but it's a clear picture of where my head's at these days, thanks to Kincaid: seeing closet monsters, boogeymen who punish bad kids for sneaking demon liquor and trying to cover it up with Trident.

I'm the last one out of Song's. I don't look at Kincaid as I pass him, but he brushes close by me as he releases the door handle, his lips near my ear—"Nice coat"—before reuniting his board with the sidewalk.

"Thanks?" It's a bombardier jacket, fake brown leather with a fake shearling collar, a grommeted waist cinch I never fasten. Not something I get a lot of compliments on.

Still crunching his fortune cookie, Trace sticks his hands in his pockets as the breeze whips around us. He paid for everyone with crumpled ones and fives, yesterday's booze money—I guess that's what they meant by "covered"—leaving an untidy stack for Daisy before she even had a chance to bring the bill. "You coming with us?" he asks Kincaid.

"Nah." Kincaid steps on his board and leaves without a

goodbye, his head angled up like he's watching the skies.

Bree whispers, "Think he's going home?"

"Probably. Crap." There's never a good time for us to follow him.

Trace holds up his phone. "Tick-tock. We got three minutes."

We run.

We cross back onto school grounds at a different place, cutting through the woods that separate it from the house next door, scaling a chain-link fence, and dashing across the field to a basement-level door. We're already late—even using every trespassing shortcut they know, it's still a five-minute run from Main Street up to school—and it's now officially two minutes past the bell, class time trickling away, our seats conspicuously empty.

Trace fumbles in his pocket, pulls out a key, and jams it into the lock, letting us go ahead of him down the dim stairway into the basement before locking the door behind him. "Where'd you get that?" I whisper.

"Office. Took it when I was waiting to see Crack one time."

As we cross the concrete floor, I keep expecting a custodian to spring to full height in front of us like one of those punching-bag clowns, but it's just a big basement with a little daylight filtering through low windows, the air vibrating with the low-grade roar of a boiler. We go up another flight of stairs to a door, easing it open to peek out at the empty English wing hallway.

Trace takes the main hallway, heading back up the stairs toward the art room. Sage and Bree go toward Hyde's English class, and I turn left, toward study hall, four sets of footsteps fading to mine, alone.

Klatts pins me with her gaze as I step into room twelve, people turning in their seats to stare. "Sorry." I fumble the door shut behind me. "Had to go to the bathroom." I feel like a complete idiot, but the girls said it was their best line. *If they give you a hard time, start going into detail*, Bree said. *No teacher can argue with explosive diarrhea.*

Klatts sniffs, nods, observes me through her triple-power bifocals as I sit and reach into my coat for *A Clockwork Orange*. Last time I read, Alex was home, enjoying classical music after an evening of beating and raping. I've only got about a hundred more pages to catch up on, but so what—I've got all study hall to read. Just an off-campus lunch. Not like I blew off actual English class or something. I picture myself trying to sell that line to Ma, and my stomach curdles. Precisely why I'll make sure she never, ever finds out.

In my pocket, something crinkles against my fingers. A lump in a plastic wrapper. I pull it out partway and see a fortune cookie. Kincaid, brushing by me in the doorway of Song's. He slipped me his cookie.

My smile takes over, the feeling of being chosen, made special, erasing any worry of people noticing the signs that I was out in the cold fresh air a minute ago, my hair windblown, my hands chapped. That I was tasting the real world instead of the stale gerbil pellets of this place all day.

Nobody looks twice. Nobody questions it.

Tearing the seal on a food wrapper in study hall is like using a can opener around a pack of hungry dogs. I wait until I'm at my locker, the door blocking people's view as I break the cookie open and take the paper slip out.

Fortune favors the brave.

ELEVEN

BREE'S MOM'S JEEP is in the lot when I step outside the next afternoon.

I hesitate, glancing at their stoop. Sage and I are supposed to show up at Bree's place at four thirty, bringing whatever we volunteered to hunt down from Trace's list. I've got the Jell-O; we've had a couple boxes in with the nonperishable pantry stuff for at least two moves now. Berry Blue.

Bree's mom is just the weaselly excuse I need to turn around and go back inside where it's warm and the kitchen smells like Ma's baked chicken, sizzling in the oven. Kincaid's fortune mocks me from my pocket; I've been having serious second thoughts about joining Trace's siege tonight.

I should've asked more questions, found out what we were really getting into instead of sitting there wondering what the hell was going on with Kincaid. But Bree. She's waiting.

I knock, sticking the Jell-O boxes into my coat in case her mom answers. Instead, it's Hazel, who says, "Hi," in a hushed tone, moving back so I can step over the sneakers piled on the mat.

The house is quiet except for the sound of the dishwasher running. Sage sits on the kitchen counter; Bree leans nearby beside a big mixing bowl and a bag of water balloons, Sage's contribution. Bree holds her hand out for the Jell-O. "My mom's sleeping, so. You know. No raves."

I've never made Jell-O bombs before, so I do as I'm told. At Song's, all this was just talk over chop suey and dumplings, but now we're wrist-deep in serious prank material. Hazel has the honor of mixing fruity-smelling powder and water; Sage squeezes the balloon necks tight to the funnel as Bree pours in the blue goop, careful not to overfill; I tie them off, dividing them between two grocery bags for easy lugging.

Bree shows Hazel Trace's list. "You probably have some of this junk lying around, right?"

Hazel looks at Sage. "Is this for your boyfriend?" The word full of import.

Bree makes a dismissive sound. "That falls under the heading of need-to-know."

Sighing, Hazel leads us to her room. Being in there reminds me of their fight Thursday night: tears, clothes stuffed into a duffel bag, Bree's shout tearing through drywall, insulation, splitting the night air. *Dad is not an option.*

Hazel goes straight for her closet, digging around, tossing things over her shoulder. She hasn't done the big clean yet, where you get rid of every single babyish thing you own, every stray doll or kitten-clinging-to-a-tree-branch poster, driven by sheer dread that somebody at school might find out you still have it and tell the world.

A door opens in the hallway. Bare feet scuff to the bathroom. I know Bree hears, but she refuses to look away from Hazel, still sifting through geological layers. It's a standoff, a turf war over the square footage of this tiny apartment, and I exchange a glance with Sage, who looks as trapped as I feel, absently snapping a hair elastic against her wrist.

A minute later, Bree's mom passes on a nonstop from hallway to kitchen, her long, tall frame emphasized by black leggings and a clinging hip-length gray tunic. She spares half a glance at us; I get my first impression of her eyes, large, ice-chip pale like Bree's, brows plucked down to nearly nothing, then she's pulled her gaze away. Nothing to see here.

Hazel unearths the last couple things we need: a Halloween makeup kit with most of the green paint used up, and a mask. It's meant to look like Disney's version of Cinderella, or maybe Sleeping Beauty. Waves of molded blond hair, shaded cheekbones, hollow eyes.

Out in the kitchen, Bree's mom is making coffee. She only turns when the process demands it, taking a mug from the cupboard, looking at the four of us getting ready to leave with no indication of anything: no curiosity as to who I am, or what we might've been doing ransacking Hazel's closet. Bree has the mask and makeup kit hidden inside her fleece, and her gaze settles on a random corner as she grinds her feet into her sneakers.

"How's it going, Faye?" Something in Sage's fresh, smiling face makes it clear that she's giving Bree's mom shit, using her own friendliness to call Faye out for not making anybody feel even remotely welcome.

Faye returns her gaze, leaning languidly against the counter as the mini Keurig machine whirs. "Oh, you know, Sage. Nothing caffeine and a lobotomy can't cure." Takes her mug, watching the artificial sweetener dissolve as she stirs, adding in a different tone, "That trash should've gone out days ago," on some closed mother-daughter frequency.

Bree looks over. "I'm the only one capable of taking out the trash?"

A beat. "Take it when you go." The curtain of Faye's hair falls, and we might as well already be gone. She carries her coffee to the living room.

Bree drags the bag from the can, another from the closet, slamming things around. As Sage and I each grab a bag of Jell-O bombs, Hazel says, "Can I come with you guys? Please?"

Bree's no is a given, but then her gaze flicks to the living room. "Okay. For a little while." Another territory gained; Hazel, as war profits.

We walk down the hill, Bree and I together, Hazel trotting along ahead of us, talking to Sage a mile a minute. "She seems okay," I say quietly, nodding to Hazel when Bree looks over. "After the other night."

"Oh." Bree shrugs. "She's fine. She just freaks out when she feels like nobody sees her."

There's something so spot-on about that; absolute truth. I pause. "Where does your mom work?"

"Lots of places." Her brusqueness punches an awkward hole between us. She speaks quickly, filling it in, showing her anger isn't for me: "Forever 21 in the mall. Part-time. She's a bartender at Carrigan's Pub, too. Most nights."

I make a small noise. "Sounds busy."

Bree says nothing for a moment. "It's really that she doesn't want to be here. She could come home a lot more than she does. She says being here messes her head up. Makes her think about Dad, something stupid like that." She gestures to herself and Hazel. "It's us. We remind her. Like, that she was married and procreated and once owned a waffle iron, you know?"

I nod, saying slowly, "An inconvenient truth?"

She looks over, like maybe I just hit that same sweet spot,

the no-bullshit bull's-eye. "Yeah. Basically. Whatever. She does her thing and I do mine, mostly. It's just"—a shake of her head—"she pisses me off. That's all."

Sage falls back a step, glancing at Bree. "Have you seen that?"

We're near the base of the hill, at the low unit numbers. I follow their gazes to 3B, where a bedroom window covered in a Bruins beach towel glows with the light of an electric candle sitting on the frame. "Deb told my mom that she's going to leave it burning in his memory." Sage sees my look. "That's where Gavin Cotswold lived."

"Ugh." Bree stares for a moment, maybe looking for signs of life, but the apartment is dark and still. "God, that's sad."

"You said you live across the street?" I say. Sage nods.

"Middle apartment." Warmly glowing windows, a patterned welcome mat at the front entrance. It has a neat, put-together look that reminds me of Sage herself. Someone left the outside bulb burning: another light to guide the way home.

The skate park has a shrinking effect on Hazel, reducing her to the size of a figurine, maybe one of those ceramic shepherdesses you see in china hutches. She sits way back against the fence, huddled over her phone in her puffy coat and a pair of fuzzy earmuffs she must have smuggled in her pocket, because Bree sure as hell never would've sanctioned them, sneaking looks at the skaters and rapid-fire texting with a friend—*OMG @ skate park with hotties*, something to that effect.

When Trace finally shows himself, darkness is coming down, a deeper saturation as the days grow shorter. The boys are more wired than I've ever seen them, Moon swinging out of the passenger-seat window, drumming his sticks down the length of the hood, Trace tossing Sage up in the air like she weighs nothing, catching her as an afterthought, walking with her hanging over his shoulder. Kincaid's last out of the car, finding a streetlight to lean against instead as he watches the park as if through a soaped pane. It makes me reluctant to go over, even though I'm bursting with the need to pin him down about the cookie, his bit of $8.99 unsolicited wisdom.

Trace catches sight of Hazel, sitting between the bags we brought. His wolf canines appear.

Bree steps in to intercept. "Leave her alone. I'm serious."

"When are you not?" He dodges her outstretched palm, walking toward Hazel, who draws back when she sees him coming, her shoulders pressed against the chain link.

I think of the kid blocked in the tunnel, the transgressor, straying too far from his driveway, and raise my voice. "She's the only reason we could find the stuff you wanted, you know."

Never breaking eye contact with Hazel, Trace hunkers down over the bags, paws through, says gravely, "Are you a helper elf?"

Hazel stares. "Yes?"

He bounces back on his heels, nodding. "Okay, then. Sweet." Finds the princess mask, turns it over in his hands. "This"—his laughter starts low, from the belly—"is mother-effing genius."

"Don't get caught," Hazel says later, leaning into Trace's backseat after we let her out at the Terraces, a blast of wind furling her hair around her neck and shoulders, her gaze on Bree. We rode over from the park with five of us crammed into the back, Sage and Bree sitting on laps so Hazel could wear a seat belt. "Okay? Promise."

Bree, her neck flushing because Kincaid's in the passenger seat, says, "Everything's fine. Don't worry."

"I'm not dumb. I know you guys are going to do something bad." Moon mutters about the cold, but I've got to give Hazel props—she stands her ground, refusing to look away from Bree. "Just promise."

"Promise. Now go inside." Bree catches the door handle and slams it shut, but Hazel doesn't go. She stands where she is, watching us back into the street, her image continuing to shrink in the side-view, small enough to fit in a thimble, then to dance on the head of a pin as we go—

—gogogo—

TWELVE

—CRUISING THROUGH THE night in our bubble of heat
and music and laughter, the greasy smell of monster makeup
in my nose as I layer it on, my reflection crammed into the
mirrored lid of the makeup case with Bree's and Sage's as we
do our faces up like death and decay.

Must be true what they say about smell being linked to
memory, because at once I'm trick-or-treating in elementary school, riding through a black velvet night in the warm
confines of Ma's car. But now it's a different car, Bree beside
me instead of family, and instead of candy, we have beer, a
six-pack stolen from the fridge of Moon's older brother while
they were stealing the weaponry now on the floor of the

backseat, Bree and I drunk-giggling already because Kincaid's here, so close, and anything, literally anything, could happen—

—and too soon we're braking, crawling at a sloth's pace into the new quiet, grit crunching beneath tire treads until we're idling alongside a curb. Hushed residential streets come into focus again, most people at the homecoming football game, semiformal dance to follow, for those who give a shit about such things. The street sign on the corner reads *Prefect*.

And maybe I'm more scared than I thought.

"Which house is his?" Moon, low, keeping one paintball gun for himself, handing the other up to Kincaid, who did some insane two-minute masterpiece on his face, a Day of the Dead–style skull, eyes bright in black hollows, teeth neon against his lips, and maybe he is the guerrilla artist after all, maybe he painted that date on the rocks just to fool us.

"Don't know. I couldn't ask anybody without being obvious. Obviously," Trace says, then giggles. He pulls the princess mask down over his face. Too small for his head, the plastic oval seems to hover in the darkness, shiny and dimpling, a baby doll with a Mohawk and a disconcerting hole punched in the center of its pursed lips, and it's all I can look at, that hole. "Hit everybody. That way, we'll know we got Spicer."

A queasy disintegrating feeling flutters through my

stomach as Bree lifts a bag of bombs into her lap, and I close my eyes, fingers finding the slip of paper in my coat pocket. (*Fortune favors the brave.*) Behind my eyes waits Kincaid from Friday, sunshine and storefront shadows casting bars of darkness, then light, across his back as he left us outside of Song's, slaloming down the sidewalk, away. Brave. I want to be that. Anything but ordinary, to see the whole alarm-school-homework-bed drudgery as optional, not *life*. Maybe this is my chance. Cement myself with these guys, make real friends, no exaggeration or wishful thinking. They're trusting me enough to want me in on this. I absolutely, positively cannot choke.

Trace turns to look at us in the backseat. "Ready?"

We murmur yeah. Sage says, "Babe? You're a freak show. You know that, right?"

"Sure. I know." Gradual pressure on the accelerator, turning onto Perfect. Slow and easy, the old-man car's license plate number hidden under smeared marsh mud provided by Kincaid.

Bree, Moon, and Kincaid power their windows down. The street stretches out in front of us, lit windows through lace curtains, gleaming bumpers in driveways. Kincaid and Moon raise their guns, barrels on windowsills, fingers squeezing triggers, forcing air through PVC pipe—

Bang! Bang! Bang! as paintballs connect with aluminum garage doors, the sides of minivans and SUVs, orange and black paint vomiting all over white clapboards and mailboxes.

Faster now—Bree heaves her bombs out the window, and I haul the second bag up from the floor, dumping more artillery into her lap, Bree swearing, fumbling. A smash of broken glass—one of the paintballs must've hit a window. Trace is laughing, yelling something.

Flash of a porch light turning on ahead, a woman stepping outside in a white bathrobe, clutching the collar closed, grabbing our attention for an instant—

Then we're over the curb, up onto the sidewalk, hurtling at a stunned face in the headlights. Reflective patches on the man's ski jacket lighting up like phosphorescence, hand trailing a leash in midair, the dog at the end lost in shadow—

Trace jerks the wheel and *thump*, we're back in the street, fishtailing around the corner, burning rubber, the stink filling our noses. Trace floors it to the stop sign, gasping, "Hol-y *shit*, hol-y *shit*," then takes us left, faster, faster down Oak until town fades to woods, until we're officially on Anson Pond Road and away.

We can breathe again. And once we can breathe, we can laugh.

"—*shit*, man, I really thought—"

"—didn't even see him—"

"—they called 911 or—?"

We ride the adrenaline high through the night, going

over it again, rehashing the details until it feels like legend, like Ricky Sartain or Dabney Kirk, but this time, I'm part of the telling, clamping my hands to my knees because I don't want anyone to know I'm shaking with reaction.

Trace takes us over the Derby line—nothing but overgrown pasture, woods, quiet houses set far back from the road—then follows a different system of twisting roads into Pender again. The clock in the dash reads 8:32. Our laughter dies down a bit at a time, and Perfect Street's on my mind: the woman in white coming out onto the porch, fist at her throat; the man in the ski jacket, almost roadkill, taking Fido out for one last sniff-and-pee around the neighborhood before settling in for the night, until we came roaring along like Death with a six-cylinder engine. What if Trace hadn't turned the wheel in time? What does it sound like when a ton of fast-moving steel slams into living tissue and bone? But all I say is, "Wonder if we hit anything good with the bombs."

"You hit somebody's front steps." Kincaid speaks from the turned-up collar of his coat. He's been quiet tonight, but he still sounds steady enough, like he won't be losing any sleep over the dog man or the splattered mailboxes.

"Really?" Bree laughs. "That's awesome. I was throwing them so fast I couldn't see where they landed."

"You know we made their year, right? The Perfects?" Trace rests one hand on top of the wheel. "We gave every

Man of the House an excuse to bust out their power spray-
ers and tool sets tomorrow and talk manfully over the fence
to the clone next door about beefing up security. Then they
can go blow money at the hardware store on motion-sensor
lights and fencing and shit, and their Martha wife will get
all tingly and give them their annual Valentine's Day lay four
months early because they're such a good goddamn pro-
vider." A pause, then: "I should go home." Followed by, "I
don't want to go home."

Silence. Sage leans forward. "You can come to my house."

"Nah. Your parents hate me." No argument from Sage.
The mask sits on the center console now, smiling blindly at
the roof. "I'd better." Trace nods a little. "Just to check in.
Then I'll drop you guys back at the park."

No one speaks. I settle back and wait, my makeup feeling
itchy and thick, pores starved for air.

I've never been to the limits of Pender before. It's a lot like
what I saw of Derby, hinting at some long-gone past before
the paper mill, when people must've made their living farm-
ing out here. Leaning fence posts, faint moonlit outlines of
barns and equipment sheds.

Trace's place is an old farmhouse sitting at the top of a
sloping driveway, with a huge Quonset hut barn and possibly the biggest outdoor light I've ever seen mounted above
the haymow door, spreading the whole dooryard in a flat,
artificial green glow. I see a tractor, a chicken coop, lots of

pasturage behind. "One sec," Trace tells us.

"Babe—" Sage.

"Leaving it running. See?" Trace climbs out, key ring swaying in the ignition.

We watch as he walks up the driveway. Dogs—looks like hundreds—explode from the darkness, barking their heads off, leaping and jerking at chains, tails lashing around, answered by Trace's booming "*Shut up.*" Apparently, he's their human, because they sit immediately, whimpering and wriggling as the door bangs shut behind him.

Time ticks by. A lot of time. Kincaid reaches over and turns off the engine.

"He said he'd be back, right?" I scratch at my makeup.

"It's his mom." Bree stops, meeting eyes with Sage, the first time I've ever seen her defer to Sage for permission.

"She's different," Sage finishes.

"Shocker." I wait. "How different?"

Moon snorts as he opens the last beer. "Like totally bizarre."

Kincaid speaks to the windshield. "She used to be the Sunday school teacher over at First Presbyterian. Sweet Ms. Savage, everybody called her. Always brought her own Bible to church with her because she said it helped her feel closer to God."

"Were you in her class?" I say, but he doesn't seem to hear; he's back in storyteller mode.

"For a long time, Sweet Ms. Savage really was sweet. She directed the Christmas pageant. Ran the bake sales. Always had Trace by her side, making change or handing out tracts. Suit, loafers, side-parted hair, the whole ventriloquist dummy look."

"Come on," I say, but Bree shushes me.

"It was the kids in the congregation. They just kept getting worse. Mouthing off, acting up, no respect for the church. People say they broke her spirit. Sweet Ms. Savage went sour. Started talking to herself, quoting the Bible all the time. Old Testament stuff, fire and brimstone."

I look up at the house. The curtains reflect the greenish hue of the outdoor light, the panels pressed right against the glass like some gale-force wind is blasting nonstop inside.

"Then little Billy Berwick brought a dirty playing card to church. Kept flashing it at his friends during the lesson, under the desk, you know. 'What do you have there, Billy?' Ms. Savage said." Kincaid's impression of her voice is high and prim. "'Nothing,' he said back. 'Well, perhaps you'd like to share this nothing with the rest of the class,' she said. So he held it up for everybody to see, right there in the church basement. And it was bad—I mean *bad*. Like, triple X."

"Oh, shit," Moon says.

"Yup. She snapped. Grabbed that Bible of hers and just started whaling on him, *whamwhamwham*. Knocking him out of his desk, stomping him while the other kids tried to pull her off." He props one mud-coated sneaker against the dash.

"Finally, the pastor heard the screaming and ran downstairs. Had to put her in a choke hold until the ambulance got there. Church fired her, of course. Nobody's seen her much since then."

We're quiet a second, then Sage cracks up. "You are such a liar! His mom never taught Sunday school—where'd you hear that?"

"I don't know," Bree says. "Trace is starting to make a lot more sense to me now."

Kincaid nods slowly. "I speak the truth." He picks up the mask, peering through the eye holes at the night.

We all jump when the front door of the house bangs open. "—yeah, yeah, okay. Okay. *Okaybye!*" Trace clomps down the steps, the dogs going nuts again, but this time he does a kind of presidential crowd greeting with them, petting heads, getting slobbered on—"Hey, buddy, hey, bubba, how you doing"—leaving them barking and wagging and wanting more as he jogs back to the car.

"Anybody want some jerky?" He's got a big square of it wrapped in tinfoil, homemade stuff that smells like spices and smoke. Nobody speaks up. "Okay. That's cool. More for me." He eats it as we go.

Tonight, we follow Kincaid.

We all agree to go straight home after Trace lets us out at the park, to wash the evidence from our faces and lie low.

Still, when Trace's taillights flash, taking Sage wherever they go for privacy at night, and we hear Kincaid's wheels hit the parking lot, Bree and I look at each other. And there's no question. It's now or never.

We're smart about it, pulling up our hoods to hide our painted faces, waiting until his board sounds distant before we follow, edging up our pace a little at a time, afraid of losing him.

Ahead, Kincaid passes under streetlights, taking the same route Bree described to me on the bus that morning. Down to the corner of Maple, a right onto Summer. We try to hurry without running or tipping him off to our footsteps. It's like I'm cursed with it now, this need to know where he comes from, as if it will somehow be the key to everything: why he clouds the truth with urban legend, how he almost made me believe in the Mumbler the other night, just for a moment.

A rattle as he hops off in one of the dark places, moving through a side yard bordered by hedges. We keep low, hustling after him, boxwood raking our clothes. The hedges end, and Bree stops so suddenly that I run into her back. "Where is he?" she hisses.

Ahead, I can make out the shape of a garage, another backyard. I listen to the night sounds, cars passing down on Main Street, people probably heading home from the football game. "He's hiding. Has to be." Nobody could disappear that fast. Why would he hide? I could understand him jumping out from behind a tree, trying to scare us, pay us back for stalking him, but instead he's trying to throw us off his scent.

I narrow my eyes, trying to pick him out from the shadows and shade trees, the same way his face appeared in the marsh woods that day. Search for the planes of cheekbones and forehead—the skull shape, and how appropriate, painted like he is tonight, not a woods elf but a headhunter, watching us from the bushes, features framed by long hair.

"Do you see him?" Bree asks.

There could be something there, in the brambles dividing the property lines. Too motionless to be human, too tall and bent, like an alder tree choked by vines. I think of the marsh, the shape on the opposite bank, the soft sway of something like hair among the branches. Think of my closet door. Open. Then closed.

"No." I step back fast, catching her sleeve. "He's gone. Let's go." Because all I want to do is get out of here, my skin cold and rigid, and I don't want her falling even one step behind.

Bree isn't one to be pulled, but she must've picked up on some of what I was feeling back there, because she doesn't shake loose until we're safely back on Summer.

THIRTEEN

HE GETS TO me in my dreams, the man with the dog. Our car, like a skidding ice boat, sailing over the curb with no sense of impact, no sense of time except for the endless stretch of my horror. His featureless, light-blasted face floats before the windshield, and there's little sense of the others around me—Bree, Sage, all peripheral—all of us bracing for impact, a contraction that squeezes me down into a fetal position beneath my comforter, where I wake, neck and shoulders aching with tension, head pounding, not sure I'm back in reality until I hear Ma's laughter from the kitchen.

I'm almost sick with it at breakfast on Monday morning, my generic squares taking on milk fast as they sit untouched.

Dad's already gone; Ma moves around me, a hum of one-sided conversation that I can't seem to grasp.

I didn't expect to feel this scared. Going back to school makes it all real again, somehow. It rained yesterday and I didn't go out. Both parental units had the day off, a rarity, so we made a real Sunday of it, lounging around eating and watching the Pats beat the snot out of the Jets, while I did everything I could to avoid local news and social media, not wanting to know what people were saying. It hits me now. We could get caught. We really could. What if the cops gather up the scraps of water balloon and dust for prints, tweeze fibers, run them through the lab? We should've worn gloves, hairnets, been smarter. I wonder if any of the others are doing this, dying of dread over breakfast?

At the bus stop, Sage has her usual Pop-Tart, winking at me as I come up; she's taken Trace's flannel back, and the hem bags past her coat. Bree looks the same as always—knew she would—and Hazel's busy with Toy Blast on her phone. "Did you look it up?" Bree asks softly.

I shake my head, really afraid I might barf. She hands me her phone, the video clip from Sunday morning's local news report already cued up.

"*A street in Pender was vandalized last night during the town's annual homecoming festivities. . . .*" Footage of various houses on Perfect, siding splattered with Halloween-colored paint; a broken pane of window glass; a close-up shot of one of our bombs, frozen to the pavement overnight, the shredded balloon fluttering in the wind like a tiny flag of surrender. *"Police are looking for the driver of a vehicle eyewitnesses say drove through the neighborhood firing paintball guns from the windows, and nearly struck a—"*

I hand the phone back, my lungs limp, wasted as that balloon. Bree doesn't notice, an enigmatic half smile back on her lips as she puts her phone away. "God. Trace is going to be insufferable today."

"Ha. Yeah, he is." Sage examines the sprinkles in the pastry glaze. "Did Landon text you guys at all?"

My "No," blends with Bree's "Like I talk to Landon."

Sage shakes her head at her. "Right. Your 'everybody hates me' delusion."

"It's not a delusion. It's keen observation of other people's words and body language. Called being perceptive. Probably means I'll be an extremely successful artist someday."

"Or a paranoid cat lady. Since when do you care about art?"

Somewhere, in another galaxy far, far away from the hellish guilt dimension I'm writhing in, the hoodies are coming, shoulders hunched, sleeves tugged over their raw knuckles to fend off the cold.

"Since always. I just suck at it." Bree reaches down, straightening Hazel's hood, which was tucked into her coat collar. Hazel makes a vague shooing motion without looking up. "So, what was Landon's issue? Drugstore ran out of Essie

Wicked and she needed an emergency mani before school?"

My gaze is locked ahead, seeing splattering paint, the stunned face of the dog man. Green Hood stares at me as he goes by, saying nothing, apparently speechless since Bree neutered him with a pair of pruning shears in front of a live audience.

At school, everybody's talking about it, dividing the population into kids who think it's hilarious and kids who don't, primarily ones who live on Perfect or streets like it. I pass through it all, glazed over, telling myself that the flashing arrow pointing at my head is a by-product of no breakfast and too little sleep, that Ma will not be seized by a craving for Jell-O Jigglers, discover the boxes missing, and put it all together in a stunning mental leap. Nobody knows. Nobody is looking.

I don't see anybody worth seeing until lunch. Bree, Sage, Trace, and—Kincaid, unbelievably. Packaging reduced by 35 percent: no board, no coat, hands in his jeans pockets. Trace goes straight to the hot-lunch line and pretends to muscle his way in front of the last guy in line, starting a laughing shoving match that ends in a teacher swooping in, cawing.

Kincaid splits off and drops onto a stool across from me at the flotsam table. His T-shirt's black, faded, worn over a white thermal undershirt, the collar of yet another shirt visible under that. He reaches across the table, and for a split second I think he wants to hold hands; my arm moves a quarter of an inch before his fingers land and start tapping a signal on the laminate between us. The close call with total mortification coats me in panic sweat, making me force the cheese crackers I was holding into my mouth all at once. He watches with interest as I struggle to chew. Hard swallow, sip of iced tea, then I rasp out, "You actually came to school."

"I wanted to hear what people were saying."

"Do your teachers remember your name?"

"Did you like your fortune?"

I give him a long look, showing him that I'm onto him, his whole shtick; that maybe Bree isn't the only one who spends their whole day defending personal barricades. I know he was hiding from us in the darkness last night, just out of reach. Which, if you ask me, is way weirder than the stalking ever was. "I think it was meant for you."

"You're still not seeing it." He leans forward, and I'm close enough to make out sunbursts around his pupils, some cracks of gold in those murky irises—and we're right back in the marsh, him holding me, me reaching out with my eyes shut. "No mistakes in this world. Not for us. You opened that fortune; it was meant for you."

Us—as in me and him? "You don't even know what it said."

He scratches his elbow, pushing up his sleeve to examine a scab there. Road rash; I guess even he wipes out on his board sometimes. "Destiny. Responsibility. Pretty soon, the universe is gonna test you, and you better be ready."

I drop my hands to the table, staring. That cookie was vacuum-sealed; I remember the puff of vanilla-scented air escaping when I ripped it open. It takes me a second to say, "Oh my God. You know what you are? I just figured it out."

His whole face lights up—genuine, intense interest blasting away the perma-stoned soothsayer act—and for the first time I see how deeply bored he usually is, with school, maybe with all of us.

Of course, everybody chooses that moment to reach the table, trays and soda cans touching down. "Fellow vandals," Trace greets us.

"Told you." Bree looks at Sage. "Insufferable."

"I can't believe we're sitting at this table again." Trace bites the head off a flaccid burrito, his tone low. "Anybody ask you guys about it?" We all say no. "Nobody acting suspicious?"

"Everybody's suspicious," Bree says. "Not necessarily of us."

"Nice. Should've heard Spicer in shop this morning." Trace screws his face up, sobs out, "'They broke my mom's birdfeeder, man!'" We laugh. Trace nods at me. "Anybody ask Clarabelle about the other thing?"

And this is it. I can feel it. The dark and massive thing I've sensed riding my back since morning; stretching, blocking out all light, some huge black bat at full wingspan, jaws lowering down on my head—not just our stupid Saturday night prank, but something hungry and idiotic and cruel, and it's starting. It's starting right now.

My voice is separate from my body: "What?"

"You didn't hear, huh." Trace's coyote eyes widen. "Toxic Twins." Nods toward the cool table. "Ivy ran away Thursday night. Guidance and the cops are asking around to see if anybody knows anything."

"What?" again, but softer, an echo. Ivy, knitting up a storm at the park; being cool enough to give me a heads-up about the unspoken rules, helping me avoid the girlfriends' claws.

I turn, looking at where we sat last week to hear the story of Dabney Kirk's head. Landon sits separate from the rest of the skaters, picking at her food with a pinched, abstracted look on her face. Her hair is down—free of its usual slick twists, it's a pedestrian shade of light brown, unexpectedly curly—and she isn't wearing any makeup, rendering her strangely vulnerable. She senses us looking, returns the stare for a moment, then goes back to sporking her burrito to death. "Ran away where?"

"They're not sure yet. There was a big fight at her house Thursday night—her stepmom again—and I guess she bolted," Sage says, shaking up her strawberry milk, and I can't tell if she senses it, too, the sudden wrongness of everything, if that's why her expression is so closed. "That's the reason Landon texted me yesterday. She didn't say anything about Ivy running away, just asked if I'd seen her. I figured Ivy's dad took her phone away again."

I remember the assembly Friday, spotting Landon sitting by herself on one of the top risers, combat boot bobbing, keeping time. Waiting for Ivy. "Thursday was forever ago." Glance at Kincaid, who's listening closely, rubbing his knuckles over his road rash.

Trace shrugs. "Cops and her family kept things quiet over the weekend. Figured she was just hiding out and she'd come back on her own. Now they're thinking maybe she caught a ride down to her mom's place in West Virginia." Trace nods over at Landon. "You know her stepmonster was always weird about them. Finally drove Ivy out the door."

"Without her other half?" Bree shakes her head. "Can't see it."

"Maybe they got in a fight, too," I say, half listening, and the words drift and evaporate under lunchroom white noise, as they should, because I don't know them, Landon or Ivy, and the new kid is the last person who should be floating theories.

On my shoulders, the dark thing flexes its scaly feet, folds its wings, and continues to wait.

FOURTEEN

AFTER THE LAST bell, I linger in front of the school, wondering if I can catch a ride with Trace, or if they've left for
the park already; taking the bus seems so bourgeois now. I'm
about to give up when I see Kincaid push through the glass
doors. His gaze finds me, and in an instant, I know he was
looking for me.

It's been a long, strange day, and I'm not sure I've got the
chutzpah to finish what I started with him at the lunch table.
I turn, moving toward the street at what I hope looks like a
casual pace, jogging over the crosswalk with my backpack
beating my backside—very slick, nice form. Down the sidewalk, trying to look like I have a destination, checking over

my shoulder once all the buses have roared by, contorted faces and flailing hands beyond the filthy windows like some view into hell's furnace room.

Kincaid follows at a distance. Riding the flat gray horizon, not waving or calling for me to wait up. Just tailing on his board.

Despite my mood and the doom creature riding my shoulders, that damned smile is back, the one I can't keep off my lips, and I turn on the speed—won't run, but neither will he, pushing off and coasting, keeping that long stretch of sidewalk between us. I'm ready for this role reversal, letting him be the one in pursuit for a change. My mind's scrambling— where to go? I don't want to walk all the way to the Terraces. Main Street it is. Straight shot down the hill.

The wind's fierce, but I keep up my barely restrained speed walk past the post office, Song's, and the gas station, ending up in the lot of D&M, where the Blazer sits in its usual spot. Good enough—how does Kincaid know I don't need antifreeze and scratch tickets?

Inside waits the usual old convenience store stank—stale cigarette smoke, coffee, pizza congealing under heat lamps. The cashier, a guy with a mop of reddish hair, glasses, and an immobile expression of snark, barely lifts his gaze from the pages of a college chemistry textbook on the back counter.

I wander over to the two-bags-for-a-dollar gummy spinner, warmth returning to my face and hands, counting silently, waiting to see what Kincaid will do next.

A couple minutes later, a jingle of entrance bells, and Kincaid's beside me, gusting in on cold air. "Hi." He's out of breath, smiling.

"Hi." Now that I'm caught, I can hardly keep the laughter out of my voice; it's tight in my lungs, making me feel buoyant, ready to float up to the water-stained ceiling panels.

"You came all the way down here for gummies?" Kincaid nods to the cashier, who nods back. "Thought you were trying to lose me."

I clear my throat, keeping my gaze on the selection. "What do you think? Sharks, watermelon slices, or hedgehogs?"

"Easy. Hedgehogs taste like Pepto."

Not sure if that's an endorsement or not. I grab two bags of sharks and go to the counter, glad Ma gave me money for supper before I left for school this morning; Dad must've told her I probably wouldn't be home in time to eat with him. Ma's gotten stuck with this eleven-to-closing shift lately, probably because she's the only one willing to work it.

The cashier's gaze is acidic, like my purchase is too small to justify the basic motor functions required to make change for a five-dollar bill. "So." Beside me, Kincaid coughs, still congested. "You were going to tell me what I am."

"That's why you're following me?"

"One of the reasons." His gaze flickers over me, physical as a touch.

My body floods with heat, adrenaline, and I can't look away from the peeling decals on the countertop. He's returning fire. Oh my God. I have no idea what to do.

The cashier slides the cash register drawer shut with a *ching.* "Okay, kiddies. Take the pubescent mating rituals outside." He and Kincaid do a fist bump; the cashier nods at me, telling Kincaid, "Remember to wrap it up, buddy. Last thing I need is your skate-rat progeny coming down here, trying to steal the Bic lighters."

Kincaid laughs. I leave, face flaming.

Back on the sidewalk, I set the pace to hyper speed. Kincaid rolls up alongside, skating backward, hands in his coat pockets, zigzagging. "So?" he says to me. "What am I?"

"Other than a big show-off?" He laughs again. "How did you not kill that guy just now?"

"Owen? He's Trace's cousin."

"So it's okay for him to trash you?" *And me,* I think, but my pride won't let me say it.

"He's the reason I can drink." Looks back at me. "If he didn't buy for Trace, then Trace couldn't sell to us."

"Supply and demand, huh."

"I guess. Anyway, he didn't mean anything by it. That's just how he is." Considers me. "I've never seen you pissed before."

"Yeah. Well. It happens." What I'd almost said to him at the lunch table was probably too personal, too harsh, but I'm feeling thorny now, so I say, "You really want to know what you are?" He raises his brows. "Snake-oil salesman. Flim-flam man. You think you can sell people on anything. And usually, you can."

"*Really.*" Intense interest.

"Hey, you came all this way. The least I can do is insult you." I rip open one of the bags and hold it out. "Shark?"

His gaze doesn't waver. "But not you. You're not buying."

"Nope. Told you." I pick out a gummy, wincing at the occasional stray raindrop striking my face, hard as a pellet of buckshot.

"Then you won't be scared to go back out there." Kincaid squints at the clouds. "It's daylight. Things usually don't try to eat you in the daylight."

I recognize his brand of teasing now, and I snort. "What is it with you and that marsh?"

"It's a good place to be alone."

"And you want to be alone with me." Too late, I realize how it sounds. Oh, shit.

The last thing I expect him to say is "Yes."

It opens a pocket of silence between us, the unspoken thing we've just acknowledged. My heart races and my body feels anything but still, yet we walk without discussion up a side street I've never taken, another shortcut, another steep hill that starts a fire in my quads. At an intersection of quiet

streets, Kincaid scales the slope to an old cemetery surrounded by chain link. Ignores the gate, hops the fence. I
follow. Inside stands a massive oak, leaves turned yellow, a
blazing hand of glory against the sky.

We enter the woods on the far side of the cemetery, where
the gravestones are sparse, forgotten-looking, a stone lamb
for a lost child. Kincaid takes more care to make sure I'm
keeping up this time. We follow two shallow gullies layered
with blowdown and dead leaves, then come out in a familiar
place, the ledge above the murals. He reaches out, holds my
hand. My fingers feel small in his, oddly unfamiliar, and I
can feel my pulse everywhere, every place I'd thought was
private, untouchable.

He stashes his board in the weeds by the path, where his
bag already sits; must've been there all day. Then we walk to
the railroad bridge.

"How could anybody be under there?" By the time we climb
the last slope to reach the railroad tracks, nerves have gotten
me talking again. "I mean, I've seen the bridge. It's not like
there's anything to hang on to in those tunnels. It's stone."
I pause to catch my breath, watching him make the tracks.
"Just saying, your Mumbler origin story needs some work."

"He doesn't follow rules like that. He can go anywhere."
Kincaid takes a few big steps, touching only the ties, arms out
to the side for balance. "You've seen the painting. With those

hands, he could probably stick on like a spider and crawl."

A flash of white buzzes by my head, and I watch it spiral away, fluttering. "God." I smooth my hair, imagining little insect legs tangling there, frantic. "I'm like a moth magnet lately."

He looks up, watching it go. "Lace-border moth. They're all over the marsh this time of year."

And my closet, apparently. "What is he, then?" I say, actually finding the Mumbler a more appealing subject for once. "Where'd he come from?"

"I think we made him." Kincaid keeps his gaze down as we follow the tracks, chin in his collar. "Like, people. How shitty we are. Poured out of the vials of the wrath of God, right. Where's Trace when you need some good blasphemy?"

It has the ring of a bad charm, said aloud out here, in the isolation. Like an invitation, pushed beneath the door to something forever with its eye to the keyhole, its pupil a reptilian slit.

My hands are ice, freezing air leaving a taste of iron in my mouth as we cross from land to granite, the wind blasting us again now that we're on the bridge platform, stripped of tree cover. Our jack-o'-lanterns still form a line along the railing. I hug my coat around me. "Crap. Don't tell me this is becoming 'our place.'"

It's a risky joke, assuming too much, but I want that concept out of my head, vials of the wrath of God. He smiles slightly but doesn't look at me, giving a slow nod. "You're very funny."

"Wow. Add a little pat on the head, and I'd feel super special." I cut my eyes at him. "And since when aren't you an easy laugh?"

The corner of his mouth goes up a bit more. "I think you joke around to cover how you really feel about stuff."

"Kind of like why you tell stories?" He doesn't answer. I shrug, looking off at the water, slate-colored under the overcast sky. "Maybe I just keep myself to myself, you know?" I don't have to say *just like you*; he turns to me, and we bump into each other, his hands steadying my shoulders. I look into his eyes as another one of those steel raindrops spikes my lashes, making me blink. "Not that I'm mysterious or cool at all."

He lowers his head to look at me closely, the teasing light in his expression again. "You. You are an unknown quantity."

Our noses are nearly touching; wonder how he broke his, why he didn't bother to make sure it healed straight. "Well," I say, "that new-kid smell wears off after a while. Fair warning." We both laugh a little, and his hands cup my face, crossing beyond friendly touch, and oh God, I'm going over the edge again, maybe not so different from surrendering to dreams, that warm pull of sleep, how our heat blends as we kiss—his lips as chapped as his hands, like I knew they'd be, because he's always outside, the wind always taking from him. At first, it's soft, both a question and a confirmation, then harder, our heads angling together to go deeper, his fingers in my hair.

We pause for breath, me looking back at him, so dazed that I say, "Do you even know my last name?"

He's quiet a moment. "Do you know mine?" Honestly curious.

"Is it Kincaid?"

"No."

We laugh again, and all we can do is kiss, and all he wants to do is get his hands under my clothes, which is fantastic except for the shocks of goose bumps leaping across my skin every time my shirt rides up. "It's so cold," I say in his ear.

We cross the bridge to the far side, the couples' side, where I've never been. And we're not picky—the ground works. Off the path, partly shielded by the branches of a blue spruce. He takes his coat off and lays it over us, his heat enveloping me, his weight, his kisses on my stomach, his fingers finding the hooks of my worn-out bra with the skill of an experienced bra finder, a worry for another time, and there are so many parts of him I want to touch, to kiss, to know.

After we hit the point where I whisper, "We should stop"—the last thing I want, but still—he groans and drops over onto his side, nuzzling under my jaw, kissing down my throat, tickling, making me laugh.

As we cross back over the bridge together, he holds my hand in both of his, rubbing my fingers, warming them as we move together, like I'm holding him up. I feel flushed, rumpled, thoroughly explored. I don't know how far is too far for the first time touching a guy, how much I should've given him, why it even needs to be played that way, like awarding points or something. All I know is that I inhabit an entirely different skin from the one I wore before, one that never knew the feeling of his lips kissing just below the line of my underwear.

Our row of jack-o'-lanterns grins back at us, beginning to wizen, black mold speckling the corners of their mouths and eyes. "Where's Ivy's?" I'm not sure I've even spoken aloud until I feel Kincaid's new stillness, his head leaned against mine. "Her pumpkin. It's not there anymore."

We stop by the space where it once sat. "Somebody probably knocked it off." Sounds like his thoughts are still back there, in the trees.

"Do lots of people come here?"

"Not lots. I find beer cans and stuff sometimes."

I go to the railing and look down, as if the jack-o'-lantern might still be bobbing below us, then examine the next one, Trace's. "What the hell?" I laugh. "Somebody stole our offerings, too."

The jack-o'-lanterns have been completely cleaned out. Even the cold sore treatment is gone. Kincaid rests his forearms on the railing, his gaze keen as he watches me. "Guess he must've been pleased. Maybe he'll go easy on us this year."

I look back at him, trying to gauge how much shit he's giving me, if he's really shutting me out of the joke again. But then he smiles, and impulse brings me in for more kisses, sliding my hands inside his open coat, around his waist, into the back pockets of his jeans, hardly able to believe I get to touch him like this, know the pattern of his ribs—too easy to find—the few scattered moles on his chest.

We leave, passing my jack-o'-lantern, first in line. Ours, I mean. Mine, Sage's. And Bree's.

FIFTEEN

I DON'T KNOW what to do.

A dam's burst, letting all the consequences through, sweeping away my floaty, spinning feelings, leaving nothing but this roaring in my ears. I'm practically silent on the walk back, searching for words—*don't take this wrong, but*—*can we not*—*at least, not in front of*—but it's impossible, the idea of pushing him away, turning him down when we're so new, just born together.

I'm sick with the thought of Bree, flat-out nauseous by the time we reach the park. Everyone's here, like they heard a rumor that we were handing out free Fireball or something. Bree's talking with Sage, Trace, and Moon. She doesn't notice us coming out of the trees, doesn't look over until she hears leaves crunching beneath our sneakers. I'm quick to split off from him, and now who's in the killing jar, beating their wings as everything goes dark?

"Hope you're ready for this," Bree says to me. "Trace wants to pull another one." But her heat-seeking gaze follows Kincaid, watching him get on his board and do a couple slow laps to warm up. I force myself to look anywhere but at him. We didn't cheat. There's nothing to cheat on. But still.

Trace shows Sage something on his phone, and I take in all the details: how she sits with her hip pressed against his, their shoulders touching, things that were just vaguely discomfiting PDA before, but now, over the span of one afternoon, I can so totally understand, and envy. What I did in the woods with Kincaid was the farthest I've ever gone, a giant leap from that first, chaste little kiss freshman year, with the boy who only dated me because he knew it couldn't last.

"There's a crapload of stuff you can do to a car like that." Trace grins. "Crack picked the wrong ride." He points his phone at each of us. "You'll get a text letting you know when. We've got to change up the day we hit, so there's no pattern. Human brains want a pattern. We want them scared." Two skaters, underclassmen, stray close to our spot, and Trace stares them down until they move on.

"What's the plan?" I say.

"Operation Hide the Bug." Bree puts her hands up at my look. "That's all he'll say."

I sit cross-legged on the ground, making the gummy bags crinkle in my coat pocket. I toss one to Sage, the other to Moon, stealing the moment of shark enthusiasm to drop, briefly, into a flashback of the woods. How I let his tongue in my mouth, something I always secretly thought sounded gross and intrusive, but isn't at all. With the right person, maybe you can never get too intimate, never go too far. I open my eyes. Kincaid is watching me. I watch back.

He slows, hops off his board, holds it out to me. "Ever done it?" And it's there between us, all the heat, his hands sliding over my bare skin. A smile plays at his lips. "Try."

"So you can watch me fall on my ass?"

"Damn, really? No faith." Kincaid puts his board down, steps up with the spectators. "Put one foot on, push off with the other. Easy."

I exhale, looking over at Bree, who's watching with the rest of them. I put one foot on the board, push off on the concrete with the other, rolling along with embarrassing slowness, making me push off again, harder, getting some speed under me, following the edge of the flat bottom so I don't wobble into the paths of the pros and sabotage somebody's trick. Kincaid walks with me, calling out, "Goofy leg." Gestures down. "You ride with your left foot back. Not many people do."

"Always knew I was special." Trying to act like this is all impulsive, indicative of nothing, cursing and laughing as I almost run into the rail. "How do you, like, steer?"

That's when I notice the small, dark figure coming down the sidewalk toward us. As she draws closer, she develops mid-calf boots, a black watch cap, a purposeful gait as she crosses the parking lot, then the dead grass. Landon, her face still and guarded.

She stops at the first group of people she sees, talking low, not lingering long before moving onto the next, then the next.

"—okay? Forget it." Landon turns away from the girl-friend bench, leaving them whispering, shooting looks in her wake. She stops a few feet back from us—Trace scrapes a fin-gernail gouge down a shark stomach, saying, "Look. Gummy surfer body parts," making Sage laugh—and you can feel it: Landon doesn't really see us as friends. Even though we all hang here almost every day. Maybe Ivy is the buffer, the one whose presence makes this place belong to them, too. Kind of the way Sage and Bree are my passports to . . . well, pretty much anywhere. I step off the board, needing to feel grounded, my nervous stomachache back again.

"Do any of you guys know where she is?" Landon's voice is a little below normal speaking range, brusque, like she's making herself do this just to cover all the bases. She's working the fingers of one hand, concentrating her nervous energy there.

We glance at one another. After a pause, Bree says, "You don't?"

"No, I don't. That's why I'm asking." Landon's gaze is fixed beyond us, on the street, fingers ticking, ticking, counting off. "Look, did any of you hear anything? Did she say anything to you? I'm just trying to figure out what happened."

Trace and Sage look at each other, Trace finally giving a shrug. "She seemed the same as always on Thursday. That's the last time I saw her—standing with you, in the parking lot. They think she went to see her mom, right?" Landon nods. "Then . . . sounds like you just have to wait. She wouldn't do anything stupid like hitch with some skeeve, would she?" Landon glances down, shakes her head. Trace sits forward a little. "She's either riding with a soccer mom, or she took a bus. She'll call."

Landon's quiet a moment. Then she says, "Yeah," walking past us toward the next group of people hanging out on the playground equipment, not looking back at Sage's quiet "Sorry, hon."

She's so stiff, Landon, so deep inside herself, that I find myself scanning my memory of Thursday for anything I could tell her, but it's hazy, lost under a blood wash of Fireball and Kincaid butterflies—make that lace-border moths. I remember Ivy's hands, her fingernails tipped with black polish, carving the pumpkin, protecting it from Trace's kick. Her words about black cats and Halloween. That's all.

Bree waits until she's gone. "Such crap." Sage raises her brows. "That she doesn't know where Ivy is. Bet you anything it's like Clarabelle said." I look over, surprised. "You know. That they got in a fight and now Landon's having serious guilt spasms."

"I didn't say that." Only I kind of did. "That's not what I meant."

Bree shrugs. "Then maybe Landon's helping her hide out so they can stick it to Ivy's stepmom. Cops will probably find her in Landon's attic, like, living off Hot Pockets and bottled water or something."

Sage focuses on adjusting her gloves. "I believe her." Her calm, immovable stubbornness hangs in the air, something I've never heard before. Bree looks at her, but Sage won't acknowledge it. Trace watches them, says nothing.

I grab Kincaid's board before we have a chance to spiral any deeper. "Your turn." Hold it out to Bree.

She pulls her attention from Sage. "Yeah, right."

"Hey, I tried it. You can't be as bad as me." Plus, I want to share him—God help me, I don't, but I do—hoping it'll be enough to smooth that off-chord that's still reverberating around us.

Bree glances at Kincaid, who smiles, unbothered by any of it, sinking down into a crouch to watch. She takes it from my hand, a little rougher than necessary, applies foot to board, and pushes off, upright, steady as she goes.

SIXTEEN

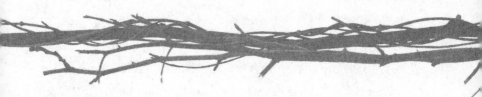

WE CAN'T KISS goodbye. We can't touch. I take one look back at him as I leave with Bree to follow the trails home, freaked over hurting him, not being able to make him understand without words.

But he's coasting. Gaze on the burning strip of early sunset edging the trees, thoughts a million miles away. So maybe words aren't something he needs from me.

A hard frost covers everything the next morning, turning the world into one of those panoramic sugar eggs, my leopard-prints crunching over the spiky crust coating the grass at the base of our steps.

A pumpkin is propped against my bedroom window.

An origami jack-o'-lantern, specifically, orange paper folded to create a stem, slanted eyes, zigzag mouth, the features carefully shaded with a black marker. Written on the back is *Happy October* in an almost unreadable scrawl. So Kincaid.

No frost on the paper—he was just here. I run to the parking lot and look down the hill, but he's nowhere in sight, nothing but ugly houses all in a row and the usual gaggle of malcontents at the bus stop.

My first impulse is to tape the jack-o'-lantern inside my locker door, but I don't want anyone asking questions I'm not ready to answer. Instead, I leave it in my coat pocket along with the cookie fortune, the beginnings of my own private Kincaid collection. Private (*fortune favors*) for now (*the brave*). Until I figure out how to tell Bree without destroying everything and losing her.

Maybe I won't have to tell? Maybe it'll become obvious on its own, that he and I are a thing now, no formal announcement necessary? Maybe she'll get that it just happened, him liking me back. I launched myself into this yesterday, hurtling down a steep slope, hands in the air, headed for a drop-off, and so far, this is my best plan? To close my eyes and hope for the best? Maybe there's a reason none of my friendships have lasted. Maybe I was never worthy of the Nica Plecks

I've known, and somehow, they sensed it.

But I didn't steal him, did I? We're not cheaters. How can you cheat on a crush? How do you even navigate around one? I should've checked with her first, before Kincaid and I did anything. *Bree, are you okay with this? Bree, do you mind?* I think of her: bitten lips, pale stare, the vulnerability of her laugh. The shape of her silhouette, solitary and erect against the window shade. My guilt is a bruise-colored flower, unfurling with excruciating slowness. If she said yes, she minded, *Please don't do this, it hurts me*, what then? Give it all up, tell Kincaid we could never be anything but friends? Friendship, so elusive and precious, all I ever wanted from this place. Until what I experienced with Kincaid in the woods, so intense, something I've been waiting to feel my whole life. How can I pretend that I don't want him?

I slam my locker door and see Kincaid coming through the crowded hallway toward me. He doesn't just walk up; he stops so close our toes touch, looking down into my face, not caring who sees, and how the hell am I going to keep all this under wraps? "Hello," he says.

"School two days in a row? Watch out. Somebody's going to think you're a student here."

"I didn't come for the classes." His smile is an inch away from mine.

"You know, a Halloween gremlin left something outside my house this morning. I didn't even have a chance to thank him." I shouldn't kiss him here, I know this, but all I want to do is wrap myself in him, breathe in everything. "So, thank you. I love it."

He nods slowly, says, "How're you liking the book?" I realize he's looking at *A Clockwork Orange,* which I'd forgotten I was even holding.

"It's good. Disturbing, obviously, but I'm guessing that's the point."

Kincaid leans against the lockers, banging the back of his head lightly, deliberately, off the steel sheeting as he studies the ceiling. "Holds all the truths."

"Such as?"

"How free will separates us from the animals. How a person having the choice to steal, rape, kill, whatever, is more important than whether they commit the crime. How every day, we all make the choice." He pauses, meeting my gaze. "Be moral, or be a monster."

I let his words settle around me before pointing toward the English wing. "Can you come teach my class now? Because you made that sound way better than Hyde ever could."

"You don't have to go." Straightens. "Come with me. I just walk out. Nobody cares."

Tempting doesn't begin to cover it, but I'm carrying around enough guilt and worry for one day without adding skipping school to the mix. "Interesting approach to senior year. Just disappear, and hope they print out a diploma for you on graduation day?"

He smiles, only fifteen watts, and I wonder if I've failed some test, if he was expecting more from me. Or maybe less. "Okay." Lifts off from the lockers. "See you after."

After class? After school? But he's leaving, a head taller than most of the other kids he moves through, everybody hurrying to get where they're expected to be, where routine demands. And I guess I'm one of them, part of the hive mind, an ant with a bread crumb. "Hey," I call after him, because I don't want to leave it like this, "how'd you know where I live, anyway?"

He doesn't turn. "I asked Trace."

I can't help but laugh, remembering Sage's advice on the bus that day while Bree and I schemed together. But that means the guys have talked about me. Which means Trace knows more about Kincaid's feelings than I do.

Trace's text is waiting for me at morning break: *Tomorrow. 6:30 p.m. Behind the teachers' lot.*

It's the next evening. Dusk. I know I shouldn't be here, that this can't be leading anywhere good. But Kincaid's meeting us behind the school, and my need to see him trumps all. Trace has the princess mask tucked into his back pocket. Not a good sign.

Trace leaves the old-man car in the athletic field lot; then we hurry down the footpath leading behind the middle school, through the smokers' woods, and out behind the high school teachers' parking area. I'm telling myself that if Trace has anything too crazy planned, I'm out. They'll have to fill me in on how it went at the flotsam table tomorrow.

Kincaid is already there, sitting on a log dragged up alongside the path. His head is down, hands in his coat pockets; he looks huddled, deep in some internal process, until he hears our approach and looks up. I saw him at the park yesterday afternoon as usual, but we haven't been alone since Monday. After I failed the skipping school test yesterday, I wonder what he's thinking, if he sees me differently now, as some Goody Two-shoes. I've been wondering about the girlfriends at the park, too; if they jump whenever their boyfriends snap their fingers. Because you know what? I've decided that's not me. Not even close. And maybe that's not what Kincaid expects, either—impossible to find out, since we don't seem to be able to steal a second to ourselves. "About damn time." His eyes are on me, but he speaks to Trace. "You were right. Crack's still here."

"Every night, man, every night. I've driven by and seen his car parked out here at, like, ten." Trace grins. "This is what he gets for being an eager little beaver."

I glance over at Bree, chewing gum, her breath mingling with Kincaid's in the chill air. Still don't know how to tell her what's going on. If she hates me, Sage might hate me, too, and then what would stop everybody else from piling on? No more friends. No more park. A leper wearing a big scarlet S pinned to my chest; S for slut, S for stealer, the boy-friend variety. I fell asleep in knots over it last night, gazing back at the origami jack-o'-lantern sitting propped up against my bedside lamp, the paper aglow with light.

Now, Bree glances over at the school. "Can you tell us what the hell we're doing here?"

Trace and Moon trade looks, laugh like a couple of eight-year-olds. Bree glances at Sage, who shrugs, but I get the feeling she already knows all the details. Interesting, how info finds its way into these little inlets and eddies among a group of friends. Never know who knows what, who told who when. Who's being left out of the loop.

Trace points to the two remaining teacher vehicles still in the lot, an SUV and a light-colored VW Beetle, the old kind. "Crack's going for a little ride. He just doesn't know it yet." He points to us. "This time, you guys are lookouts. That's all. We get caught, this could mean serious shit, so just be glad Moon's willing to take one for the team."

Moon digs in his coat, brings out a flathead screwdriver, a metal slim jim, and his phone. He's sporting a bruise on his cheekbone today, thanks to his older brother, who caught him trying to replace the paintball gear and figured out what happened. Moon says not to worry, his brother's basically cool, would never tell anybody what we did, but I still wish a few less people knew our secret. "Okay," Moon says, "I've never done this before. Like, any of it. But old cars are supposed to be way easier to hot-wire, and I got the WikiHow pulled up. If it doesn't work in, like, ten minutes, we get out of here."

"Good man." Trace claps Moon's shoulder, shaking him down to his shoes. "I'll see you get a commendation for this, soldier." Moon's salute ends with the middle finger.

I stand silently, chewing my lip as the rest of us get our assignments—I'm posted along the drive that winds around the school to the teachers' lot—but we wait until we're sure Moon can get into the VW, watching from the trees as he fiddles with the slim jim, wobbling and flexing it and trying to peer down between the rubber window seal and the door to find a way to work it in. Hesitates, frustrated, then tries the handle. Unlocked. Tosses a grin at us and climbs inside.

I catch Bree's sleeve before she splits off with Sage. "Maybe we shouldn't." She stares at me. "Isn't this, like, grand theft auto?" Another pause. "As in a felony?"

"That's the general idea, yeah." She pulls loose, smiling a little. "Hey. We're only lookouts, right? Nobody can give us the chair for that."

Then she goes, heading around the opposite side of the school with Sage, while Kincaid ducks low, running beneath the windows in front. I'm the last one left standing, rooted to the spot, and I finally race for my post. Whether I'm loving this or not, I don't want to be the one Crackenback sees first if he decides to step outside for some night air.

I'm wearing gloves and a hat, still freezing right through my jeans as I press myself back against the fence that marks school property, glad nobody on staff cares enough to tame the climbing vine that's grown wild through the chain link, providing me with cover.

I dance a little from foot to foot, straining my ears for the sound of an outraged teacher or a shrieking car alarm. Do cars that old even come with alarms? Debating what I'll do if all this goes to hell, who I'd text first with the news that we're all about to get busted. Makes me realize that I've never seen Kincaid with a phone in his hand, never heard him say he'll text somebody later, nothing like that.

Time crawls. I check my phone. Ten minutes gone by.

I google Ivy's name. No news. School's buzzing about how it's been almost a week, and nobody's heard from her. If she were headed to West Virginia by any normal means, she would've been there by now. The doom creature on my shoulder sinks its talons in deeper, and I lower my head, shutting my eyes, remembering Ivy, her fearlessly short haircut, how she loved her cat enough to knit him a present. It doesn't feel right that she would leave a pet she was that crazy about, especially if her stepmom and dad might give him away to the Humane Society or something.

Tires crunch over asphalt. I jerk up, ready to text, when

I realize it's coming from the wrong direction, back by the teachers' lot.

They're driving without headlights, maybe ten miles an hour. It's Crackenback's VW, looking like some fugly little insect on a set of narrow tires. As I watch them pass, I see the princess mask smiling at me from the shadows behind the steering wheel, Moon ducked so low in the passenger seat that I can only make out the top of his cap.

Can't believe step two of plan A is happening—meeting back up at Trace's car, victorious instead of shitting bricks, ready for further instructions. I race through the dark smokers' woods and follow the footpath alone, glad when I come out on the sloping green behind the middle school, where moonlight can reach. A pair of dark shapes appear at the crest of the hill—Bree and Sage, running all out. I run to join them.

Their laughter's infectious, as always, and it's like their little difference of opinion over Landon on Monday never happened. Best friends forgive and forget pretty easily, I guess. But even as I lean against Sage, shoulder to shoulder, there's no *click*. I don't fit with them, not like before, walking the trails that night with jack-o'-lanterns in our arms and demon on our breath. Maybe secrets have changed my shape, made me different. I click with somebody else now, Bree's boy. The one I've maybe stolen. And suddenly, it's not so easy to laugh.

Speak of the devil: Kincaid's already there when we reach

the dirt athletic field lot, sitting on the hood of Trace's car, grinning as if in private conversation. He points at something in the distance.

Way off beyond the baseball field, a pair of taillights glow, moving along at an uneven pace as the VW follows the grassy ridge along the woods' edge.

"What're they *doing*?" Bree steps forward, arms folded tightly against the cold. "There's no road there."

"I told him. . . ." Sage shakes her head. "They're going to get stuck."

We watch as the VW pulls a lazy, difficult right, the headlights now on, giving a glimpse of trees as they seem to turn directly into the woods. And disappear.

"Where'd they go?" I ask.

The only answer I get is Kincaid's laughter.

When Trace and Moon reach us ten minutes later, it's from out of the dark, the mask bouncing around Trace's neck from its elasticized string. We pile into his car, all except for Kincaid, who shoves off down the hill in a slight crouch, tunneling into a speed that makes my heart rise in my throat, watching as he's swallowed by the night. Wouldn't be surprised if he makes the park before we do.

As Trace backs out, Sage, riding shotgun, says, "Did you really do it? The last part?"

Trace reaches into his pocket, pulls out a wrapper, shakes it. "Big enough to accommodate the larger man."

Sage places a hand over her grin. "Oh, my."

"What—?" Bree reaches forward, snatching it from him and holding it up under the dome light. The package reads *Trustex Dual Color Orange & Black.*

She curses, flinging it away. "Oh my God! Trace! You are so disgusting!" The rest of us crack up. "I can't believe you let me touch that!" Wiping her hand furiously on her jeans.

"What? It's just the wrapper." He laughs as she lunges forward and pounds his shoulder, jolting his words: "It's a—responsible—way—for two adults—"

"You assclown! Now I've got freakin' lube or whatever on me—"

"No." He holds up a hand. "I went for style, not comfort. We're trying to make a statement here."

I laugh. "We are?"

He's quiet a second, taking care to come to a complete stop at the bottom of the hill, scanning his mirrors for cops lurking in turnarounds. "After four years of mind-numbing bullshit, I want PDHS to know exactly what it can do with its driveshaft."

It's hard not to rehash every detail of the night when we get to the park, but caution demands it. Looks like I'm going to have to wait until the news hits tomorrow to find out what they actually did with Crackenback's VW.

It's nearly eight o'clock now, so cold that almost nobody's still at the park, just a few diehards who never seem to leave,

Kincaid being one of them. Like that day Bree told me about, last summer, when he skated in the rain until he was soaked through, water streaming from his hair, then took off down that shortcut through the houses. He hasn't stopped moving since he got here, and there's a deliberateness to it, like he's trying to keep warm.

After Sage and Trace leave, Bree nudges me. "I'm calling it. Can't feel my toes. Let's go." She springs up and down a bit to keep the blood flowing.

I hesitate. "Actually, I think I'll hang out for a while."

She looks at me. I've never done this, stayed without her. "Aren't you cold?"

"Not too bad. I'll see you tomorrow, though." It comes out sounding weird, like I'm throwing her a bone or something, and I force a laugh. "For the big Bug unveiling and everything."

She snorts, nods, and goes, crossing the park. Once she passes the picnic enclosure, her phone flashlight is the only thing I can see, heading toward the trails home. I feel like such an asshole, making her go alone.

Even worse is the fact that I'm still excited for it to be just me and Kincaid, nobody left at the park now but one other couple doing their own thing, and some girls I don't know sharing a cigarette. Kincaid's gaze finds me, anchoring us as he does circuits, taking the half-pipe a couple times, then slows when he sees me walking toward the trees, turning on my own flashlight. I'm hearing Ivy's words: *Anything you don't want an audience for, take it into the woods.*

He meets me there. It's like no time has passed; we lock together, him covering my face and throat in kisses in a way that confirms everything, kills every doubt, but his hands are icy, startling. "Holy crap," I say, "you need gloves."

"No, I don't." I jump as he glides his hands up under my shirt, across my back, hugging me to him, but it takes only a second for our temperatures to blend. It feels good to be able to give him some comfort, and we stay like that for a moment. The congestion's still there, a slight rattle in his chest. I say, "Can I ask you something?"

He doesn't speak right away. "Probably."

"When did you figure out I liked you?"

I can feel his smile in the dark. "A while ago."

"Smug bastard." He laughs, and I don't want to do this, ruin the moment, and expose Bree's secrets, but I don't see any other way. "Do you know Bree likes you, too?"

A beat passes. "She does?"

"Yeah." I go slow, not wanting to open the vault door more than a crack, displaying all the details of how we obsessed over him, how he was almost all we talked about. "I feel bad. She doesn't know—" I gesture between us. "I don't know how to tell her."

He pulls back a little, looking down at me. "I never hooked up with her."

"Yeah, but she liked you first."

Another pause. A slight shrug. "Act like it's no big and do what you want. She'll get over it."

"Have you met Bree? Or, like, the world?" He snorts, pressing his face against my head. "No. I've got to suck it up and tell her. I mean, she put herself out there for me. She didn't have to be so nice." I hesitate. "I probably never would've even met you if she hadn't asked me to come hang out."

"You would've." He holds my chin. "Told you, Clarabelle. No mistakes."

"Uh-huh." I stand on my tiptoes, kiss him. His beard's coming in a little, right on the verge of scratchy. "Well. Grasshopper has to go home now."

"Sensei's going to walk you."

On the trail, he hugs me to his side, and I slide my arm around his waist, as close as we'd be if we could spend the night together, share a bed. How amazing would that be, a whole night in the warm dark with him?

"You really can't stay out any later?" he asks.

"Not without my parents killing me." I catch his look—distracted, frowning slightly, and I'm not sure what it means, how the tone of things changed so quickly. "You better get back, too." We've reached the fork in the path that leads to the Terraces, the stretch to the trailhead partially lit by the streetlight at the bus shelter. "Summer Street's, like, halfway across town. I took you pretty far out of your way." He shrugs. "Do you have a phone? You need a light." I hold my phone out.

He moves a step back from me. "Nah. I'm good. You're going to miss that."

"I can survive one night without tweeting. Go ahead. I'll get it back from you tomorrow."

When our kisses end, he presses his fingertips to my lips as his goodbye. I stand, watching him leave. "Hey." Calling after him again, not ready for it to end. I hear his footsteps hesitate, waiting. "Confess. When did you start liking me back?"

"I've always liked you." And that's it. He goes.

I could fly back to our unit on those words, and I practically do, my steps light, my nose already full of phony floral fabric-softener smell gusting from the vents of the laundry building.

In time—how much, I'm not sure, but no more than a minute—I hear the other. The follower, mirroring my steps almost exactly, leaving enough of an overlap that I don't register the sounds at first, just sense something off. I glance back. The woods are blackness.

"That you?" I say. My voice too loud, alien.

No answer. Kincaid would say something—he wouldn't mess with me like this. I don't think.

Somewhere, in that inky tangle, a twig snaps.

Panic snaps with it, spurring me forward, my walk turning to a run. The streetlight's ahead, but it's my dream become real—trapped in an endless moment of gut-sinking dread, the cold in my bones making me brittle, my skeleton turned to ice.

When I burst out of the tree line, my breath explodes—I've been holding it all along—and it's like I can feel the hands (*impossible fingers, wriggling black snakes*) stop just short of my shoulders and reduce to vapor as I spin, stumbling back, staring at the trail. No one.

But the woods are alive with new sounds. Crackles and rustles, either from my own sprint or from something receding, moving away through the trees, now that I'm out of reach.

I run the rest of the way home, pausing on our stoop to catch my breath so I don't blow through the door looking like the devil's on my heels.

And it's the second night I fall asleep with the lamp on, Kincaid's jack-o'-lantern glowing with a look of infernal delight.

SEVENTEEN

MY WORDS COME out, "Can we talk?"—so similar to how I approached Kincaid last night that it's a physical stab in my chest, making me press my lips together, cringing inside.

Bree gives me a skeptical look. "You okay?"

She cares if I'm okay. I should be shot. Granted, she said it in her usual deadpan way, with a trace of distracted annoyance, but again: Bree doesn't lie. She wouldn't waste the words if she didn't care. "Yeah. I just need to talk to you later."

We're at the cool table this time, our usual lunchtime vibe disrupted by Trace's unsinkable grin. "You better wipe that off your face," Sage says, holding out one of her hot-lunch delicacies to him, a plastic cup of what's supposed to be a trail mix but is mostly pale, unsalted peanuts and withered raisins. "Crack takes one look at you, he's going to know something's up. You're never this happy at school."

"I can't help it. It's so funny." He ducks his head, snorting laughter, something he's been doing periodically since we sat down. Tries to compose himself, which only gets him laughing harder. He digs his fingers through the cup. "I only like those raisins covered in Elmer's."

Nobody seems to know about the hidden Bug but us—none of the students, anyway. Trace checked out the window during gym class; the VW still isn't back in the teachers' lot. I guess the administration and the cops must be keeping it hush-hush while they search for it, figuring drama is exactly what we attention whores want. I lost some sleep over it last night, the dread of getting caught, though it wasn't the only thing preying on my mind. Crackenback made it to work today anyway—I heard his rusty tones over the intercom this morning—and if the teachers' gazes are a little sharper, it could also be due to the general unease laying over everyone like the thin fog from a February thaw.

Everybody's gossiping, not about the principal's clunker getting stolen from school grounds last night, but about Ivy. The seven-day mark seems to have shaken everyone, the Lucky Number tearing through all those platitudes about runaways, kids hiding out somewhere nearby until they get too cold and hungry, then coming home, tail between their legs, desperate for mac and cheese and a free Wi-Fi connection. Word is, Ivy's mom in West Virginia still hasn't seen or heard from her. So that leaves darker explanations. Hitchhiking. Murder. Shallow burial in some interstate drainage ditch. We've all seen enough trash TV to know the score, and it's chilling. Sickening. Thrilling.

"About what?" Bree brings me back to the now, picking her sandwich into pieces as she watches me.

I hesitate when I notice Sage watching me, too, her gaze intent, a faint line between her brows. A silent signal to change tactics? I'm so close to spilling everything in totally the wrong place and time that I can almost taste the words, and I sit back, as if from the edge of a precipice.

Obviously, Sage knows about me and Kincaid. Trace must've told her, maybe gave her a heads-up that there was a nuclear detonation due any day now, and she might want to duck and cover. Kincaid isn't here today—apparently not even hanging out with me can make school tolerable for more than a couple days. I could borrow somebody's phone during break and text mine, hoping he'd answer, but that would open a can of worms I'm in no way ready to deal with. Besides, I know what he'd say if I told him about what I sensed last night, on the trail. More smoke, more flimflam.

"Have you ever had anything weird happen to you on the trails?" I say to Bree, as if this was where I was going all the time. "The ones behind the Terraces?" My yogurt requires stirring. Vigorous stirring. "Seen any animals or anything?"

"Squirrels."

"Deer," Sage puts in. I think I hear relief in her voice.

"You've seen deer out there?" Bree says.

"No, but there are some. They come up from the marsh." Sage surrenders her tray to Trace, who's still grazing.

I turn my spoon over. "Do deer ever, like . . . attack?"

Trace chokes on another laugh as whispers ripple through the room, making all of us look up in the direction of the double doors that open onto the main hallway.

Landon's come in, walking through the tables, making heads come together so fast half the school will be sitting down to our next class with subdural hematomas. It's obvious she's been crying hard, her face puffy, splotches of red on each cheek, usually a sign that somebody's just been released from Guidance. She doesn't have lunch or a backpack with her. Her gaze is fixed unwaveringly on us.

She lowers herself slowly onto the chair beside Sage, like a deep-sea diver navigating the dark, silent ocean bottom, the sights and sounds of the lunchroom only reaching her distantly, as whale song echoes.

Silence falls over us, stiff, uncomfortable, drying up any thought of condolence. We all stare at the tabletop.

Landon speaks flatly, not letting tears get in the way of what she needs to ask us: "Do you think she could have gone back?" I realize she's trembling, a low-level shudder affecting even her knotted fists pressed against the table edge. "That night?"

I meet eyes with Bree, then look to Trace. He's the only one facing Landon, his expression serious, but not pitying, or pained, like mine. "Back where, dude?"

"The marsh." She takes a breath, releases it slowly, trying to keep control. "Maybe she went back"—sharp gesture—"after the fight, after she left home."

"Why would she do that?"

"I don't *know*. Maybe she thought she lost something. Maybe she just wanted to get away from people for a while."

"It would've been really dark," Trace says.

"Yeah, and she doesn't know those trails. We've never been out there without everybody else. Maybe she got turned around, and"—she shakes her head helplessly—"I don't know. I don't know."

No one speaks. Sage shifts in her seat. "Lan. Maybe you should ask to go home."

Landon bangs her palm down, then again, harder; all of us flinch. Gets to her feet, in motion again, no longer interested in us. "I'm going." She walks around the end of the table. "I'm going to find her."

The cafeteria watches in stunned silence as she goes, shoving through the double doors with a teacher right on her heels, Sage's quiet "Now?" fading without response.

● ● ◐

I catch a ride with Trace after school. Nobody has much to say. The princess mask is nowhere to be seen, maybe hidden in the glove compartment, or under the seat.

First, we pick up the bag of demons at D&M. It *is* Thirsty Thursday, after all.

But when we reach the park, there's no skating, no hanging around bullshitting while everybody gets their buzz on. Because you can hear her. Landon. She's in the woods, not far off. Calling for Ivy.

It's horrible, like listening to some animal call for her young after a poacher has already done his damage. Kincaid's here, and I keep my distance. He looks, but doesn't approach, not with Bree so nearby. This sucks. I know what I need to do, but not how to do it—and that isn't a good enough excuse for silence anymore. A friend would tell Bree the truth, straight up. Because I know from experience that if I was lost in the woods, Bree would go looking for me.

Once the booze has been sold, Trace says, "I'm going to help her."

Most of us follow, pairing off in twos, which we all agree is the way we've seen people do it in the movies. Partner up, so nobody else gets lost.

We find Landon on the trail to the marsh. She's exhausted beyond crying, her face pale and drained, eyes deeply shadowed. She doesn't speak when Trace asks, "Where have you looked?" instead gesturing vaguely in the direction we came from. That leaves a lot of woods, more than the eight or so of us can hope to cover, but we're going anyway, into the marsh.

Bree and I pair together without words, without a plan, dovetailing down a slope covered in knee-high water grass bleached to a dry, autumnal blond, following muddy flats where standing water rises over our sneakers.

The others are already out of sight, their voices echoing back to us. Kincaid's walking with Moon; last I saw, they were climbing the ridge above the murals, going to check out the woods that stretch that way, off toward the cemetery.

"Gross." Bree stops, shaking mud off her laces. "You know, I bet real search parties wear things like boots."

"Do you really think Ivy might've come out here?" I say.

"No. Why would she? The night was over. We all know she got home in one piece. Of all the places she could've gone after a fight, she comes back here? It would've been pitch-black out, not to mention subzero." Bree sinks, swearing as the cuffs of her jeans get dunked. "I think Landon's lost it, personally." She hesitates, looking up ahead of us, her tone softening. "Look at that bird."

It's the egret, or a close relative, standing like a monument to patience. One leg bent, the other a stilt.

I say, "Bree," and, at my tone, she glances back. "Remember

I said we needed to talk?" She turns, the embankment of pitch pines and brush providing a stark backdrop, and maybe there's no better place for this, no better time, nowhere more solitary. "It's about Kincaid."

The topic seems to surprise her. "Yeah?"

I rub my eyes. "We kind of . . . he and I have been talking, and . . ." My stomach is acid, and my mouth suddenly tastes bad, metallic, like old pennies scraped off the bottom of a wishing fountain, and I spit out the last of it because there's no other way: "He likes me back."

The silence goes on. Her face, looking back at me, inscrutable, eyes a fraction wider than normal, taking me in. It's Bree, so she'll give me nothing, I know this, but it doesn't stop me from babbling, cramming the silence full of words to the point where I'm begging to be put out of my misery: "I'm sorry, I never thought he would, but he says he does and—" A small, weak laugh escapes me, and I wish I could stomp it. "Is it okay?"

She stands in her spot as if rooted. I rush on, hating how I sound, like one of Those Girls, a whole different species from me, ones who would choose boys over their friends. But that's what I'm doing, isn't it? I could've broken it off with him after that first time in the woods, stopped things before we went too far, put Bree first. But I wanted Kincaid. Even now, trapped in this torturous moment, I still do. "I'm so sorry, I didn't want to hurt you. I'd never do that.

187

You know that, right?" *You're my friend—maybe my best—I'm pretty sure you're my very best—* "It just kind of happened, and I know that sounds like the biggest cliché ever, but it's true." I could slump to the ground right now, sink into the mud, be buried forever without complaint. "I'm just really sorry."

I look back at her, wincing, bracing for an explosion, for her fist crashing into my face. I can almost see her internal adjustments, a pattern of slight movement from her throat, to her jaw, then her eyes, some fast blinks before her gaze settles on distant trees. Maybe the direction Kincaid went off in. "Why? I wouldn't be." Rough sound in her throat, signaling her sharp turn away from me. "He's hot, so. Enjoy."

She walks off, fast, and I follow because I don't know what else to do. No chance that I've been forgiven, but I don't want to make things worse by leaving. Ditching my partner.

We're the only ones not calling Ivy's name. Nothing here but the sound of our feet splashing through the shallows, and the heavy beat of the egret's wings as he takes off in search of calmer waters.

She's ditching me. Or trying.

I almost fall twice, following her up an embankment so steep that falling would mean rolling all the way back down to the flats in a battered heap. We clutch roots and clumps of bushes with our hands, reaching the top of the slope with our knees soaked through, our palms raw.

Bree pushes straight into the woods, letting branches snap back, one whipping my cheek so sharply that I stop, check for blood. "Will you slow down?"

"Why? We're supposed to be looking." The remoteness of her tone lands the punch that I was waiting for, forcing the air from me.

I watch her go, plowing a one-woman path through the undergrowth, then start after her again. Not sure where to draw the line—how many ravines should I fall down to pay penance? But if Bree fell, got lost, I'd never forgive myself. It'd be my fault, no matter how hard I'd tried to call her back.

We're in unfamiliar woods, no sign of a trail, no sign of anything but the usual maze, and I wish I could call Kincaid. I could describe a tree, and he'd give me directions home. Bree's breathing hard, I can hear it, and it's not until we hit the next gully that she snags her shoulder on one of those jagged pitch-pine branches, catching her fleece on it and swearing, giving her no choice but to stop.

"Let's turn around," I say, breathless, supporting myself against a trunk behind her. "Come on. We don't know where we're going."

She hesitates, looking ahead, shoulders moving as she breathes. "How long have you guys been hooking up?"

I don't like that she called it that—"hooking up"—even though everybody does; Kincaid just said it last night. But it's like saying that he and I aren't real, like what we've done in private is some cheap, disposable thing. "Only a couple days."

"Have you had sex with him yet?"

Another internal objection, this one stronger. My voice sharpens. "No. I just said, it's only been a couple days."

"Sorry. Didn't mean to offend."

I press my lips together, trying to absorb it, the snark, remembering that I've got a lot to make up for. You can't say, *Oh, hey, by the way, I stole your dream date*, and then get pissed when the person acts upset about it. "We should find the trail. I'm sure everybody's back at the park by now."

"Go, if you want." She's starting down the bank, sliding on mud and dead leaves, grabbing anything for a handhold, still showing me only her back.

I breathe out through my nose, going as far as the edge to watch her descend to another muddy cove, my sense of responsibility dulled by exhaustion. I could go back alone. Secure my spot in the Worst Friend Hall of Fame now and quit screwing around.

Instead, I follow. I'm not letting myself walk out on this. I'm part of the way down, eyes on where I'm stepping, when I hear her call my name. Just "Clara," no "belle." I'd think she was punishing me, but her tone is all wrong. Faint, disbelieving.

She's standing at the edge of the flats, looking down. It's low tide, the water receded far beyond my line of sight. "Yeah?" She doesn't answer, doesn't turn. It strikes a cold note. I start to hurry, skidding on my heels, falling on my ass at one point, smearing mud up the back of my coat, wet and cursing and miserable by the time I reach her. "What?"

When I see what she's looking at, I stop, staring, transfixed, just like Bree.

It's caked in mud, the denim jacket, like it's been submerged for some time and was only recently dislodged by the tide. Stiff, the embroidered band patches barely legible, one sleeve up, the other down, both bent at the elbows like there could be arms inside, like that's how she fell, and was swept away.

EIGHTEEN

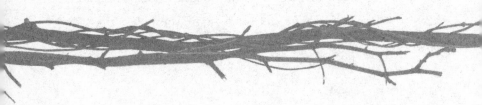

IT ISN'T UNTIL after, long after, when I'm in bed, Ma down in the kitchen making me undeserved hot chocolate and peanut butter crackers, like she used to when I was little and played outside in the cold too long—that I realize Kincaid managed to disappear himself again.

I can't say exactly when. Sometime after Bree and I raced back, panic calling a truce between us as she led the way to the trail—turned out I was the only one who was lost—and told everyone what we found. Landon got hysterical, the girlfriends actually surrendering their bench so she could huddle there, weeping, her head in her hands while Sage rubbed her back, murmuring comfort as we waited on the cops to answer our call. By the time they arrived, Kincaid was gone.

"You good?" Ma's in the doorway, watching me.

"Yeah." I sit up. "Just reading." *A Clockwork Orange* lies open on my lap. Alex is being strapped to a chair in the screening room, eyelids forced open, ready to begin his treatment.

She nudges the origami jack-o'-lantern aside with the mug and plate, not sparing it more than a glance. Part of me wants her to see the message on the back, ask who wrote it, who would be giving me October gifts, while the other part of me doesn't have the first clue how to begin the subject of Kincaid. I won't kid myself that he's the kind of guy my parents would love seeing me with. His brand is anti-school, anti-authority, and that would get Ma's back up about as far as it can go. I'd never get her to believe that anarchy isn't contagious. She checks out the cover of *Clockwork*. Flames, a screaming mouth. "Looks fun."

"Caught me. I was trying to throw you off. I've got a stash of your Harlequins under my mattress."

"Now that's what I'm talking about. Finally showing some taste." We smile a little, but the moment fades fast. "They're sure it was this girl's jacket? It couldn't be a mistake?"

I shake my head. "It was hers. One of a kind." After the chaos and the crying and the general evacuation of the skate park precipitated by the word "cops," Bree and I led the

193

officers back to Ivy's jacket. It seemed to take no time at all, as if the doom creature carried me there, releasing its talons and dropping me back to earth like a flailing fish not worth the trouble. Then questions, a million of them, and a call to Ma, who has the night off and came to pick me up.

Ma reaches out, squeezing my hand. "I'm sorry."

"I didn't really know her." But that's a cop-out, an easy trapdoor to avoid all these awful feelings, to avoid thinking about how Ivy seemed like a really cool person, somebody I would've liked to get to know better. "She seemed nice. And funny."

Ma squeezes tighter, her eyes glistening a little. "God. Her parents. I can't even imagine." Sighing, she puts the mug in my hands. "Here. Drink. Pretend it's got marshmallows, because we don't have any." She sits forward, as if to stand, then stops with her hands spread on her thighs, gaze on the carpet. "Promise me you and your friends won't go out there. To that marsh. It sounds dangerous as hell, and if one kid drowned . . ."

This may not be the time to mention Ricky Sartain and Dabney Kirk. "We won't go." Tiptoeing around so many lies with careful word choice, and hating myself for it—not actually saying *promise*, because I can't swear I won't go back into the woods. Like it or not, the woods are Kincaid.

Ma's sharp. She fixes me with a hard look, and thank God Dad chooses that moment to come down the hall and look in on me. "How're you doing? Need anything?"

I lift the mug. "Got it covered. Thanks." Though I don't think I can touch these snacks. Ten-year-old Clara earned them; the current version has spent this day hurting people and telling half-truths. I watch as Ma gets up and goes over to him, the way his arm finds its way around her shoulders like it belongs there. She doesn't push me for more answers, not now, but she lets her gaze linger on me as they go.

I read for a while, soothed by the sound of my parents' quiet conversation from behind their bedroom door, even though they're most likely talking about how worried they are, how next time, it could be our family, their kid.

I go down the hall, take Ma's phone from the counter, bring it back to my room, and shut the door softly behind me, sending Kincaid a text to my phone. I can always delete the conversation from Ma's phone after we're done. Sneaking around is getting old fast, but I hope now that I've spilled to Bree, I can get back to being a basically honest person again.

Hey. He's seeing Ma's name on the screen right now. *It's me, the unknown quantity.*

Wait, wait. Bloop—quote bubble. *Hey I still have your phone.*

I muffle a snort; uh, yeah, I know. *Where'd you go today? Not a big fan of cops.*

I consider typing *who is?* It would've been nice having him around, is all, after the showdown with Bree, and seeing

Ivy's jacket hardened in the mud like that. I wonder if it ever occurred to him that I might've needed him. *They think Ivy's dead. Cops didn't say so but you could tell.*

Wait, wait. *A jacket's not a body.*

I straighten, watching the cursor blink. *Do you think she's alive?*

Not really

The words, unanchored by a period, seem to hover and sink, like some forecast seen in the haze of a crystal ball. He has an odd, tilting way of coming at a subject, even in writing. Try a different topic. *Are you at home?*

Where's home.

A pause, exasperated. *Are you drunk?*

FUBAR.

Is this a game—I take one step forward, he takes one step back? *Should I let you go throw up in peace?*

Lol miss your face.

I want to say something about Bree, but I'm pretty sure that was his way of signing off, and I hate the thought of the message *I told her about us* waiting on the screen for him tomorrow morning. Was he serious about being drunk? Does he ever go home? Wonder about his family. Wonder how hard he's going to make me work for these details, if it should have to be work at all. If that's a warning sign of a hookup.

◑ ● ◑

Friday motif: strange sense of unfulfillment.

Everybody's heard the news about Ivy, but the general mood is quiet, charged, discussion kept to close-knit groups of three or four, comparing facts, trading tragedy. Lips move in near-silent formation: *Mumbler's Marsh. Mumbler's Marsh.* Linking Ivy and Gavin Cotswold together, too coincidental— two kids who went missing only to turn up dead, out there, in the wilderness. The Mumbler's MO.

It doesn't matter if people really believe or not—it's an affirmation of superstitious dread that does nothing to improve the gloom of Spille's bourbon-clouded lecture, or distract from the misery-guts drama queens rushing out of classrooms to Guidance, where they can gasp about how much they miss Ivy already and how it really makes you think—at least until they've killed most of the school day and get to go home. In my last school, two seniors died in a car accident; these same people were there, behaving the same way. Different faces, different names, same opportunistic bullshit.

Not like Landon, who's broken. Her absence isn't mentioned. Who knows when she'll be back?

And everybody's seen the pics, courtesy of some Raging Elk whose ass must be suspension-bound for uploading them to his social media and tagging half the school before telling his coach what he found on yesterday's practice run.

Crackenback's tan 1971 VW Beetle, parked blocking the cross-country trail, bookended between two trees so tightly that the front bumper cut a visible gash into the bark.

Then, the money shot: the driver's-side door hanging open for a close-up of the stick shift, sheathed in a giant orange condom with a perky black tip.

Seventh-period assembly. Wish I could close myself up in my locker, in the peaceful dark, and wait it out.

The bus stop was worse than awkward this morning. Whatever anger Bree felt yesterday seems to have cooled into a barren, icy wasteland between us, with her barely acknowledging my presence, and me too emotionally sapped to argue my case, if I even wanted to. Sage, stuck in the middle, eventually gave up on conversation and looked at her phone instead. I don't want it to be like this, and I have no idea how to make it better. Hazel knows something's happened, and spent her time studying me, like the answer might be obvious on my face, some freakish overnight transformation into her sister's worst enemy.

Now, as I reach the gym, I don't look for anyone to sit with, just troop up the bleachers, watching for Kincaid, trying not to compare myself to my memory of Landon up here, toe tracing the air as she waited for the girl she might never see alive again. Wonder if this is my future here. Life without friends, because I botched it. And a boyfriend who may or may not exist.

I glance over as a stack of pamphlets printed on slick paper are placed in my hand. Mr. Mac stands over me, today's casual Friday ensemble consisting of relaxed-fit jeans, a tucked-in polo in a shade of chick-fuzz yellow. "Do me a favor and pass them down, please?" The title reads *You Are Not Alone*, and there's a photo of a hoodie-wearing girl with her face pressed against her bent knees. As I hand them on to the next person and the stack works its way down the line, most of them waft to the floor and are ground beneath shifting sneakers.

Somebody taps my shoulder. I turn to see Trace lower himself into the space beside me, never mind that there isn't enough room and he almost sits on somebody's hand. I don't see Sage—she must be with Bree, somewhere. "What up." He passes me my phone.

"Why do you have this?" I look back, scanning the rows. "Is he here?"

"Was. For like a minute."

Unease is stealthy, spreading through my body with slow deliberation. "Why didn't he give it to me himself?"

"Probably because he wanted to get out of this shithole ASAP before they start the your-friend-is-dead-but-that's-no-reason-not-to-learn-about-the-hypotenuse-of-a-triangle speech." Raises his voice: "Today should be canceled," making heads turn. Hyde glares, but stays at parade rest between Klatts and Tourneau, cutting us that much slack to act out our grief and inner turmoil. "Seriously. Like Ivy didn't rate an early dismissal." Trace stays quiet a second, head and knee bobbing to some internal beat. "You and Kincaid, huh."

I nod slowly, wonder if I'll ever not feel that stab of guilt, like we've been caught. "So it would seem."

"You and Bree have your little talk? Thought I felt a cold front coming down." Lower: "She's had a lady boner for Kincaid for pretty much ever."

"I wasn't trying to steal him."

"Hey. You can't make a play, hang up your jock, that's what I say."

I glance at him, curious to know what Kincaid said to him about me, but struggling not to ask because, considering what's happened to Ivy, it shouldn't matter. "I guess. Thanks." Trace gives a chuff of laughter, rubbing his face with his hands, and there's something comforting about him, bigger and more substantial than anything in our surroundings on this strange awful day, and I'm okay with the fact that he's sitting too close and his dirty untied bootlace is lying on my foot.

Crackenback begins, Mrs. Mac standing nearby, her eyes moist and glittering behind her glasses. Crackenback delivers a brief, no-frills summary of what we all know about Ivy—presumed drowned, police searching the salt marsh—then pauses a moment, as if, somewhere inside that dry husk, a tear has formed. None of us blinks; we're riveted by him, a museum exhibit in tweed and a red carnation, giving this single drop of precious, genuine emotion time to evaporate before saying, "If you'd like to share your thoughts and prayers with Ivy's family, Mrs. Mac asks that you write them down and hand them on to her, and she'll see that they get them. The Thayers should be given privacy at this time."

Soft sounds of muffled crying in the bleachers, echoing up to the rafters, festooned with sports balls forever wedged between the steel beams and the ceiling. "And finally." Crackenback's translucent gaze rises to our faces. "The theft and defilement of my antique auto is hardly news to any of you, I'm sure. All I'll say is this. We're aware of you pranksters. We're highly anticipating your next move, because it will be your last as students enrolled at Pender District High. Anyone"—his gaze sweeps across the bleachers—"named in connection with what happened on Prefect Street, or to my car, will face expulsion. No appeals. No second chances."

I spot Kincaid as we sweep down through the double doors toward the main hallway, the general confusion forming the perfect distraction for his escape. Black coat, light hair, slipping past the office windows—where the secretaries dwell like supreme beings surrounded by frosted glass, Keepers of the Files, their distorted voices filtered through pipes and grates—right out the front doors. I want to stop him, pull him back, make him talk to me. Really talk, not play games and dance around the truth.

"Trace—" But he isn't beside me anymore, and I start

to hurry, cutting between people, trying to catch up to him. I want some affirmation of Kincaid and me, proof that I haven't lost Bree for nothing. Him passing off my phone feels like a brush-off, like he didn't want me to trap him in another conversation. If that's how I make him feel—caged, smothered—then I sure as hell shouldn't be the last to know.

I'm not totally clear on Trace's schedule, but he headed in the direction of the art room the last time we used the basement entrance to get back in time for seventh period. The bell hasn't rung yet—he's probably in there, killing the last few minutes before the class change to eighth period.

The art room, air thick with pottery dust and paint fumes, is a battlefield. The teacher hasn't made it back from the gym yet, so bits of broken pastels and colored pencils soar through the air; a lead point bounces off my cheek, making me swear and smack my hand over it. Trace lounges in a chair by the window, paying attention to none of it as I come up to him. "Can I borrow the key to the back door?"

"What for?"

"I just need to get out of here." I hold out my hand, keeping my expression as blank as possible, trying for a Bree face; I don't want him knowing how scared I am of getting caught, or how worried I am about what Kincaid will say when I catch up to him. "I won't lose it or anything. Promise."

After a second, he takes his key chain from his pocket, pressing the basement key into my palm. "Don't forget to lock it behind you, going *and* coming back. Custodians usually don't come in until two o'clock, so you got time, but if one of them figures out what's going on, bye-bye Key to the Kingdom. Got it?"

"Got it."

The bell rings as I go down the east hallway, trying not to run—I'll never catch Kincaid at this rate—stopping at the blank door that conceals the steps down to the basement. Take a breath, put the key in, hesitate a moment until traffic's light, then sweep myself inside, laying my shoulder into the door, waiting just a moment to see if some teacher will try to follow me through. Doesn't happen.

I go after him, locking up behind me.

It plays out one way in my mind: catching up with Kincaid, how happy he'll be to see me, how he'll put all my fears to rest, be real with me. Then our kisses right there on the sidewalk in full view of the world.

But this is how it really goes: I run down the hill, hope sinking fast, seeing no sign of him. Standing despondent on the corner of School Street and Main, lost as to where to go, other than the park. I'm already running the risk of getting busted for skipping last period—being spotted on Main Street could hurt my chances of convincing them I was in the bathroom the whole time, barfing straight through to the bell.

I'm about to turn around when Kincaid pops out of the shelter of a doorway down the street, the old Strand movie theater, which looks like it's been closed for decades. A familiar adjustment of his coat, then pushes off on his board. I know what he was doing—using the shadows for a quick sip of Fireball, a fifty-milliliter bought fresh from Trace yesterday before everything happened.

Kincaid takes off, rolling across the bank parking lot without even glancing over at the sedan that nearly hits him, the driver stomping his brakes, mouthing unheard curses.

I could call Kincaid's name; he'd probably hear me from here. But now I don't want to.

I follow, my pace determined. He's not going to lose me this time, like he did the night that Bree and I followed him after our assault on Perfect. I want to know what he does, where he goes, how he manages to spend almost every day doing whatever the hell he wants, no one asking uncomfortable questions. Except me, of course, but he dodges my attempts so easily, clouding the issue with tall tales, every trick he keeps up his sleeve. I should know these things. Because we are not just hooking up. Of that, I'm almost sure.

For a time, Kincaid seems aimless, just cruising the town, jumping a curb here and there. Business owners must be used to seeing him roam all hours of the day. Halloween decorations are everywhere, wraiths with plastic skulls and ragged shrouds hanging from the street signs on Main, cardboard cutouts in windows, pumpkins on doorsteps.

He heads up the street we took the day we walked back from D&M, pushing hard uphill. I stay as far back as I dare, rounding the corner as Kincaid passes the halfway point.

When I reach the crest of the hill, I'm not sure what direction he went in; there's a four-way intersection of streets, the old cemetery visible with the blazing oak on the left. Then I hear it, plastic wheels grinding over concrete.

We take Summer, a bolt of excitement passing through me. He's going home. I force myself to keep the same slow, measured pace, letting him have a big lead, careful not to tip him off to my presence. There's got to be a reason why he didn't want Bree and me to see where he lives. Just having a crappy house isn't enough; we all have crappy houses.

He cuts through the hedges at the usual place, then continues through the next yard, doubling back down an offshoot called Lorimer, a dead-end sign standing at the foot.

I'm not sure where to hide myself as he goes to the last possible house, a little brown chalet-style cottage surrounded by dead hedges overwhelmed by bittersweet vine, woods closing in at the back. There's a car in the driveway, a maroon compact that seems somehow too low to the ground, as if all four tires are losing air in tandem. A mailbox with the name *Nevers* on it.

I step back behind an old ash tree in the neighbor's yard, really hoping that nobody chooses this moment to gaze out the window at the foliage. At this point, though, I almost don't care if Kincaid catches me. Knowing is all I care about.

Kincaid goes past the driveway to the wooded turnaround, into the trees. For a long two minutes, I can't see him.

Then he crosses the lawn—no board, on foot—moving at a fast clip, skipping a couple steps as he lets himself in the front door, his shape visible through the glass panes of the sunporch for a moment before he moves deeper into the house.

I wait, but in what feels like no time, he's back, going briskly down the steps, over to the tree cover where he stashed his board. He doesn't emerge right away. I look around the other side of the tree, trying to get a better view. I think he's just standing there, mostly hidden by woods, looking up at the house.

Then a silhouette moves past the first-floor windows of the house, onto the sunporch, drawn by the sound of the front door closing. It's a woman, wearing gray—a sweatshirt, faded jeans. As she opens the storm door and screen, looking out, I see her short-cropped hair, pale brown, something that was maybe once a style, since ignored, allowed to lose shape and creep into her collar.

She stands with the screen door open a few feet, not wide enough for anyone to fit through, should they try. Waiting. From nowhere, I hear an echo of my own words from the other night on the trail—*That you?*

Finally, she steps back. I watch her progress through the house. Her silhouette appears at a front window—kitchen, probably, standing at the sink—where she continues to look out at the world for a time before receding from view.

Kincaid will skate back down the street now. There's no way he could miss me coming from that direction, so I'll confront him, ask if that's his mom he did an end run around, and why. But he doesn't come. That hint of him I could see through the trees is gone now. He left through the woods.

NINETEEN

THEY'VE GOT DEACON POSEY, the little wannabe skater boy, on the rack this afternoon, stretched on his belly on top of the monkey bars with one guy holding his arms, another his legs. Moon warms up his drumsticks, *ratatatat*-ing on a seesaw, then runs under the monkey bars, pummeling Deacon from forehead to toes before skidding across the cedar chips on his knees, sticks crossed over his head. "Thank you and good *night!*"

Deacon howls, then giggles wildly when the other guys laugh.

I watch from the sidelines, sitting closest to Hazel, my phone balanced on my knee. As if Bree hasn't banished me,

I'm just deeply engaged in a rousing game of Toy Blast.

Maybe not banished. But whenever I look up, Bree's giving me her sharp shoulder or her profile or her back, and there's so much unacknowledged tension among all of us that I'm surprised the park isn't crackling like a power station. Everybody obviously knows about me and Kincaid and Bree; nobody's letting on what they think. Nobody's talked directly to me yet since I showed up at the park after school—except for Trace's "Sweet," when I returned the key—and it's ridiculous, how much it matters, how I'm dissecting every movement and word for meaning, wondering if people will start taking sides. He's here, Kincaid, following the circuit, off in his own world again.

I didn't go back to school for eighth period. Instead, I killed time wandering the side streets until school let out, lost in thought, sitting on the curb for a while, watching fallen leaves blow around yards and storm drains. I used to fantasize about cutting class all the time, wondering what it would be like, spending all day out in the world, free. But maybe there's a point where freedom just becomes loneliness, living without a compass, lost in your own life. That's what I saw today, watching Kincaid. It haunts me, the way that gray woman on Lorimer peered out her door at the world, maybe waiting for him, maybe not. Never once calling his name.

"Makes no sense." Sage shakes her head as she watches the torture of Deacon Posey without really seeing it, her eyes swollen from tears. "I couldn't sleep at all last night. I just kept thinking about it. Why would she have gone back out there?" Ivy's on everybody's mind, and I'm ashamed of worrying about my stupid drama, particularly the nagging thought that, thanks to skipping, my backpack is now trapped in my locker all weekend, my homework with it.

"She wouldn't." Bree stands with arms folded, obviously avoiding looking at Kincaid. I never meant to make her feel like she couldn't look. It's crazy how much I want to tell her what I learned today, about the little brown chalet house, how Kincaid snuck in and out like a thief. "I guess . . . when they find her, they can test her blood and everything, see how drunk she was. But even then."

"She only bought one little bottle from me." Trace, his tone sharp. "Same as always. Nobody's getting drunk off that. And if she was acting wasted, wouldn't her parents have told the cops that?"

"People think the Mumbler got her."

Everyone turns to Hazel. She looks frankly back at us, shifting her laptop, hair blowing around her earmuffs. "It's just like the song says. He buried her where the milkweed grows. Like those other kids who got killed. Like Gavin Cotswold." She's starting to show signs of wavering under Bree's stare. "They'll probably never find her because he took her deep down into the mud."

"Who thinks that? Your friends?" Bree waits until Hazel

nods. "Yeah, well. Your friends are also, like, two years out of light-up sneakers."

Kincaid slows to a stop, and it's strange, seeing him through this new filter, a mortal with a mother, a home. I probably have as much personal knowledge about him as anyone now, and there are about ten different things I wish he'd say to me, none of which start with, "We saw him that night. Didn't we?"

"Saw who?" Bree says.

"The Mumbler." Kincaid. "He was out there."

"What? When and where did this happen?" Sage's attention is focused on me.

"When I got lost, and Kincaid found me." I shake my head, holding his gaze. I see it now, how he uses these stories to keep me at arm's length, to cast everything in a distorted light. "He pretended he saw something on the bank across from us."

"I never pretend."

"Yes, you do." I raise my voice. "You were messing with me. Again."

"What exactly *didn't* you see?" Trace is waiting.

"I don't know. Kind of like . . . a head. Some shoulders. But it was just bushes and trees and stuff." I point at Kincaid. "He's the one who made it something else. To scare me." Wish I hadn't tacked that on; sounds petulant and little-girl-ish. "Okay. New subject."

"Do you think it really was somebody?" Sage looks between us. "I don't mean the Mumbler, but a real guy? Somebody who got Ivy?"

"No," I say, even though the idea of it makes my stomach churn, the thought of someone standing there, so unnaturally still, watching Kincaid and me together.

"A kid in my class saw the Mumbler once." Hazel sounds thoughtful. "Outside in the trees behind his house. Just watching. He said his eyes glowed white."

"Ew, Hazel," Bree says distractedly, but Hazel goes on.

"And I know a couple kids who think he came into their rooms, back when they were little."

"Came in? How?" I ask.

Hazel shrugs. "Under the bed. Through the closet. You know. The monster tunnels." I jerk slightly, touched by a cold finger, seeing my closet door; first open, then shut, a movement ever so slight. "Everybody says you should leave your jack-o'-lantern burning all night on Halloween, until the candle's gone. He likes that."

"Should we tell the cops? About there maybe being somebody in the marsh that night?" Sage asks.

"Not somebody. Him." Kincaid sounds unperturbed, reaching down to smooth the peeling corner of duct tape wrapped around his board. "I know the signs. He was checking us out. Trying to tell if we were ripe."

"That's bad, Clarabelle. Really bad." Hazel shakes her

head. "The Mumbler knows who you are now. Maybe he put his mark on you. You'd better stay home on Halloween. And be super nice to the trick-or-treaters, too—don't give out anything sucky like root beer barrels, or he'll probably kill you."

Kincaid laughs, and the fact that I could strangle him right now kind of blurs behind how clean the lines of his jaw and throat are when he tips his head back like that. "I like you, helper elf. You can stay."

Hazel smiles hesitantly. I aim a kick at him but don't follow through, letting him skate off because I'm afraid it'll look like cutesy couple fighting. Because Bree. Of course.

I don't know which comes first, the dream or the sounds. Maybe they grow together. One moment I'm on the verge of sleep, then I'm standing at the foot of my bed, feeling very much awake, very here, the carpet beneath my bare feet and the closet door before me. The light is on inside.

Faint sounds—*tickaticktick*. Better make sure nothing's in there. Because closets are not to be trusted.

Behind the door stands Kincaid. He takes up the doorway, silhouetted by light, head tilted at a slight angle, looking down at me, gaze steady, no smile, which isn't like him. "Hi," I say, vaguely registering the muffled, distant quality of my voice. Anxiety begins to constrict my chest. Something's wrong about all this. "What were you doing in there?"

He keeps looking, staring so deeply into my eyes that I'm compelled to look back. I'm missing it, whatever it is, whatever he's imploring me to see. A rush of emotion, the warm tangle of everything I feel for him all at once, and, "Come here," I whisper, reaching out, just wanting to heal it, whatever it is. He stoops to me, letting me slide my arms around him.

Tick. Tickaticktick. Those sounds, right by my ear. *Moth.* The word's in my head, on my lips. His back is hot and moving, not the rise and fall of breathing, but squirming. Alive. I pull back, disbelief rendering me slow, stupid, as his coat slides open.

I see them, hundreds of them, lace-border moths, crawling and twitching and fluttering, nothing inside but moths.

I scream, and they explode, a whirlwind of moths pounding through me, my hair, my clothes, battering my eyes and mouth with papery fury, my ears full of the roar of their wind until—

—my brain throws some internal overload switch, and I'm out of it, awake, the storm of moths fading, trickling to the faintest *tickticktick. Ticka-tick.*

I stare at my closet door. The space beneath the door is dark. The clock face glows red: 2:37 a.m.

Tickatick. The sounds are real enough, the rest of the dream some rancid, shameful cloud that I try to clear from my mind as I sit up. God. Kincaid, as some thing. Some creature.

Turn on the lamp, stare hard at the closet, then grab *A Clockwork Orange* from the nightstand—my best protection, some skinny little paperback. Go to the closet door, test the knob, compelled to repeat the dream's pattern.

The light from my bedside lamp casts a dim glow inside the closet. Nothing but the stain. The shoebox. But I hear another *tickatick*. I pull the chain to the closet bulb.

They're walking the ceiling. Moths, at least half a dozen. The light sends them into motion, one dive-bombing me, driving me back against the door with a gasping curse.

I dart out, slam the door, hearing them battling the bulb now—*scritchscritchscritch-tickaticktick*. I jump into bed, yank the comforter over my head, eyes wide in the soft, crumpled dark.

It's Saturday, and I'm scratchy from lack of sleep, from lying awake listening to the sound of insect bodies bouncing off a lightbulb, wondering if my nightmare somehow ripped a hole in reality to let those things in.

I shower, inhale breakfast, then drag Ma's vacuum cleaner into my room, grab the hose, and throw open the closet door, jabbing the nozzle to the ceiling before their tiny bug brains have a chance to register fight or flight.

When it's done, I think I stand a chance of sleeping in this room again.

Ma comes out of the bathroom, does a double take at

the door when she spots the vacuum. "Whoa." She puts her hands up. "Sorry. Thought I saw you cleaning for a second there."

"Must've been all that acid in the sixties."

"Ha-ha. Don't even joke about me being that old." She leans on the doorframe. "I'm heading to Bangor. Groceries and stuff. Want to come?"

"Nah. I've got plans." With Kincaid.

After lunch, I ask Dad if I can borrow his car, then head out, casting a look over at Bree's window. No obvious signs of life. Faye's Jeep is in the lot, so I'm guessing Bree's probably hanging out in her room, avoiding her mom.

You ride high in Dad's Suburban, and it's strange, looking down at the street from up here, seeing all our shortcuts and escape routes from a bird's-eye perspective. Wonder if this is sort of how Kincaid feels most of the time, flying above the sidewalk on his board, rarely touching down.

The dream left me spooked, begging for an analysis I'm not sure I want to make. But I'm sure I want to see him, make sure he's okay, then finally get some answers.

I check the park first—almost nobody around this time of day on a weekend, but plenty of cop cruisers parked along the curb. Out there in the marsh, searching for Ivy.

I drive around for a while, thinking maybe I'll find him skating down some random street. I end up in a neighborhood

I recognize, the one with the old cemetery. I park the Suburban on the grassy shoulder, and continue through the stones on foot, stopping to read inscriptions, particularly the ancient ones made from black slate. Crazy to think about being dead and buried for almost two centuries longer than you lived.

I didn't plan to go into the woods, but I do. Gingerly at first, lots of stopping and listening, as if I might hear his footsteps far off, some hint that it's worth braving this place again to find him. It's quiet, peaceful. A bird sings, then falls silent.

I choose a direction and go, moving fast, hands in my pockets, senses working overtime. Even in the daylight, it's scary being here, but maybe I want to prove to myself that I can take on Kincaid's demons, anything he can throw at me. And maybe I'm still trying to figure out what he sees in this place. *It's a good place to be alone.* Like the egret, standing sentry.

I walk until I reach the ledge above the murals, not straying as close to the edge as Kincaid did the day he smiled down at me. From here, you can see the view spreading out for miles, the boats of the searchers bobbing on the water like small colored specks, dragging the depths for Ivy's body. I didn't intend to watch this. I leave quickly, gaze on my steps as I follow the jagged circumference of the ledge, carved by some glacier millions of years ago.

Maybe forty yards away, I step on something that crunches underfoot. A cellophane wrapper with a paperboard tray, the kind Twinkies or Devil Dogs come in. These woods are strewn with trash, but the next thing I see is the distinctive blue of a tarp, rumpled, just visible around the base of a lichen-spotted granite boulder.

I round the rock, see how a piece of old cedar fence paneling has been propped up between the boulder and some trees to create a makeshift wall to block wind, the tarp there to shield from the rain. It's a shelter. No blankets or newspapers on the ground as a cushion, but it's been worn to dirt, as if the sleeper takes his bedroll with him each time he leaves.

TWENTY

I WAIT AT the park until he shows, sitting on a bench where I can watch the street, refusing to budge when one of the girlfriends turns up with her boy. She glances at me, sits on the opposite bench, and makes herself busy with her phone, apparently acknowledging my right to take up space now.

Kincaid appears, so far away that I'm not even sure if it's him at first. He jumps off the sidewalk, coasts in the break-down lane, then jumps back over the curb before repeating the whole process. Even with the skill involved, there's a weird, unsteady rhythm to it, like he might lose control at any moment and bite pavement.

He sees me and comes over, dropping down on the bench

so close that our thighs touch. I'm aware of the other girl-friend watching us from the corner of her eye. "This, here?" He gestures to me, on the bench. "Prime example of kismet. I was just thinking about you."

Whiskey bristles the air between us. "Well. You're . . . aromatic today." I watch as he laughs, nodding slowly, like his head feels so light it might drift away. "Wasted, huh?"

"Yes." His own solemnity makes him laugh again.

"It's three o'clock."

"That late already? Shit."

"Any chance I could get some coffee into you? Maybe try to talk?" I can't catch his gaze. "Kincaid?"

He comes back to the moment. "Yeah. Definitely. What-ever." Stretches, groans, rests back on the bench, eyes closed, feeling the thin autumn light on his face. "Wherever you want to go, Clarabelle."

We end up at Song's. He kept his eyes closed during the ride in the Suburban, neither of us speaking, me glancing over at him now and then, wondering how to begin, thinking about those marks on the dirt, the impression of a sleeping body.

Even at an off time on a Saturday, quite a few booths are taken as we seat ourselves in Song's dining room. Kin-caid opens the paper napkin and gets to work folding—first halves, then thirds. I watch him, the feeling of the nightmare coming over me again, shifting, unreal, like déjà vu. If he makes an origami moth, I might scream.

Daisy appears eventually, holding menus to her chest as she watches Kincaid, engrossed in art, his face inches above his work. She glances at me. "I'm guessing this is one of those savant things."

"Can we have some coffee?"

Kincaid looks up. "Tea. Please. For me."

When I change my order to ask for the same, Daisy goes, not bothering to leave the menus. She knows if we're eating, it's buffet. I found a couple loose dollars in the center console of the Suburban, and I have a little left over from the cash Ma gave me this week.

After we get our food, I settle back into the booth and sip some tea. I understand the appeal, particularly for Kincaid; they lace it with so much sugar here that my body gets an instant buzz. The origami sits half-finished, creation unrealized. Time to wade in. "So. I've been thinking about the fortune you gave me. How you made me think you knew what it said before I even opened it. But you didn't. You guessed. What are there, maybe three basic subjects? Love, money, fate. Right? When you asked me how I liked my fortune, you watched my reaction, then picked the one you thought would be most likely to bother me. Fate."

He eats an egg roll, hopefully sponging some of the demon from his system. "Says a lot about a person. Those three subjects. You're already lucky in love." I laugh. "Don't give a shit about money. It's just fate that gets you. Facing the unexpected." He studies me. "Why?"

I fold my arms on the table. "I guess because I'm scared of it. I hate the idea that we can't control our own lives."

"Is that what the fortune said?"

"Well, no. Not exactly." I glance up, catch his intensity as he conducts a two-second postmortem of my expression. My mouth moves in a reluctant smile, and I shake my head. "I'm giving you everything you need to play me, aren't I?" His smile broadens, and he sits back against the booth, caught. He seems better now, back in the moment with me. That's when I drive in my first nail: "Do you live on Lorimer Street?"

Kincaid's smile fades. His brows are still raised, eyes on me.

"Down at the end? The brown house?" Nothing. "Nevers. That's your last name, right?" He doesn't speak.

"Jesus, Kincaid. I just want to know you. Why do you make it so hard?" Shake of his head, his gaze finding the exit behind me. "You don't go home sometimes, do you? You stay out all night." I've got him, wings pinned to a board, but it doesn't feel good, no payoff for making him feel this trapped. "I found your bed. Out in the marsh."

He holds still, but maybe I'm picking up some skills from him, because my answers are all there, in his silent exhalation, the set of his mouth. He wants out of here, away from me, and maybe I'm ruining what we have, but I can't stop now. "You really sleep there? God. That's crazy." Silence.

"Your parents don't even care? Did they kick you out?"

More silence. As good as a yes. "She doesn't know." Pause. "She doesn't want to know."

She. No dad. I try to keep my voice level. "Is that what you meant, when you talked about being scared so much? You meant sleeping out there, alone. With nothing. How long have you been doing this?"

He rubs the side of his head distractedly, one of his braids surfacing, the end coiling on his shoulder, fastened with a plain rubber elastic. "Since summer. It wasn't bad, at first. Anyway. I've got what I need." He touches his coat, where the inner pocket lies, heavy with whatever's left of the bottle. "I sleep okay."

"Kincaid. That's how people freeze to death. Can't you stay with Trace, Moon, somebody?"

He shrugs, looking out the window. "Sometimes I do. But it's not like their families need another problem."

I exhale heavily, trying to control my frustration, not show how much it hurts, thinking of him alone in that makeshift shelter, just trying to get through till morning. "The night Ivy went back out there. Did you see her?"

He leans on his elbows, rubbing his eyes with both hands. "See all kinds of things. Hear things. Half the time I never really know. . . ." I can fill in the rest: he doesn't know what's real, and what's some bad dream brought on by too much fire demon to drive out the chill.

"If you saw Ivy, we have to tell the cops."

"No. I mean . . . I don't know. Maybe there was something." Shuts his eyes, gives his head a slight shake, loosening a memory. "Like a light. But it was there, and then . . ." Breathes out, opens his eyes. "Maybe it wasn't even that night. It all kind of blends, you know?"

I reach across the table and take his hand, squeezing his fingers, which somehow still feel cold to me. "Why did your mom kick you out?"

He pulls his hand back. Bounces in place a little, ready to move. Because as long as you keep moving, nobody can pin you down, right? "Want to go? I can pay for us."

I sit back, folding my arms, forcing myself not to keep pushing as he digs money out of his wallet, tossing it down where Daisy can see it the next time she wanders through. I add two extra dollars to the tip, as if that will somehow raise us in her estimation.

When we get back into the car, I begin, "The money," focusing on fastening my seat belt, remembering how he went into the house, coming out a minute later, before his mom could follow. Enough time to get into a purse.

He stretches his legs out in the space under the dash. "I go home sometimes, take what I need."

"Think she wants you to have it?" I shift into drive, glancing over when he doesn't answer right away.

"I don't know what she wants. But she doesn't want me

there with her. She said so."

"During a fight?" I glance at him. "Everybody says stupid stuff when they're mad. I'm sure if you just talked to her—"

"She changed the locks."

And I've got nothing. "Really?"

He nods slowly. Then he reaches over without looking, sliding his hand from my knee, along my inner thigh, between my legs, and my pulse is there, meeting his touch. I've learned so much, gotten so many answers, but somehow it comes back to this, the two of us, and I move into his gentle pressure. "I just want to be with you." His voice is quiet.

I breathe out, trying to focus on the road. "Where can we go?" Not the woods. That's cold estrangement to me now; we deserve better.

"I have a place." He rests back, doesn't move his hand. "You know how to get there."

My stomach is churning by the time we reach the end of Lorimer and the little house. There's no car in the drive this time. "You're sure she won't come home?"

"Not anytime soon. She works Saturdays." He's got my jeans unbuttoned, edging the zipper down.

"But the locks . . ."

"Only so many places to hide an extra key."

The street is hushed, the daylight beginning to fade as we go inside together, Kincaid letting us in with the key he pulled out from the gap under the front steps, holding my hand the whole time. She didn't leave any lamps on. *We shouldn't be here*, I think, but don't say. This is his home; and there's nowhere else for us to go.

As we pass through the dim kitchen, I get a quick impression of the private nature of his mom's life. Bare surfaces; a spoon rest by the electric kettle, a jar of instant coffee; small plate and fork in the dish rack. Faint odor of dust.

He leads me upstairs. He has a room, of sorts; a bed with a metal frame, a bureau and trunk, a few personal things left around like whoever once slept here has moved on, left for college or something. There's a closet door by the window, a mosaic of treetops visible beyond the glass.

We don't turn on the light. Our coats drop to the floor. He peels my jeans down over my hips, easing me back onto the bed, his lips finding my ear, kissing harder down my neck. The coverlet is cool beneath me, the mattress soft, broken in. I help him pull off his shirts—he wears three, two thermals under a T-shirt—and then mine falls beside them.

TWENTY-ONE

AFTER, I WATCH him get dressed, glad he stays shirtless because it keeps him as vulnerable as we just were to each other, exposing his lean arms, the faint remainder of the summer sun not quite disappeared from his skin. We didn't go all the way, but far enough for me to sense that invisible line, how easy it would be to cross; even in this bare, too-quiet house, I feel warm, in touch with him in a way I'd started to believe I never would. "Where are you going to go tonight?" I wait as he picks up his shirts, shakes them out. "What if we just stay? Try talking things out with your mom?" I think of her standing in the doorway yesterday, waiting. Listening. "I bet she misses you."

"Doubt it. There isn't much about me that she likes."

"What did you guys fight about?"

"Everything. Anything." He pulls his shirts on. "She wants me to be somebody else. Did the same thing to my dad." He shrugs. "I'll find a place tonight. Don't worry about it."

"Like where?" I wish I could bring him home with me. As if my parents would go for that. *Hi, guys, meet my first boyfriend—can he move in with us? I'll take care of him myself, promise!* Cut to Ma beating me severely around the head and neck. "Promise me you'll stay with Trace or Moon."

"Promise." Kincaid puts his hand on my thigh, holding my gaze. "We should get going." Meaning his mom will be back soon. The last thing I want is her coming home before we're ready, finding us up here, figuring out what happened between us.

He's first out of the room, trailing his hand back for mine, and we lace fingers.

It's only later, once I'm home, that I realize we never straightened the sheets.

A text kicks off my Sunday morning: *Heads-up. Cops coming your way.*

It pops up on my phone around nine thirty, from Sage to all of us—Bree, Moon, and Trace. I'm in the kitchen getting breakfast, moving slow, seeing everything through the grayscale filter of yesterday afternoon. Being with Kincaid. I want to spend my day lounging in it, gradually wrapping my mind around everything we did together, who it makes me now. Trying to figure out how to heal the damage between Kincaid and his mom, even though I don't know exactly where the break is, how to find it if he won't give me more details. Maybe the real question is how hard to push when somebody you care about is sending signals that they want you to stop.

But. Now the cops are coming, and I shoot a question mark back, adding to Bree's.

They're in the Terraces, just left my place. Asking about Ivy. Next bubble: *Talking to everybody again, trying to find other people who might know something.*

Trace's emoji response—smiley face with no smile— appears.

Can somebody get in touch w Kincaid?

Tactful, Sage. Not coming out and asking me specifically, because Bree's on here, too, and the whole thing is still so raw. I miss Bree. Think of her sitting alone in her room, right next door, yet here we are, not-talking through text when we could be dealing with this together. I think about saying I'll find him, then think about letting Trace field it instead, when the knock at the never-used front door wipes my thoughts clean.

I go over, almost opening up until I hear another door

open outside—the knock was actually at Bree's place. I peer around our shade, watching as Faye lets a female uniformed officer inside with a languid sweep of her arm.

When it's my turn, I'm glad Ma's working a morning shift, because she'd probably never let me leave the house again after some of the questions Officer Donohue asks. Dad takes it easier, offering coffee, sitting with us at the kitchen table, arms folded across his chest, not showing much as Officer Donohue asks if Ivy was using drugs, if she ever talked about running away, about hurting herself, about being in trouble of any kind. Did I get a sense of what her home life was like, her relationship with her dad and stepmother? I answer mechanically—mostly, "I'm not sure," because even though I've gotten a pretty good feeling for Ivy through what people have said, it's all secondhand, passed down from a friend of a friend—and my attention sharpens as the questions move on to somebody else. Somebody unexpected. Gavin Cotswold.

Dad speaks up. "We just moved here a few weeks ago. If that kid ran away last year, then Clara never met him."

Donohue looks at me, as if his word isn't enough. I shrug, shake my head.

"What about Ivy's relationship to him? Did she ever mention him? How she felt about his leaving?"

An echo of myself, rebounding: "I don't know. Not to me." We never got that close. Never had a chance.

After Donohue leaves us with her card and our promise that we'll be in touch if we think of anything else, I wait at the window until the cruiser drives past, leaving the development. Then I get ready to go see Bree.

"Maybe you should stay in today." Dad watches me go down the back steps, propping the door open with his shoulder. I can see him mentally debating what Ma might say, whether he should put me under house arrest until she comes home. I'm anxious to face Bree, though, get this stuff off my chest, no matter how much her response will burn.

Before I can answer him, Bree comes out onto her stoop, probably on her way to the park. She stops when she spots us, then turns away, shutting the door behind her.

Dad raises his voice a bit, lifting a hand. "Hey. How are ya?" Bree looks over at him. "I'm Jay. Clara's dad. You must be Bree?"

"Hi." Her voice is low, posture still, watchful, as if his introduction is a lead-up to him bitching us out for something.

Dad picks up on it, says lightly, "Listen, you two are going to stay together today, right? That cop made me jumpy."

"Yeah," I say quickly, not allowing the silence to stretch out. "We'll be fine."

Dad nods, says to Bree, "Nice meeting you," then goes back inside, wanting to give us our space. Smart guy, my dad.

I walk over to her, stopping at the base of the stoop.

"So . . . what did she ask you?"

At first, I think she might not answer. "Same stuff she asked you. I'm assuming."

"Any chance we could not do this anymore?" I return her stare. "The fighting-without-fighting?" Long pause. "This sucks. I miss you." I hear her soft snort. "It's true."

"Why?"

"What do you mean?" She comes down the steps, moving past me; I fall in with her. "Because I have fun with you. I miss talking."

"Kincaid talks, doesn't he?"

"Not the same thing. You think somebody gets a boyfriend, and they don't need friends anymore? Like they just write them off?" My exasperation's showing. "Is that what Sage did?"

Bree looks straight ahead, her fists in her fleece pockets, walking at a fast pace toward the street. The hoodies hang around the corner of one of the units on our left, slumped over their handlebars as they watch us go, whispering to one another. I take a breath, try again. "You said you weren't mad." Nothing. "It wasn't like I wanted to steal him from you. He followed me to the store after school one day, and we started talking . . . he told me he liked me. We never wanted to hurt you. I wish I'd talked to you first, though. I should've." Still stonewalling. "You said I shouldn't be sorry. That you would've done the same thing." My patience snaps as we reach the sidewalk. "So you lied."

"I did *not* lie."

"Well, you weren't telling the truth. You're so pissed you won't even look at me."

She looks over, proving she can, then faces forward, saying, "I wouldn't," half under her breath, clinging to the last of her stubbornness.

"Wouldn't what?"

"Need friends. I wouldn't need anything."

If she had him. I'm quiet a second, slightly stunned. Wondering what that means, that she'd give everything, but I wouldn't.

She walks ahead of me the rest of the way to the park.

"Did the cop ask you about Gavin?"

We're comparing stories, Trace holding a massive carryout coffee, warming his hands. I hardly noticed how cold it is today during my walk down the trails. Too busy trying to find a path to healing things with Bree. Won't be overnight. Might not be in this lifetime. Kincaid isn't here yet, and even though most of me is dying to see him, it's also a relief. No six-foot-two reminder with a do-what-you-want philosophy of life breezing back and forth between us. Wish he had a phone, though, so I could at least text, see if the cops tracked him down with their questions yet. Make sure he spent last night somewhere safe.

Trace nods at Sage's question. "Yeah, asking if Ivy was friends with him or whatever? I was like, no, he was a sophomore. Just because Cotswold hung out at the park sometimes doesn't mean we were all BFFs. Little ankle biter was annoying as hell." Takes a sip, chokes, swears.

Sage grabs the Styrofoam cup from his hand, holding it out of reach. "Just let it cool down! God."

"Ow-ow-ow-ow." Fans his mouth. "Tongue grafts, stat. I'm suing Dunkin'."

Moon pries an earbud loose. "Hey, puppet master. Is the prank war still on, or nah?"

Trace thinks. "Guess not. With Ivy and everything."

"Yeah. Plus, getting expelled senior year would kind of suck."

"Little bit."

They grab their boards and head for the ramps, Trace pausing to trash his coffee. I stop him there, keeping my voice low as I come out with the question that's been eating at me since yesterday. "Did you know that Kincaid is homeless?" Trace looks down at me, then up at the sky. "How could you not say anything?"

"Doing the couch tour of your buddies' houses isn't the same as homeless."

"But his mom kicked him out."

"Yup. A while ago. Like back in June?" Trace rubs his neck. "I dunno. Stuff was said. 'If you walk out that door,' whatever. It's not like he and his mom have anything in common. She's strict as hell. Maybe she thinks if she doesn't back down now, she'll squish him into that straight-As over-achiever mold after all. Who knows."

"Where's his dad?"

"He left a long time ago, before they moved to Pender. Kincaid said something like his mom doesn't want him talking to his dad, something like that? Anyway. I guess Kincaid finally got sick of her shit after she started ragging on him about coming home smelling like weed, something stupid like that, and told her off. She kicked his ass to the curb, changed the locks."

I think of the Sweet Ms. Savage story Kincaid made up the night we blitzed Perfect, how he wove bits of his own truth into it—the ventriloquist dummy son, the mom gone sour. I push my hair back, giving a sharp laugh. "Well, I get why he hardly goes to school anymore. And the whole not-having-a-phone thing makes a lot more sense."

"Look. Kincaid wants to do his thing, and his mom doesn't like that. They'll figure it out."

"It's getting below freezing at night now," I say. Trace feels the burned spot on the tip of his tongue. "Do you know that when he's not crashing on your couch, he sleeps out there in those creepy woods? He made a shelter."

"Clarabelle . . ." Trace exhales. "He doesn't want people getting all up in his shit. Okay? That's why he didn't tell you in the first place." He steps down onto the flat bottom. "Trust me on this. He doesn't want you to fix it for him."

Kincaid never turns up at the park. I go home alone in the late afternoon, defeated, missing him, without a clue how to help, knowing I have to, even if that's "getting in his shit."

When I come through the door, Dad says hey from over by the counter, coating chicken in bread crumbs. I go to the fridge for something to drink, looking back when he says, "You get takeout yesterday?" Jerks his head toward the table. "Found that in the car."

It's a fortune cookie. Kincaid left me his again. I break into it immediately, hoping for any nugget of wisdom.

For good health, eat more Chinese food.

TWENTY-TWO

WE THOUGHT THE war was over.

As I walk to my first class, a kid opens his locker and is lost in an avalanche of orange and black Ping-Pong balls. They bounce and skitter across the hallway, ricocheting off people's legs and feet, rolling into open classroom doors. One girl steps on them, goes crashing down onto her armload of books.

Spille's room reeks of liquor. Like, worse than usual. Everyone's whispering about it as he harrumphs, gaze glued to his desk as he tries to find his place in Friday's stream of thoughts about the Civil War. One smart-ass asks to open a window, gets barked at.

It isn't until five minutes before the bell, when Spille opens his top desk drawer for a paper clip and brown liquid sloshes out onto his arm and the floor, that the prank hits home: somebody's emptied a bottle of cheap bourbon into each drawer.

Hyde opens her mouth to begin her lecture, hands clasped behind her back—and the fire alarm goes off. We file out and stand around the parking lot in the freezing cold, watching leaves detach themselves from trees while we wait for the fire department to arrive. Nearly a whole class period later, the verdict comes in: false alarm. Somebody pulled it. Prank Number Three. Low points for originality, high marks for honoring tradition.

"Swear." When Trace just laughs, Sage shakes her head, grinning. "I knew you were full of shit yesterday. What'd you do, recruit people?"

"I swear on a whole crap-ton of Bibles that *none* of this is me. It's freakin' inspirational, though, isn't it? We grew baby pranksters. They're like little birds leaving the nest for the first time." He links his thumbs, winging his hands through the air. "Fly, fly, Starling. Fly, fly."

Bree shakes her head. "Don't quote Hannibal Lecter while I'm eating."

I want to ask if anybody's seen Kincaid since we talked

yesterday, but I don't. I haven't seen or heard from him since what we did in his mom's house, and I spent last night worrying about him, wondering if he was in the woods, in the dark, flirting with hypothermia, hoping he's smarter than that. I know he stays with the boys most of the time, but if he even thinks he's a burden to their parents, he'll bolt. Now, sitting here in the hysteria the prank war hath wrought, I come clean with myself: it bothers me. A lot. I'm officially pissed that he did not come to school today.

"Young Master Savage." Crackenback, death warmed over, stands at the end of the table, watching as Trace's bird hands descend to earth. "A word, if I may."

"Okay. Here's a good one—*ablaqueated*."

Crackenback points in the direction of the main hallway, and his office. "Right this way, please."

Trace's glance is disinterested. "What's over there?"

Sage sucks her lips in, finding something else to look at. Crackenback's smile forms as slowly as skin on pudding. "Your destiny."

For a long moment, Trace stares back at him, not moving. Then he jumps up and walks toward the doors, letting Crackenback catch up.

After school, I walk straight to the park, not bothering to wait to catch a ride, since Trace is probably in detention, anyway, or worse.

Kincaid's not here. Two days is unheard-of—since when doesn't he live on the half-pipe?

Maybe since me. Since I figured out what's really going on with him.

Tension settles into my muscles, solidified by the cold, making my stride swift, rigid, as I walk on. Next stop, Lorimer Street.

The little brown house is quiet. Car's in the drive, meaning he's definitely not inside. I watch for a couple minutes, anyway, in case he might come out the door at a run, but nothing moves. Picture his mom in there, sitting at the kitchen table. Silence, dust, a cup of weak instant coffee by her hand as she waits for something to change, looking out the window at the woods.

I walk on, taking a guess at how to get over to the old cemetery from here. Cross through the graves to the woods, pushing through dry brambles, taking gullies faster than necessary, making myself breathless.

When I reach the boulder, I stop where I stand. Kincaid's shelter is gone. He's taken away the tarp and fencing. Not a hint remains that anyone ever slept here, except for the faint, S-shaped bare patch on the ground where I know his body once lay.

After that, I run. To the ledge, clambering down so fast that I don't know how I manage it without falling. Find the path, checking for Kincaid's bag in the weeds—not today—then head down the trail with something like fear fueling me.

Why would he move his shelter, other than to throw me off? Maybe Trace warned him that I was freaking out, that there was a chance I might tell somebody? "Kincaid!" My shout echoes across the flats, and I want to pull it back—too much like Ivy all over again.

The Mumbler mural grows as I close in on it, swelling, stretching across the rock. I make myself stare at it as I pass. *You don't scare me.* No face. No eyes. *I don't believe.* Hands a snarling nest of snakes. *You never were—can't be.* But I'm so small beneath it, lost in the shadow of the cliffside.

I keep thinking I'll follow a curve, and Kincaid will be there, ahead of me, getting his breathing room way out here where few of our friends dare to go. My backpack feels heavy over my shoulder, full of homework and reading I'm behind on, but I can't turn back, not until I make it all the way there, to the bridge.

Once I reach the railroad tracks, I can see he isn't out there on the platform, waiting for me to figure out that this is the only place he'd come. Our place. But there's no one. Just our jack-o'-lanterns, facing east.

I walk all the way to the far end of the platform, where my steam runs out. Squeeze my eyes shut against stupid tears, frustration, the creeping knowledge that I've messed everything up, crushed our fragile beginning like a dried aspen leaf.

Open my eyes and stare without seeing for a time, the

jack-o'-lanterns not really coming into focus until the wind sends another blast through my clothes, jolting me. I'm directly across from Moon's creation, an oblong-shaped pumpkin carved with giant, joyful features. There's more rot showing now, black mold stealing like a rash across the orange shells, each pumpkin beginning a slow collapse into itself.

My gaze travels past the gap where Ivy's once sat, to Kincaid's, like a neat, rounded skull, shaped by decay and the elements.

But the next space is empty. My jack-o'-lantern is gone.

I head home, not really feeling safe until I pass the usual dump sites and know that I'm only minutes from the trailhead. I keep seeing the place where my jack-o'-lantern used to be, hearing Kincaid's words, that some partyers must've knocked Ivy's off the bridge, that other people go out there all the time, do their own share of vandalizing.

Slog, slog, up the hill of the Terraces. I'm envisioning our futon, TV, whatever's left of the ice cream in the freezer, being a completely selfish waste who doesn't worry about anybody, when my senses give me one second's warning. The sound of metal chains working through gears, the zing of air through spokes. I look up. The hoodies, coming at me.

"Christmas Barf. All alone." Green Hood, doing a half-standing pedal, letting the incline bring him toward me. "No friends." Behind him, Blue Hood drops against his handlebars, fake-weeping. "Where's the bitch and the hottie today?"

I fix Green with a flat stare, keep walking toward our unit.

He snorts. "What're you looking at, you shitty-haired freak?"

"A douchebag on a little girl's bike." I don't slow down.

Green Hood's expression darkens, reminding me of when Bree slammed his wheel with her foot—oh, right; bruised ego, score to settle, all that—but the words are out. No time to do anything but flinch back as he drops to the seat, blowing by me, snagging my backpack as he goes.

I curse, spinning before he pulls me over, yanking free of the strap even though my whole everything's in that bag—then Blue Hood slams into me from behind, forearm like a crowbar across my shoulder blades, sending me down.

Pain. Above me, laughter, more of those metallic, blade-like bicycle sounds as they circle above me on the slope so they can charge again. I get up at a run. They swoop after me—one glimpse of them standing on pedals, suddenly huge, grizzlies on their hind legs.

I try to dart across a yard. Green Hood cuts me off— "Nope, sorry"—and I throw my elbow into him, hitting bone. More pain shoots up into my shoulder, and he swears, almost pitching over.

I break into a sprint, knowing the paved hill is like a cattle chute: nowhere for me to go but right where they're driving me. Somebody's got to be seeing this out their window and not doing anything about it, not stepping in. Not like Bree would.

Yellow and White burn by me on either side, one ripping a handful of my hair, making me shriek and swear at them as they crisscross into my path at the base of the hill.

I go left, head for the open doorway of the laundry building, one glance showing me that nobody's inside before I reach back and drag the door shut behind me, the cinderblock doorstop thudding over onto the dirt.

I dig my heels in and hold the door shut, engaging in a short battle as one of them tries to get in, can't; leverage is on my side. A hail of rocks batters the door and wall, gradually petering off to the sound of silence.

A scrape, then a thud against the door. More laughter.

Shit. I think that was the cinder block. They must've wedged it between the door and the ground. I stay where I am, listening, fingers aching against the handle. "Have fun," one of them calls.

Slowly, I straighten, giving the door a tentative push. Won't move. Go to the window, standing on tiptoes to watch as they pedal back up the hill, stopping to dump my backpack out in the middle of the road, books and notebooks tumbling everywhere. Green Hood kicks my phone across the asphalt.

I hit the glass. "Asshole!" But they're at the crest of the hill now, then out of view.

TWENTY-THREE

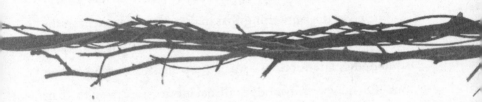

SILENCE IS MY enemy. Not only because it drives home how alone I am, but because it means none of the washers or dryers are running. Which means there's a good chance nobody's coming to get their laundry anytime soon.

Still stoked on adrenaline, I look for an obvious way out. Two small windows covered in wire mesh on the wall facing the hill. A back exit that I test and find locked. Washers beneath the window, dryers against the far wall. Two molded plastic lawn chairs with curling magazines stacked beneath, a folding table.

I bang on the door for a while, yelling for help, not holding out a lot of hope. The closest thing is the deserted bus shelter;

the laundry building's set back from the units, embraced by the woods.

I sit in a chair, tapping my legs, facing a wall clock—4:10. Dad won't be home for another hour at least, maybe two. Ma, not until seven thirty. I've been skidding in right at curfew most nights lately, so they won't worry until after eight. I go to the window, look out at the trailhead, only a stone's throw from where I stand. Bree and Sage will come that way, eventually. Probably. Unless Trace gives them a ride home.

For now, the only thing that makes sense is switching the lights on and off, like an SOS. Should be enough to catch somebody's attention, eventually, especially as it gets darker out. Or maybe somebody will decide to stop in with their dirty socks and towels. Hopefully before tomorrow.

For the first hour, I pace from the switch plate to the windows, periodically checking for any sign of Bree and Sage. My palms and knees sting with scrapes from hitting the pavement, and I've got a patch on my chin, too. Maybe Kincaid and I can compare road rash. If I ever see him again.

Around five, cars start turning into the Terraces, people coming home from work. I flash the lights, bang the door, yell for help, look to see if any brake lights come on. Nobody stops. I growl frustration in my throat and kick a washer. Seriously, people—look up!

When I cross the two-hour mark, I grab a magazine.

Woman's Day. Dated two years ago, featuring a photo of a mom who lost one hundred pounds on an all-soup diet, beside a headline advertising the perfect Easter layer-cake recipe, inside! I slide down the wall into a sitting position beneath the switch panel, turning the light on and off as I page through.

Laughter. My head snaps up. Boys, somewhere nearby.

It's the hoodies. I watch them thread around one another down the hill. Coming to make sure nobody's let me out yet, probably.

They laugh some more, call a few insults down to me, then tires pass over dirt as they turn down the woods trail. No more sounds.

More time passes. I keep flashing the lights. Full dark outside now.

The whisking of pedals and gears draws me back to the glass: one hoodie emerges from the trees, Yellow, from what I can see by the streetlight glow. Maybe he's the only one with a curfew. He doesn't spare my prison a glance, taking his time riding up the center line toward home, steering with one hand, using his phone with the other.

I rest my forehead against the glass, breathe out, leaving a fog. When something else moves along the tree line, I don't react right away, expecting another hoodie to pop out.

The movement's not on the trail, but in the bushes, a shadow that shifts, goes still. Something's over there.

I stare, trying to convince myself it isn't real, more space junk drifting through my mind, but something stirs in me, an instinctive prickle. Big beast coming.

It moves farther out, clear of the trees. Takes a couple steps.

Tall, broad silhouette. A hood up over its head, maybe, or long hair, I can't tell which. Staring up the hill, where Yellow Hood has disappeared. Another step, turning back toward the woods, ready to blend into the night again.

Then it hesitates, like maybe instinct tapped it, too—the primal sense of being watched. It looks toward the laundry building, where I stand, frozen, unthinking, the light framing me in the window. Slick, pale gleam off the face, somehow too small for the head, misshapen, like a crumpled paper plate.

I jerk back, lunging for the light switch, sending the room into darkness, praying I ducked in time, that maybe you can't see as much from the outside as I think. Hold my breath, counting seconds—only reach nine before I hear a heavy footstep on dead leaves. It saw. It's coming.

I whirl, eyes half-adjusted to the dark, only the white lawn chairs having any distinction. I lift one, jam its leg through the door handle and across the frame as hard as I can—the leg's too wide, only slides about two inches through before it sticks. I hear the scrape of the cinder block being pushed away from the door.

I stare at the chair, wedged horizontally, as if by levitation.

Praying that thing out there will test the door, think it's locked from the inside, give up.

It tries the outer handle; the door moves, as if with a breath. Stopped by the chair leg.

Counting seconds again: one, two—another tug, harder. Go away. *Go away.*

Thud, thud, thud. Harder. Sensing some give, working at the leg. I've got nothing to fight with, nothing but light, so I slap the switch again, casting it all into brilliance. Fine curls of plastic peel up from the friction of the handle; he's making headway, working it down, widening a gap to show a sliver of darkness beyond the jamb, so little space between me and it.

"Leave me alone." My voice. Shaky, but there. "Get out of here." Louder, shouting: "Get out of here!"

The door saws back and forth, the leg developing a sickening bend against the frame.

I run to the folding table and push, skidding its rubber-stoppered feet over the floor until it slams across the width of the doorway, bracing my palms against the edge, teeth gritted, leaning my whole weight into my barricade, as if it'll do anything once that thing gets through the door.

The gap of darkness widens—then holds in place as it looks in at me.

The wetness of a single eye. Face coated in peach-hued plastic, showing a slender, painted eyebrow. A mask.

The head tilts, face bobbing in the gap. Pink lips with a hole punched in the center, a circle of airbrushed blusher on the cheek. I know it, of course I do, but there's no time to process—too busy screaming, *"Leave me alone!"* Turn, seizing the first thing I see—trash can—heaving it at the mask. Garbage explodes. Grab the magazines, pelt them at the door, heave the other chair, grab it on the rebound and throw it again. *"Get out of here!"*

When I stagger back, gasping, the mask is gone. The door is closed.

I breathe, waiting. It worked. I scared him off. Then headlights flash through the windows, the real reason he stopped trying to get in: someone's coming down the hill, slowing, signaling a left turn.

I run to the door, start to yank the chair free so I can make a dash for the road, flag them down. A spiderweb-thin strand of chill adheres to my spine. I look over my shoulder.

The princess mask is there, in the far window. Just looking. I stare back, hands locked on the chair, unable to do anything but watch as it gives a slow, condescending dip of its head . . . and leaves.

TWENTY-FOUR

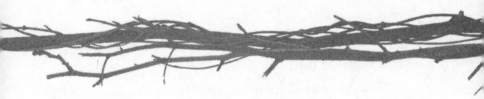

COPS MOVE AROUND our kitchen, visible to me only from the waist down as I sit, head bent over the cup of coffee Ma made me out of desperation, the need to do something. Face bathed in steam, blanket around my shoulders, I watch legs clad in navy uniform slacks pass back and forth. Outside to the cruiser, back in; outside to the stoop to make some clandestine call to the station. Back in.

Murmured conversation among the adults. I've answered the same questions enough times to write the cops' script. *Did you get a look at him? What was he wearing?* I described the mask; didn't say who it belongs to. They're already thinking Halloween prank gone wrong, another gotcha on par with

Jell-O bombs and Ping-Pong balls; one of the hoodies, probably, coming back to finish the scare.

The eye, though. That damned eye glittering in the recess behind the molded plastic—the iris was dark. Not Trace's coyote greenish-gray. If that guy has the mask, maybe he hurt Trace before he took it. All I want is my phone so I can text a quick *you ok?* at him, but it's still out there on the street somewhere; the female officer, Donohue, is looking for it. My school stuff has already been gathered, stacked on the counter.

The next time the door opens, Dad says, "Found him yet?" his voice sharp.

"They're searching the woods." It's Donohue, not liking Dad's tone. Her footsteps, lighter than the rest, come up beside me. "Sorry. I found it in the road." She sets my phone on the table. Crushed, the screen shattered, obviously run over. "If you press charges, you could be compensated for it."

Right now, my one compensation is picturing Aidan's face when the cops knocked on his door tonight. I didn't even have to know his last name; apparently, he's acquainted with the Pender PD already.

The male cop is making leaving sounds now—still searching, etc., keep us posted—making Ma hit her *Excuse me?* pose. "What're we supposed to do until you catch this guy? What if he comes looking for her again?" She's got the officer trapped halfway out the door. "That man was after my child, and you're telling me you'll keep us *posted*? What the hell is going on in this town? You got one kid dead in that marsh—a whole pack of flying monkeys chase my girl around and nobody does a damn thing—and then some crazy person tries to get ahold of her, and you people got nothing but 'we'll look into it'?"

"He was after me." I finally lift my gaze to Donohue, tightening my grip on the blanket. "He was."

"And we believe you." She holds up a hand when the other officer starts to speak. "We're taking this very seriously. But we also have to look into the possibility that this was a stunt pulled by kids in the neighborhood who knew you were locked in there. We've got somebody speaking with Aidan and the other boys right now. One of them will probably admit to as much." I hear Ma's noise of protest; I told them about his size, how he seemed to be hunting Yellow Hood through the trees. "That said, until you hear from us, stay calm"—raises her voice when Ma tries to interrupt—"and take normal precautions, like keeping your doors and windows locked, leaving lights on. I promise you, we'll find out who did this."

When it's just the three of us Morrisons again, Ma grabs the dishrag and tosses it into the sink, staring out the window at the night. "This is some great place you brought us to, Jay."

"Didn't have a whole lot of choice, did I?"

She doesn't fire back right away, shaking her head. "Just seems to me that a kid's life goes pretty cheap around here. That's all I'm saying." Looks out the window for a second longer, then drops into the chair beside me, pulling me close for a kiss on top of the head. "I'm so sorry. I should've been there."

For some reason, after everything, this is what makes me cry.

I spend the night on the futon, sneaking into Ma and Dad's room to snatch her phone off her nightstand. Still feels safer out here than in my bedroom, with the TV flashing faces, products, and promises at me, the overhead light left on. I text Trace first. No answer for a minute, two. My fingers can't wait, blasting out a message to Sage: *Where's Trace?*

I should've told the cops everything, sent them to make sure the person in the mask didn't hurt Trace, even if it meant blowing the lid off everything we've done in the name of disobedience. What if he's hurt, what if—

Ping—Sage. *Crack gave him a 3 day vacay. Mom took his phone ???*

I sink back against the cushion as my body remembers how to breathe. Then I sum up what happened in as few characters as possible, pretty much a lost cause, but between the two of us, we come up with a plan for tomorrow. I put the phone down, stretch out, close my eyes, but there's no sleep back there, behind my lids, sure as hell no peace.

My closet, the place where bad dreams come from, waits down the hall. The memory of Kincaid—unable to speak, arms crossed over the soft shifting of his coat, the hidden movement below the surface—waits behind the door. I try not to think of him as missing; I just have no idea where he is.

Ma's on the phone to the school first thing the next morning, asking for Crackenback, giving him the rundown of yesterday, explaining that I'll be in class today because she thinks it's safer than staying home alone, but for somebody to call her at work in case of anything. I hear her agree to be put on hold; next thing I know, Mrs. Mac's got the ball, running all the way back—crap. We've got a conference scheduled for eight thirty a.m.

When we walk through the doors of PDHS together, Ma gets to see this morning's stunt: a big drawing done hastily in Sharpie on the wall beside the mascot mural. It's a slapdash reproduction of the Mumbler by some new guerrilla artist— a black outline, fingers long and jagged, mouth a gaping maw of razor teeth. A cartoon bubble stems from the Raging Elk's head; some teacher taped a piece of printer paper over it until the custodian gets in, but you can still read the words *aw shit*. The Mumbler's bubble reads *nom nom nom*.

● ● ●

Mrs. Mac has dragged an extra chair in for Ma, which means I get stuck in the egg again.

She bustles around, getting Ma coffee from the outer office. It's so weird being with a parent at school, worlds colliding in the most unwelcome way, all the people with power to destroy you in the same place at the same time, Godzilla vs. Megalon in an ultimate death match. Ma doesn't seem like she's loving it, either. She doesn't put her big purse down, instead keeping it in her lap, making a statement up front that this isn't going to take long. She is, after all, the mom; these people are only in charge of my pseudo education.

"There, now." Mrs. Mac settles behind her desk, her smile on low beam in deference to my pain. "Clara. Sounds like you had quite a scary experience last night. Do you want to talk about it?"

I glance at Ma. "It was just . . . some guy. Trying to get in at me."

Mrs. Mac's look is sympathetic, not only her expression, but her outfit. Today's sweater hue: Compassionate Coral. "That doesn't sound like 'just' anything. You must've been scared to death. The police are looking into it?" At my nod, she turns to Ma. "I really appreciate you notifying us, Rose." Ah, she's done her homework.

Ma nods, the two of us like a couple of those novelty dippy birds. Mrs. Mac folds her hands on the desk. "This seemed like a good opportunity to check in with both of you, see how Clara's transitioning into the Pender state of mind." Small laugh, fading quickly. "The past month has been hard. First Gavin, and now what's happened to Ivy Thayer. And you couldn't have missed our new student artwork in the hallway on your way in." Ma laughs a little. "Mmm. Well, it's that time of year. People take Halloween seriously around here. Mr. Crackenback's been dealing with some pranksters, handing out some suspensions. The kids always get a little"— wiggles her shoulders—"you know. Overexcited."

That's one word for it. I shift in my padded womb-chair, distracted, wondering if Bree even asked about me when I wasn't at the bus stop this morning. Really hope Moon was able to borrow his brother's truck like he said he'd try to when I texted him last night, so Sage and I can go see Trace after school. I've texted everybody but Bree to ask if they've seen Kincaid around; nobody has, but that's normal. I won't tell Trace about his shelter being gone, how he ditched me. It would be like admitting we were a hookup, and the only person who didn't know it was me.

Mrs. Mac studies my face. "Socially, you seem to be doing great, Clara. I pay attention . . . notice when somebody looks like they're making fast friends. So, kudos to you on that." Wait to see if she's going to nail me on my choice of friends, maybe mention Kincaid, but she moves on. "Grades are another story. I took a look-see at your averages, and to be honest, they're not quite what I'd expect to see from a student who came to us with a GPA of 3.52. Also, Mr. Smythe noted an unexcused absence last Friday afternoon. He says you never showed up to his calculus class." Ma's gaze cuts across me like a Ginsu knife, and suddenly, I can't sink deep enough in my seat, my gaze seeking the potted vine climbing the file cabinet.

"Granted, you're only a couple weeks in, so I don't want to cause a panic. Plenty of time for these things to even out. But I have to ask"—she plops her chin on her fist, small, sapphire eyes bright behind her glasses—"what's going on here?"

Ma adjusts in her seat to face me. "I'd like to hear it."

Godzilla and Megalon just formed a tag team. "Nothing. I"—work that new-kid angle, work it—"got overwhelmed, I guess? And I got sick. Last Friday. I was here, just . . . in the bathroom." Hard swallow. "Everything's changed so fast." Ma hasn't budged. "I started the semester late, and I was already so far behind. . . ."

Mrs. Mac nods, like I've confirmed some suspicion; Ma presses her lips together and chooses her own plant to glare at.

"I think I know what you're saying, Clara." Mrs. Mac shakes her head. "I could kick myself for not thinking of it sooner. I should've set you up in our tutoring program right from the beginning. You must've been feeling like a miner's mule, with that load on your back!" Scribbles a note to herself on a sticky pad. "This is my failing. I don't want either of you"—a shaped mauve fingernail points between us—"taking this on yourselves. Relocating is one of the biggest challenges a family can go through. We want to do everything we can to help you make this move a success."

I think we're done. Ma shakes Mrs. Mac's hand, turns to follow me to the door, jumps when Mrs. Mac gasps, "Oh!" Hurrying around the desk, shaking her basket. "Don't forget your Raging Elk pin."

Hesitantly, Ma takes one, dropping it into her purse. "Thanks."

"Pleasure's mine. Always happy to spread around a little school spirit." Mrs. Mac opens the door, just in time for us to witness a secretary race across the hall with the coffeepot and douse a smoldering trash can.

The drive to Trace's house is even longer than I remember—on foot, it would've taken the better part of an hour. I'd be lying if I said I wasn't checking out the window for Kincaid, silently hoping we'll pass him on his board somewhere, see that he's okay, that he must've spent the night somewhere safe. Because now I know that the cold isn't the biggest threat in those woods.

The driveway is steep and rutted, Moon's truck nearly bottoming out on the last hole before we park behind Trace's car. The dogs are barking, giving themselves whiplash against their chains, all of them some strange spotted mutt breed.

"So . . . this will be weird," Sage says to me as I slide out the passenger door behind her. It's strange, not having Bree with us. I don't know if Sage told Bree that I was coming here with her today, or if she told her about the guy who came after me last night. If Bree would even care. "Just warning you. His mom is—"

"Different?" I finish.

"You think she'll even let him come out?" Moon walks with us toward the paint-peeling steps. Now that we're closer, the dogs are whining, wagging tails, desperate for love. "Sounds like she's pretty pissed about Crack giving him the boot."

Sage shrugs. "We'll see." Leads the way up the steps, opens the crooked screen door to knock. In the glass pane, between limp curtains, a white macramé cross dangles from a length of yarn.

After a long time, a tall, loose-fleshed woman opens the door, staring at Sage from beneath fierce, unkempt brows shot through with gray, just like her long, brown hair. She wears a white sleeveless muumuu, the floral pattern washed to a memory, her feet in open-toed terry bedroom slippers. She doesn't speak, just takes Sage in with a beady stare.

"Hi. Is he around?" Sage has my respect forever; I don't think I could force a word out if I tried, let alone have this be my boyfriend's mom, who I had to make nice with on a regular basis. But Sage's smile is forthright, no apologies in her tone.

Ms. Savage gives a short laugh, her voice hoarse and low. "Oh, yeah. He's home. Home for three days, thanks to his fresh mouth." She gives us an agitated glance. "Suppose you think I should let him see you anyway."

"Only if it's okay with you."

As I look past Sage, I get a glimpse of the mudroom behind Ms. Savage. A big framed painting hangs on the wall, one of those blond Jesuses with a mournful look in his blue eyes and light beaming around his sacred heart. Ms. Savage shifts to the left, shouts across the yard, "Trace-y! You got comp-any!"

She shuts the door on our thanks, watching us through the pane as, a second later, Trace comes around the back of the barn, wearing coveralls flecked with dried mud and bits of hay.

He dabs his brow with the back of his glove. "Hey. Heard you guys pull up, but I was hiding from my mom." He glances over at the door; Ms. Savage steps back from the glass. "Friggin' Crack welshed on our gentleman's agreement. Goat-sucking bastard." He kisses Sage, who kisses him back, keeping as much distance as possible from his coveralls.

"Does he know?" I ask.

"Nah. I mean, he suspects. But he's got no proof." Trace shrugs, starts walking back to the barn. "Sending me home was, like. . . a preventive measure. Get me out of school for a couple days, hope the pranking will die down once the bad seed is gone."

"We wanted to make sure you were okay." Sage watches as he picks up a shovel leaning against the wall. "If I didn't know your mom had you on lockdown, I would've been freaking."

"Somebody took your mask," I say.

He pauses in the open bay of the haymow, looking back at me. As I tell him what happened, he gradually gets back to mucking out the stalls, turning shovelfuls of manure and soiled hay into a wheelbarrow. A couple of brown-and-white goats wander over to stare at us, jawing in a terminally bored fashion. "He was tall, like you—I don't know, maybe he wanted me to think he *was* you. Or maybe he just wanted me to know that he knows who we are." I try not to lose my temper as Trace focuses on scraping the edge of the shovel across the floorboards. "I think he knows we pulled those pranks." I make a frustrated sound. "He was trying to get me."

"What—you think it was one of those *Father Knows Best* drones from Perfect Street? Come on." He laughs. "Their idea of risk is letting the warranty expire on their electric hedge trimmers." I watch as he drops the shovel and walks past us, saying to the goats, "You guys have to stop shitting so much. Seriously." He goes to his car and we follow, watching him root around inside for a while before he comes out and leans against it, arms resting on the roof. "Huh."

Sage tosses up her hands. "Did you think she made it up? Some psycho got into your car and stole the mask, numbnuts. He wanted to hurt Clarabelle."

"He came out of the woods, dude." Moon's expression is grim. "Ivy? Gavin? Dabney's head? Know what I'm saying?"

"And Kincaid and Clarabelle said they saw someone in the marsh the night Ivy disappeared." Sage rubs her arms. "Maybe he started following all of us after that."

Trace stares at his house for a second, a humorless grin passing over his lips. "A serial killer. In Pender." Burst of barely contained laughter. "Letting the Mumbler take the fall for everything, when we really got a homegrown Dahmer picking off the bad-kid population. Hells yes. I can buy that." Thumps both hands down on the roof, starts back to the barn with us on his heels.

My air escapes in an exasperated gust. "What are we going to do?" My near shout makes the goats look up. "Thoughts? Anyone?"

Trace grabs his shovel, scoops another load. "Well"— pauses, hefting the weight—"this guy's a traditionalist. So, far as I can tell"—manure lands in the wheelbarrow—"all we've got to do is survive Halloween."

After we leave Trace's, Moon drives toward the Terraces. I promised Ma this morning that I'd come straight home after school and keep the doors locked; the ominous way she said, "We'll talk later," after the meeting with Mrs. Mac made me want to be extra sure I don't get caught breaking my word. I don't know if Trace took anything we said seriously; maybe that's just how he processes, by being a smart-ass. Sounds familiar.

I glance over at Sage, wedged between us in the cab. "You and Bree hanging out after this?"

She nods, watching how hard I try to keep my expression neutral. "Have you tried talking to her at all? About—" Gestures, meaning the obvious: Kincaid.

"Tried." I shrug. "I don't think I got through." Not sure how well-versed I am on the subject of Kincaid, anyway, if I'm even qualified to guess at what he really wants from me. I stay silent a second, then blurt, "I just feel so bad. I mean . . . with her parents, and being the only one watching out for Hazel and everything. I never thought—"

"That he would like you back." She smiles a little, shaking her head. "Bree didn't, either. So when he crashed your little crush party, it kind of blew everything up, right?" She holds up a hand. "Not judging. I've been there."

"You have?"

"Not with Bree. A different friend, back in middle school. Crushing on this one guy was like this game we played every day, until shit got real. I don't know which sucks more— being the one he doesn't pick, or getting the guy, losing the

friend." She pauses, chipping at the clear coat on her fingernails. "But if you're feeling bad because you think you have
things better than Bree, don't."

I give a short laugh. "Seems pretty legit to me."

"Bree having jackholes for parents has nothing to do with
Kincaid liking you. Okay? There's no cosmic connection
there. Trying to find one isn't going to make things any better with her. Sometimes you come out on top. Next time,
maybe it'll be Bree's turn." Sage rests back against the seat.
"End of speech."

"Any idea what I can do to make things better?"

"Um. You can't make Bree do or feel anything. And I'm
saying that as her best friend. Sorry." She turns to Moon.
"Don't you repeat a word of this."

He laughs, switching radio stations. "I didn't hear anything."

TWENTY-FIVE

I'M HOME BY myself when somebody knocks so quietly that I don't move right away, paused over my homework, listening.

Another soft knock, almost like a branch tapping in the wind. Ma left me her phone so I could call Dad in case anything happened, and I bring it with me as I go to the window, peeking out at the back stoop.

Kincaid stands on the top step. Relief has me pulling the chain off the door, and the chill air is in my face before I can process anything but his expression, guarded, like he wasn't sure if I'd be the one to answer. I put my arms around him immediately, squeezing; somehow, his body feels fragile to me today, impermanent, and my anger and confusion only come back as I say, "Where have you been?"

He hugs me, gaze moving over the doorway—wondering if there are parents lurking back there—then going to the scrape on my chin. "No place. Hanging around." He gently runs his thumb over the scab. "I heard about yesterday. You okay?" I nod. "Want me to kick their asses? Aidan and those guys? I'm not buff or anything, but I'll do it."

"Nah. I'm sure they crapped themselves when the cops tracked them down." I get quiet, looking at him. Remembering how it felt, running down the trails searching for him, realizing I'd been dropped. Feeling like a fool. How it made me question everything, doubt myself. My tone is flat when I speak again: "Better come inside."

He steps through the doorway, taking a quick survey of our kitchen, a glance at the hall. Tea—I know he likes that, and we have it, so I put the kettle on, grab a mug just to keep busy. Everything we did in his bedroom—it's vivid, present, a third party listening in on us. I drop the bag of Lipton's into the mug, then turn to face him, my arms folded. "Why'd you ditch me?"

He looks back. "I didn't."

"Yes, you did. You moved your shelter." My voice is tight. "I looked everywhere for you."

Kincaid shrugs, stopping beside our table, looking at the flowers painted on our salt and pepper shakers. "I always do that. Stay in one place too long, somebody will figure out you're sleeping there."

I swallow, working up my nerve. "Do you know how that made me feel? After what we did, and then you were just—gone?" He's still not meeting my eyes, not getting it. I press my hand to my chest. "Did you plan it that way? Hook up with me, then drop me?" Kincaid's gaze lifts sharply, eyes widening. "Or was that, like, payback for trying to get you to fix things with your mom? Trying to be a part of your life?"

"No. Clara." He shakes his head, hard. "I heard what you were saying that night."

"Did you? I let you know that I care about you, and you can't get rid of me fast enough. Right?" He opens his mouth, doesn't speak. "You're pissing everything away. Your whole life. And it kills me, because you're smart, and talented, and it's like you don't even know it. How bad did your mom screw up that you don't even know that?"

"I told you. We fight. It doesn't work, us living together, and I said some stuff—"

"She kicked you out of your own house. She changed the locks. I don't care what you did, that's a shitty thing to do to your kid. She's supposed to look out for you—"

"You don't"—tone the sharpest I've ever heard it, raising a hand to his brow, clamping down on his words for a second—"you don't know her. Okay?" A pause. "It's not all

268

on her." A pause. "I made things hard."

I stare at him, breathing hard, arms still crossed tightly over my chest. "Sounds to me like she matters to you." He frowns, looks at the floor. "Kincaid. She's your mom. We can fix it. I know you guys fight, but we can talk to her together." More silence. "You can't tell me that she wants you sleeping outside in the cold, especially if there really is somebody out there in those woods, going after kids. And I don't think she wants you flunking out and not being able to graduate this year."

He turns away, gripping the top of a chair. I go over, touching his back gingerly. "It's just . . . you can't go away like that. I couldn't find you. I couldn't reach you."

"I know." His voice is quiet, and he closes his eyes, moving into my touch as I stroke his cheek. "Sorry."

He kisses my temple, my cheekbone, and we go together down the hallway to my bedroom. Erase the bad-dream memory of him with this reality, him in my bed, my safe place, and this time the room is full of sun and tree shadows.

Later, I rest my head against him, tucked between his arm and chest. This is the first time my bed has felt small to me, like something meant for a little kid. Still an hour and a half until Dad's due home—plenty of time for us to stay here together. I watch the branch shadows play across the blinds as the wind kicks up. "When you say the Mumbler's real, that you've seen him," I say slowly, "do you mean it?"

"Somebody's out there." Shrugs slightly. "There are signs. And at night, sometimes . . . he's there. It's like with you, that night on the banks. I wake up, and I feel him, so close—and I don't want to open my eyes."

I glance up at him. "The person who tried to get me last night was real. Not some monster. I think that's who you've been seeing." I press my palm against his chest. "You're lucky he hasn't come after you."

Kincaid's gaze goes to the closet door. "Why do you think he hasn't?" He waits. "If he wanted to get me, he could have. Anytime. What's he waiting for?"

I don't have an answer. "Do you think one person could've killed all of them? Going back to Ricky?"

He shifts onto his side and reaches for the origami jack-o'-lantern. "That's what I've been saying for years."

I watch the folded hexagon play between his fingers. "When I went to the bridge yesterday, my jack-o'-lantern was gone. Just mine and Ivy's." I look at him. "What do you think it means?"

His gaze follows the folds pressed into the paper. "Maybe it means he's watching you."

It snows on Halloween morning. Fine powder covers every-thing. Seems like there'd be folk sayings about that, old wives' tales, calling it a harbinger of bad luck. Feels like a sign to me, but then again, I tend to look too hard.

◗ ● ◖

Candy corn coats the floor of the bus. Our anxiety turned to lethargy, Sage rests her head on Bree's shoulder; Bree's head lolls against the seat. Me, an ocean away on the other side of the aisle, keeping my distance like I know Bree wants me to, replaying memories of Tuesday afternoon: Kincaid's hair on my pillow, rippling shadows on the wall, the feeling of his lips so at odds with the words *he's watching you.*

School. Candy wrappers litter the floors, float in water fountains. Twix, Three Musketeers. I drift from class to class, taking nothing in, some amplified heartbeat seeming to follow me, forcing blood down these long intravenous corridors. At one point, a girl in a Zorro mask and cape pirouettes by me in the crowded hall, pauses, flashes the cape open at all of us, revealing a black bralette underneath. Boys roar approval, banging on lockers, and then she spins away, a teacher in hot pursuit.

I have a Kincaid sighting between classes, but when I turn, it's somebody else, nothing in common with him but dark coat, light hair. I didn't really expect him to come today; I gave him a lot to think about on Tuesday, a lot to decide. I'm not going to chase after him. In some ways, it really is like loving a ghost. And for the first time, I let myself wonder, *Is this love?*

◗ ● ◖

No Trace, so I get on the bus after school, the talking-to Ma and Dad gave me on Tuesday still ringing in my ears. *Such a smart girl—always said you were, so why—*and for the first time I didn't really mind hearing it, because it means they give a damn. About school, about me, for no reason other than they choose to. That love isn't necessarily guaranteed. So. Straight home. Keep the doors locked, the phone close. Halloween is no excuse for taking stupid chances.

I watch as Bree gets on the bus by herself, glimpses me, sits five seats ahead. I settle in to wait for the overpass and *Fear Him.*

Ma bought candy, thank God, because the first knock on the door comes a couple hours after I get home. Bree's forecast was right: one look out the window shows trick-or-treaters crawling all over the Terraces, following paved walkways to hit every apartment. It's still daylight, so moms with really little kids are out doing the rounds now. Some of the mini monsters are wide-eyed and completely in awe of me as I drop candy into their buckets; others are power-mad with their ability to get free chocolate from an almost-adult just by saying *trick or treat.* I realize we don't have any decorations up. We are so pathetic.

I tape Kincaid's origami jack-o'-lantern in the window. I think he'd like that.

◑ ● ◐

Trace got his phone back. Around five o'clock, he sends me a GIF of a twerking skeleton. Last I knew, he'd talked his mom into letting him hang out with Sage at his place tonight, too.

I'm searching for a good comeback GIF, tearing into my fifth or sixth fun-size Hershey bar, when another bang on the back door pulls me away from *Killer Klowns from Outer Space* with my bowl of treats. When Dad gets home, this is totally becoming his job.

Bree stands on the stoop. Strands of hair blow loose from her ponytail, phone in her hand like she's forgotten it's there, or like maybe she's forgotten how to speak to me.

I stare, hurry to swallow. "Hey." Wait. Carefully: "How are you?"

Thinking, *This is it, we're finally going to talk.* But what she says is, "I can't find Hazel."

TWENTY-SIX

"WAIT, WHAT—?"

"I don't know where she is." Barely restrained ferocity, no time or patience to wait for me to catch up. Bree comes in, making me step back against the door, pacing as far as the table before seeming to remember that she's Bree and would never be comfortable barging in anywhere. Gestures with her phone. "I've texted, called her like fifty times. She's just not answering."

Does chocolate slow mental processes? I can't seem to produce coherent thought, still so shocked by her being in my kitchen. "Well, where's she supposed to be?"

"Home! She had some party with her dance class right

after school, and then she was catching a ride back here. I made her promise"—sharp, dismissive gesture—"because of what happened to you the other night. I figured maybe the party ran long, or she stopped by Jasmine's after and left her phone in the car—"

"So she did get a ride with Jasmine's mom?"

"Probably. She usually rides with them. But I can't get ahold of anybody. Jasmine's not answering, my mom won't pick up—"

"Call her work—"

"No, she's off tonight. She's pissed at me and not answering, that's all. I've left, like, three messages." Her phone chimes then, and she swears in relief—"Jasmine, finally"—scanning the text, fingers flying over the keypad in response. A couple seconds later, she looks up at me, expression dull. "They dropped Hazel off around four."

I stare, unmoving, no clue what to say.

Bree texts again, reading Jasmine's response off the screen: "Dropped her off at the turn-in to the Terraces. She said she had to check the mail." I think of the two outdoor pedestal mailbox units down there. "That was an hour and a half ago."

I feel the spike of fear that shoots through her, my empathy on overdrive, thinking of Hazel. My mouth's gone dry, and it's hard to swallow. "Okay. Then she must be in the Terraces somewhere. Where would she go?"

Bree's shaking her head, hard and fast. "Nowhere. Her friends don't live here—"

"Yeah, but it's Halloween. Somebody must've seen her walk by and asked her to hang out for a while. We'll find her, okay? Everything's going to be fine." I grab my coat from the closet, pull on my sneakers, some small, shameful part of me exhilarated that I can help Bree, try to win her back. "Do any kids from her grade live here?"

"Um. There's that Peyton girl—and Jackson Adelman, I guess. He lives up in the high numbers." Bree's heading toward the door, talking like she's in shock, like deep down, she'd expected to find out it was all a mistake, that Hazel was still at the rec department after all, eating orange-frosted cupcakes and showing off her dip and step.

"Wait for me. Hold on." She's already heading down the steps, the door left gaping, so I grab paper and pen, writing a quick note to Dad, hoping to hell that I'll be back long before he has a chance to read it.

We try four different apartments, all the middle school kids Bree can think of. Nobody's home at two of them, and at the other two, our knock is answered by a kid doing what I was doing before Bree showed up, watching TV and giving out candy. Neither of them have seen Hazel.

Bree's walking faster, faster, and the sun's lower every time we emerge from behind one of the units, a fiery orb stretching out tendrils of orange and purple along the horizon. "Let's go back to my place," I say, squeezing my hands together, wishing I'd paused long enough to grab my hat and gloves. "My dad will be home before too long, and then we—"

"Do you think he took her? That guy from the other night?" Bree turns, and there are tears on her cheeks; she's been walking and crying and I didn't even know it, because no other part of her reveals a thing. "Do you think that's what happened? She's out in the woods?"

I shake my head slowly. "Come on . . . there are trick-or-treaters everywhere tonight, people coming and going—it wasn't even getting dark yet when she got dropped off."

"Was it dark when Aidan chased you?" She's got me there; I say nothing, and she shakes her head. "What if somebody grabbed her, or tricked her? Got her to go out on the trails with them?" She presses her fist to her lips for a long second, then turns and heads down the slope toward the street.

I know where she's headed. "Stop. Let's call the cops."

"Call them, if you want. I'm not waiting."

"Bree! Don't be stupid! Come back!"

She breaks into a run. I curse, kicking the ground, watching her cut by the laundry building, heading toward the trails.

Call Dad. Call Ma. But they'll tell me to go home, to sit tight while they deal with this, when Bree's running away from me now, doing something really stupid *now*, and I'm the only one here to stop her. And I'm her friend. Supposed to be.

I take off after her before she gets too big a head start.

The light fades so fast.

I sink with it, acknowledging some self-fulfilling prophecy. Of course, all this would begin and end in the woods, with Bree and me in the dark heart of this place. Everything started here, our first pilgrimage to the marsh, when everything with Kincaid was so new. His hand taking my arm for the first time as we stared down the nightmare on the opposite bank; the darkness taking Ivy, leaving only a trace for Bree and me to find.

And now maybe it has Hazel, but even as I shout her name, I'm trying to figure out how to call this off, go back before it's too late. Find a way to reason with Bree, who I know is way beyond that. I've never seen anyone cry like she is, like her chest has been torn open but her body won't stop going, won't stop calling for her sister, expecting to see her behind every tree.

At last I stop, saying, "Let's go back," my voice exhausted, flat, because I know she won't listen, watching as she keeps on going down the trail. "The longer we stay out here, the more time we're wasting. Hazel could be anywhere. We need to call the cops."

Bree does an unsteady half turn, gaze moving over the

woods to me, almost like she's ready to faint. "We haven't checked the marsh."

"She would never go to the marsh!" Déjà vu all over again: Landon, Ivy. You go if he takes you there. "I don't want to be out here, Bree. I'm scared."

"I'm not."

"We should turn around!" I'm yelling now.

"Just go, Clara!" Bree's words echo in the trees. She steps through brush onto a side trail, leaving the main path.

And I stand, hands useless at my sides. She left me. Or I left her, take your pick. I've never felt so disconnected in my life, so lost. I fumble Ma's phone out, check the bars. No service. Naturally.

I thought I knew the way. Thought I'd been down this trail with the others before, remembering a curve, a blaze-orange marker on a tree trunk, then a right turn. But there's no marker, and the curve is too gradual, with no right fork appearing as I follow it. The dark is coming down, and I have to outrun it, won't admit to myself that I've done it again—lost myself in these pitch-pine woods.

And the heartbeat that followed me through this day, the thirty-first of October, is back, my eardrums pounding with it, filling my rib cage as I turn again, and again, staying to the path in the vain hope that it will keep me safe this time, that I won't end up on the banks.

Tired, cold, trying to convince myself it isn't becoming night around me, that I don't need the phone flashlight, not yet, I stare half-blind at the trail, where anything could be familiar, or completely unknown.

When I turn a corner and it's there, a huge, dark, immobile shape in the center of the path, I can't register surprise. Because it was always leading to this.

I stop, weaving slightly on my feet, a daytime creature on this nocturnal plane, all my defenses stripped away.

He waits. I stare, my lips cold and stiff. "I'm not afraid of you." I hear the words in my head, not sure if they reach him. "I don't believe in you." Back up a few steps.

For a long, long time, no movement. Then, something unexpected—a burst of light, like a lightning storm in his hand. Whiff of ozone. I back up. Turn. Run.

Pain forks into my lower back, an electrical impulse that takes out everything, my body gone below the waist. I fall.

TWENTY-SEVEN

A WEIGHTLESS PAPER shape circles an orb of light. *Tick-aticktick.* Settles, whispers its wings, lifts off.

Focus on the moth. An exercise in concentration. I'm coming back, shedding the soft gauze of semiconsciousness, feeling a bolt of pain screwed into my lower back, my dry cotton mouth. Squeeze my eyes shut, look again. The filament in the bare bulb overhead burns like the tip of a white-hot soldering iron.

I take a breath, reach for my back, expecting to find blood, shredded skin—but what my fingers explore is a swollen lump above the waist of my jeans, like I was bitten by something small and extremely venomous. No light here except the bulb over the cot I'm lying on, and, in the far corner, the seething red grate of a small potbelly stove. The walls and ceiling are rough-hewn, exposed beams, unfinished.

The muscles of my torso jump and twitch in some delayed reaction as I realize I have no idea where I am. I remember Bree, running away from me. A hand, playing lightning between its fingers. Not lightning. Electricity. A Taser.

There's a motor running steadily outside, and another sound, murmuring and soft, like flowing water, or a conversation so distant that the words lose all form. I sit up stiffly. Someone's taken my coat.

He lets himself in, then, granting a brief glimpse of twilight before he shuts the door. I move back, knowing the big silhouette, the darkness of it, blending so well with the shadows as he goes to the stove, taking a second to warm himself. A rustle as he sheds some outer layers, a heavy coat, maybe some gloves. "There you are," he says in his soft, modulated voice. "Took you long enough."

Mr. Mac comes closer, dressed in what helps him look like part of the night: dark Carhartts, a black fleece vest over a black hooded sweatshirt. A ski cap he removes, gently squeezing it in his hands as he lowers it, never taking his eyes off me. They're a mild shade of brown.

"What . . . ?" I shake my head, and maybe I'm not fully awake yet, because I feel like I'm floating, up there with the moth, and the questions I should ask won't come.

"Go ahead and lie back." He sets the hat on an unseen shelf, carries a big metal toolbox to a bench near the cot, opens it, brings out a handful of black plastic strips. Zip ties.

My body's never given signals like this before—air traffic control with all the boards lit up, alarms blaring, flaggers signaling *go, go now*. I make a slight move to push myself off the cot; he turns, and I'm completely blocked by his bulk, my face level with the broadest part of his thigh.

We stare at each other for a moment, and then Mr. Mac sets the ties down, walks around the end of the cot, grabs a flashlight as he opens a closet door. He shines the beam straight down into a face: eyes huge, mouth covered in a strip of duct tape, dried blood all down one side of her head and neck. Hazel sees him, then me, and starts thrashing; her cries behind the strip are what I was hearing, that babbling brook.

He hunkers down beside her, glancing at me. "Okay, Clara? For every bit of trouble you give me"—he swirls the beam in Hazel's face, watching her wince—"she'll lose a little piece. One piece at a time." He sniffs, maybe a touch of fall allergies. "You think about what piece I'll start with, the next time you want to make this hard."

He shuts her away.

I'm frozen. He makes another spinning gesture at my legs. "Pick them up." I force myself down on the thin mattress pad. It's covered in a white fitted sheet that smells fresh from the package, but it's soaked into the walls, what's been done

here, a psychic assault that makes me retch, quietly, swallowing. No doubt he's scrubbed the bits and pieces away—I saw
gallon bottles of bleach on the closet floor around Hazel—but
horror is a residue, molecules I inhale. "Let me go," I whisper.
Nothing; he's busy getting his tools out. "You killed those
kids."

"Don't tell me what I've done." Conversational. He brings
out a power drill. A hammer. A plastic box rolling with nails
and screws. The light flickers overhead, and he tsks, tossing
over at me, "Generator. It happens."

I'm rigid as he kneels beside me. "Somebody will hear."

He gives a half smile, gaze traveling from the crown of
my head down to my arm, which he takes in a light grip,
looping two zip ties around my wrist, strapping it to the
metal frame of the cot. "Don't worry, nobody's going to
hear us." Jerks the ties so there's no slack; I cry out. "Used to
come out here hunting with my dad, before the state bought
up the land." Exhales as he sits back on his heels, gaze going
over the ceiling, the light, with its moth. "Camp's still here,
though."

State-owned land: we're still in the marsh. "I just want to
go home. Please." Strain my arm against the tie. "We didn't
do anything to you."

"You know what you do." Mr. Mac drops to my level,
folding his forearms on the pad, and my senses recoil from
the normal-guy smell of him: Ivory soap, coffee, toothpaste,

like some olfactory checklist of how he prepared for tonight, as if it were a Lady Elks' playoff game. "I think you know exactly." He reaches out, playing with the earrings in my lobe, flicking them. "But it's different when we're alone. Nobody laughing then."

I shake my head, tears stinging, escaping down my face. "I'm not—"

"Ah. It's okay. That's just school." He releases a sigh. "It was the same way when I went there. Everybody laughing." He looks at the wall for a second, working the sheet between his fingers. "But now I'm big. And it's so easy." Nods toward the closet. "That one there? Got right in the car when I said Bree had had an accident. That her mom was waiting for her at the ER. All you guys did just what I wanted. I've been watching you, you know. Figuring you all out." He moves down to my feet, secures my right ankle with two more ties. Pats my leg, pausing thoughtfully. "I've never done two at once before."

My gaze is riveted on the last four ties. Can't let him put those on me. "Nobody's going to believe Hazel and I both ran away."

He smiles slightly. "Maybe they'll think the Mumbler did it." He looks at me from the foot of the cot, expressionless, zip ties held loosely in his hand. Blinks rapidly, pulls his glasses off, pinching the bridge of his nose for a second. "I just—I always wonder—you know, if it would be different.

If we could just be together before. Let you get to know me. Instead of those other boys."

I clear my throat, words coming slowly. "Just you and me?"

"Or any of the others." His gaze works over my skin by the millimeter. "I really am good with kids."

I swallow. "I think you are."

His brown eyes, so close, as he leans farther over the bed. "You do?"

That's when I jam my thumb into his eyeball.

TWENTY-EIGHT

HIM, YELLING. ME, throwing my free arm up to block my face, trying to roll to the side before he comes down on me.

His fist slams my head, sending cascades of stars through my vision, but he's off target—can't see yet. I grab at the bench, trying to knock the tools down. I make contact, dragging the heavy thing to the side.

He clambers onto the cot, cursing, straddling me, one hand still pressed to his leaking eye. I scream, jerking my left leg up between us, lunging at the bench again as he draws back to hit me.

A groan of wood over wood, and tools rain down from the surface above, bouncing all over the floor and cot. This time, his fist hits me square in the mouth—lips jammed into teeth; ripe, blossoming pain; bright taste of blood—but my left hand's latched on to a heavy metal thing, and I heave my entire body into the swing.

I catch him drawing his arm back for the next punch; he doesn't have time to move. The hammer claw connects with his left temple. I think maybe I scream, horrified by the blood it brings, splitting his skin, splattering me, dragging across his forehead in a vivid streak.

His fist hangs in midair. No time—I sweep my arm back, hit him with the business end.

Mr. Mac's eyes squeeze shut, contorted look of pain, and I jerk the hammer back. He doesn't need it. Sways, eyes still closed, then slides over, a slow collapse onto the floor beside the cot.

Hyperventilating, breath sobbing out of me, I roll onto my right side, stretching my free hand for the sharpest thing I see—a hacksaw—and manage it with my fingertips.

Three saws and the zip ties on my wrist snap, then the ones on my ankle, and I'm over the cot. He's up on one knee already, head hanging low, clinging to consciousness.

I open the closet, dragging Hazel out by her arms. She falls into me; her wrists and ankles are zip-tied. "Damn it!" I grab the hacksaw from the cot, dropping to my knees to yank the blade across the plastic binding her legs—once—twice— he's getting up, using the cot for support.

Snap, the ties give. "Run!" I shove her at the door.

Sound of wounded rage as he comes at us, his hands dragging down my back, catching my clothes, bringing me down. Hazel's fighting with the dead bolt—her wrists still bound—and I won't roll over, won't give him my face, my throat, hunching my shoulders against his blows as I crawl toward the door. Burst of fresh cold air—she's out—fanning the radiant heat of the stove across me, so close. I see the silver coil of the burner lid handle above me, the disc-shaped surface for heating a kettle or pot.

I scream as I grab the handle, hot metal searing into my unprotected palm; then I wrench around, pressing the lid into his cheek.

He screams, pulling back. I'm on my feet and running, out the door, into overgrowth and reaching branches, where Hazel waits, terrified to leave, too afraid to go back inside.

The woods draw us in, covering our path.

TWENTY-NINE

THEY SAY IT'S over now.

After all the shock, the outrage, the questions, the interviews, we've been informed that we can all feel safe again. Mr. Mac confessed to the murders of Ivy and Dabney Kirk. He claimed Dabney was his first, followed by Ivy, who he picked up while she was walking home that night, ready to apologize to her stepmom and dad after their fight; Mr. Mac offered her a ride. Acting out his revenge fantasies, they say; getting back at the bullies from his teen years, the kids who picked on him, made him miserable, the same ones he couldn't separate from even as an adult, insinuating himself into the school, the community.

That's why he targeted our group, so he told the police. Because we were that kind; he could just tell. Bad kids. He was in the woods, his hunting ground, that night we carried the jack-o'-lanterns to the bridge. He stalked us through the marsh, watching Kincaid and me from the opposite bank, later seeking us out at school, learning where all of us lived, our routines. Casually asking Mrs. Mac about me, learning I was new, had fallen in with a bad crowd. A perfect candidate to go missing.

He won't admit to killing either of the boys, but you know it's coming, they say. Sometimes, these things take years, waiting for some sicko to get bored enough in his prison cell to get the press interested again with a fresh murder story. For now, Pender has to take what closure it can get. The edge of the woods near the trails has become a sort of shrine, people leaving candles, stuffed animals, cards for Ivy and Dabney. *Miss you. Love you. So sorry.*

They say she should've known, Mrs. Mac. That he was using her own files to gather information on his victims, to target her problem cases. They say somebody with her training should've recognized the signs.

What remains is a dark, empty office in PDHS. Her sign, her lamps, her doilies, all gone, making room for the next person who just wants to help the neglected, the apathetic, the belligerent. God help them.

● ● ●

They thought I'd want to get out of this town, Ma and Dad. Dad said he'd put in for another job anywhere, any place I wanted to go. I said this is where I want to be. Then I said I wanted to get some curtains for our apartment. Their going theory is PTSD.

These days, I take the sidewalk to the park, learning my way from the Terraces to Maple out here in the open. Takes about seven minutes longer, but who's counting.

It's the second week of November. Yesterday, Bree and Hazel and I walked home together, just the three of us. Bree seems to be trying it out, trusting me again. I know it isn't something she comes to easily, and that me getting her sister out of Mr. Mac's cabin has a lot to do with it. I'm just glad she's willing. I won't need a third chance. I want to be the person she comes to, no matter what. And I know I need to earn that.

Now, I hear the roll of plastic wheels behind me. I don't turn, letting him come up alongside, coasting like he does, hands in his coat pockets.

"How long have you been back there?" I ask.

Kincaid shrugs, weaving his board slightly, eyes on the road ahead.

"I appreciate you playing bodyguard and all, but it's not necessary." I glance over. "Mumbler's gone, or haven't you heard?"

He shakes his head, staying deadpan. "He'll always be with us."

I give him an incredulous look. "As long as we keep him alive in our hearts?"

A shrug. "Lots of stuff we don't have an answer to. Two dead boys that piece of shit won't cop to. Who do you think did it?"

"Sounds like you're about to tell me."

He's serious now—I recognize his barely perceptible shift from teasing to pensive. "I've just been thinking. I mean . . . those times in the woods, when I saw him. You know. Standing. Watching me. Why didn't he do anything?" He catches my look. "I mean, if Mr. Mac was taking his tool kit to girls and guys, why didn't he kill me?" Kincaid's silent a moment, looking down at his worn Converses, dragging one foot down to slow and walk with me. "Do you think it was because I was out there, hiding, like him?"

I stop, facing him. "Kincaid. You're nothing like him." I punch his shoulder lightly. "Right? That's over." Last week, I went with him to the little brown house on Lorimer, standing back a bit, just being there with him when his mom opened the door to find us on her front steps. By the time we were sitting at the kitchen table, she was crying. He's spending nights at home again, the two of them trying to find their way together, trying to give each other their space, learn to coexist even with all their differences. He's at school most days now; perfect attendance probably isn't in the cards for Kincaid.

"I guess." He looks at me, taking my hand, fingers finding

the burn scars on my palm, finally not afraid to touch them anymore, as if his gentle pressure could be enough to bring back the memory of it all.

I look around at the bare trees. "You know what? I like November. No serial killings to plan around. All-you-can-eat turkey."

"My birthday's in November."

"Wait. You're sharing information with me?" I let go of his hand, start walking backward. "Does this mean I can throw away my secret Kincaid decoder ring?" He smiles, doesn't answer.

They're waiting on us now: Trace, Sage, Moon, and Bree. Maybe Hazel, if Faye decided she could let her out of her sight. Things have changed a little at their place. Hazel's still having nightmares, and Bree told me that Hazel can't sleep unless Faye's with her. I know Bree seems a bit lighter, finally listening to me when I told her to stop hating herself for how it went that night. I look over at the trees, dark embroidery between the houses, thinking of moths and half-open closet doors. How the separation between reality and nightmares can be so thin. "Yeah. No more woods for me. Even though the Mumbler's gone."

"We'll see what happens next Halloween."

"Yes," I say, "we will." And keep on going, making him jog a little to catch up so he can hold my hand.